The Way it Was

Kentucky Edition

The Way it Was

Copyright © by Nelson Weaver, 2016, Published 2016

Interior and cover illustrated by Melinda Weaver
Cover design by Sagaponack Books and Design

ISBN 978-0-9978563-1-6 (soft cover)
978-0-9978563-0-9 (e-book)
Library of Congress Control Number 2016914529

This book may be purchased from local and on-line retailers

Muddy River Publishing
Ormond Beach, Florida

Printed in the USA
First edition 2016

This is a book of fiction. Although based upon documented history, the author took great creative liberties in the writing the book. Every event, every conversation, every incident, within every story, is a product of the imagination of the author. Although some of the characters are real, the events, incidents, and the conversations are also a product of the imagination of the author. Any resemblance of actual persons, either living or dead, to fictional characters, is purely coincidental. The reader is, however, encouraged to use their own imagination to bring realism to their enjoyment of the book.

About This Book

The Supreme Court of the United States mandated public school integration with its ruling on Brown vs. Board of Education in 1954. School Boards across the nation requested additional time to prepare plans in order to end segregation. Some school districts did not begin their integration process until the late 60s.

Russellville and Logan County, Kentucky were two of the first public school districts to integrate their high schools in 1956. Most of the facts are public record, but the mystery of the "why" always intrigued the author. The more he thought about the timing, the more obsessed he became to understand why two tiny southern school districts, a small rural town, and a small county district, would rush to integrate their public school systems so quickly after the Supreme Court decision.

An experience, while a college student in Alabama, further inspired the author to write about his home, his family, the South, the history, and the people who make it unique and special.

Readers from Logan County, from Kentucky, and from across the South will recognize many of the locations and characters.

This work is a succession of stories. They chronicle two families, a special interracial relationship, and the journey of that relationship through the times and the culture clashes of society. A society that still wears the scars of all that was the old South, even while it continues its journey to a new South.

If you are from the South, are intrigued by the South, or are interested in developing some southern charm; or if you have ever had a good friend, you may enjoy reading this book.

Introduction

This is a work of historical fiction. It tells far too much truth to be total fiction, but not nearly enough truth to be classified as nonfiction. My African American friend, Rub, is the sum of several friendships. He has become very real to me. I am blessed to have known him.

I proudly chose Logan County as the background for my story. I am fortunate that my home provided me with so much rich story material.

Some characters in the book are real. Some are not. The entire text is roughly based on historical events and the facts as I understand them. As the author, I took a giant share of creative license to bring the story onto the pages. Note: No animals were harmed in the making of this book.

It was also intended that no humans be embarrassed or hurt, or even offended. I apologize in advance for any disasters I did not anticipate.

I have spoken with dozens of people who lived in the era of the 1960s, both black and white. Some were friends and some were casual acquaintances. I have asked them all the same questions. Why were we so disconnected from our black classmates and friends? Why were our black classmates disconnected from us?

The dominating answer was, "That's just *the way it was.*"

For African Americans, it was a statement of acceptance, at that time. There was a desire for change, but many felt that change was waiting for leadership or a better moment.

For whites, it was a statement of acceptance that we failed our African American friends. Everyone said they would do things differently if they could go back and do it again.

Because the "Do Over" option is not available, there comes a time in life when we need to take inventory and decide what we can change and what we have to accept. Once that inventory is complete, then we can decide how to attack the changes, and what to do with the other stuff.

Some changes progress so slowly that they can get stuck in the wrong column. We can't remember how they started. This book is a story about two efforts. Two young boys, and later two men, who share very little except a desire to stay friends. It just so happens that the two boys are of different races. As some might say in the South, "That shouldn't make any never you mind," but, in fact, it does mean something. It means something because of where, how and when the relationship was born, grew, and survived.

In writing this book, I learned some important lessons. I came to understand that to white people, the Civil War was about many things. It was about economics and politics. It was about states' rights and cotton and taxes. And it was about slavery.

To the African American community, the Civil War was about two things and two things only: *slavery and citizenship.*

Today, differences still remain on how the two races see the past, live together in the present and approach the future. Our only hope for peace is to find common ground and grow from that anchored position.

History is written through the eyes of inspired writers. A complete history can only be understood through the reading of more than one perspective.

All history, including the history of Kentucky, Logan County and Russellville, is a mix of horrible stories and also wonderful stories. It has stories of great people and great achievements. As with most southern communities, the *total* history is not complete until all of the history is written and examined. I look forward to more books by African American writers who will help complete the picture and give us the rest of the story.

There is an expectation that we all have to be in the same place to have progress. I pray that is not true. It is our differences that define us as individuals, and as a nation. The two main characters of this book never find agreement. They find something more satisfying. They find that friendship is more important than agreement. Their friendship is worth more, and it is greater than, the issues and the differences that divide them.

The Way it Was
Kentucky Edition

Author

Nelson Weaver

Muddy River Publishing
Ormond Beach, Florida
2016

Prologue

"Down south, white folks don't care how close I get, as long as I don't get too big. Up north, white folks don't care how big I get, as long as I don't get too close."

—Dick Gregory, 1971 issue of Ebony Magazine

Friendship is a perfectly natural occurrence between young boys with common interests, unless the time is the 1950s in the South, and their skin is, you know, not the same color. I am your basic southern cracker. To be called a cracker would have been fighting words at one time in history. Crackers are actually residents of the southeast coastal region. My mother's family is from that area, so I qualify for some claim to the title.

People in Kentucky are often referred to as either rednecks or hillbillies. That is the kind of generalization that is common among the uninformed and uninitiated.

The south central part of Kentucky around south Logan, has rich, flat farmland. There are some hills but no hillbillies. Now a redneck is more an attitude than a culture. Sure, there are a few rednecks around; however, Pulitzer Prize Poet and novelist, Robert Penn Warren, was also from that area.

To truly understand the many stories of the South, especially if you are not from the South, it is necessary to get down near ground level. Forget what you think you know. Step up and take a deep breath of hot, humid air; relax and enjoy the slower pace, and a cold glass of sweet tea. Every experience, from the sounds of the crickets to the smell of the flowers, speaks to a place deep down inside. In no time, you just know that everything is going to be just fine, thank you.

A common expression amongst people of the South who quote common expressions is, "Southern folks love black people in particular, but don't care so much for them as a group."

"Yankees, on the other hand," it is said, "have no interest in black people as individuals, but love them as a group."

Short quips, as everybody knows, never tell the whole story about anything. The good white people of the South *are* defensive about the culture of the old South, and also the bumpy parts of the newer South. Most wish the world would "get over it" and move on to something, my God, to anything else.

If you find yourself swinging on a southern front porch swing some hot summer day, or if you are just passing through some part of the South, good advice you should remember in casual conversation is that some history is not discussed in polite southern society.

Because the where and when of our birth is not our decision, destiny dictates that we drop in and play the cards we are dealt. No one disputes that our environment has a major impact on our social development. We learn what we see. We repeat what we hear. Our first impressions become the foundation of all of our beliefs. I accept that I am a part of all that was the South in the '50s and '60s, and that the South is a part of all that is me. I would, however, like a few "do overs."

The outside world has a Hollywood picture of the South. They do not understand that the South has many faces. It is not a single place and it is not represented by any particular group, philosophy, or ideology. The South has, since the end of the Civil War, seen more change and has evolved farther and faster than any society in human history. However, all who suffer injustice, are justified in their impatience with the areas that lag behind.

I think people want to be proud of where they are from, don't you? It says something about us. "Where are you from?" is one of the first questions asked when getting to know people. I always say, "I'm from Southern Kentucky." Not just anywhere in Kentucky. No siree!

Southern Kentucky, my southern Kentucky, in the southern Kentucky that borders Tennessee near Nashville, is as southern as any part of the South. The first thing you may notice is the vast amount of farm land. The second thing you notice is the churches. There are churches everywhere in the South. Nothing defines the South more than the strong element of faith that is common in every community. Faith is alive and well in the hearts, minds and spirits of the South. "Jesus" is not a cuss word there. On Sunday mornings, the streets are as quiet as a graveyard because the pews are full of the faithful. Sure, the prisons in the South are full too, just like everywhere else; but trust me, it is different.

There is no Spanish moss on the south Kentucky oak trees, but don't let that fool you. The rivers flow north out of Alabama and Tennessee, and so does the culture. Jefferson Davis, the first President of the Confederacy, was born about 20 miles to the west in the next county over. In a strange quirk of fate, Abraham Lincoln was also born in Kentucky, just north and east of Logan County.

Four Kentucky Governors were Logan County residents. Governors from Florida, Illinois, and Texas also came from the land of Logan.

In our current age of terrorism, it is interesting to remember that the Barbary Coast pirates were America's first encounter with Jihad.

The pirates had kidnapped American seamen and were holding them ransom. In response to a ransom demand, President Thomas Jefferson sent the Marines to Tripoli. The first U.S.M.C. landing and the first raising of an American flag on foreign soil was led by Logan County resident, Lt. Presley N. O'Bannon. The pirates were subdued and the sailors were rescued. The O'Bannon home still stands at the corner of Ninth and Main Street in Russellville.

Also, I find it amazing that four citizens from Logan County died at the Alamo. No other county, outside of Texas, contributed so many in the famous siege of the mission in San Antonio, Texas. The 180 men of the Alamo were led by Colonel James "Jim" Bowie, Colonel David Crockett, and Colonel N. B. Travis. James Bowie was born in Logan County. The famous "Bowie Knife" is credited to him. Legend has it that the weapon became well known after he used the big knife in a duel.

Three other Logan County men died in the battle against a Mexican force of over 4,000 soldiers and led by Santa Anna. They were Peter James Bailey, David William Cloud, and William Fauntleroy.

Another dueling story also has its roots in Logan County, Kentucky. The duel was fought in the south part of the county, close to the Kentucky-Tennessee line, near Dromgooles' Station, or what is now the small town of

IX

Adairville, Kentucky. Since dueling was illegal in Tennessee, Andrew Jackson rode across the state line into Kentucky for his duel with a wealthy attorney from Nashville by the name of Charles Dickinson. Jackson challenged Dickinson to a duel because Dickinson had made disparaging comments about Jackson's wife, Rachel.

Rachel's first husband, Lewis Robards, of Harrodsburg, Kentucky, had petitioned for divorce in 1791, accusing Rachel of adultery with Jackson. Unfortunately for the Jacksons, Robards did not finalize the divorce. Jackson and Rachel were married believing the divorce to be signed and recorded. In fact, the divorce was not final until late in 1793. Jackson and Rachel remarried the next year.

By 1806, the story about Jackson and Rachel and their "sinful" living arrangement, was well known. Drunk and angry over the loss of a horse race to a horse owned by Jackson, Dickinson's mouth got the best of him. He lashed out at harshly at Jackson regarding Rachel. Jackson lost his patience and challenged Dickinson to a duel. They met at a place called Harrison's Mill on the south fork of the Red River in Logan County.

Dickinson was known as the best marksman, with a pistol, in all of Tennessee. Good thing, too, because angry drunks with big mouths did not live long, unless they could shoot. Both men stood in the early morning dew, with their seconds. They bowed and each took their pistols. After walking off the paces, each man stopped and turned. Dickinson fired first. The shot was dead-on but struck Jackson in the rib. Dickinson's aim was off due to the cut of Jackson's coat. "Great God, have I missed him?" Dickinson is reported to have said. Jackson's second ordered Dickinson back to his mark because Dickinson had stepped back a few paces after firing.

Jackson then fired on Dickinson. His weapon misfired and Dickinson had to stand while Jackson took aim and fired again. Jackson's second attempt was a success and Dickinson fell mortally wounded. Dickinson died later that evening at the William Harrison farmhouse, located nearby and just above the river valley.

Dickinson's wife heard of the duel, panicked, and left immediately by buggy for Kentucky. She hoped to comfort her husband if he was wounded. She met her husband's entourage making their return trip to Nashville. Her greatest fear was realized. She was a widow.

X

Jackson was wounded but not fatally. The duel did hurt his reputation for a while. Some thought he should have spared Dickinson's life by firing into the air or simply wounding him.

Since Dickinson fired first and had attempted a lethal shot at Jackson, Jackson harbored no guilt for the manner in which the duel was concluded.

As was the custom between gentlemen, Jackson sent a bottle of brandy to his victim as he lay dying. The brandy, it was hoped, would ease the pain. Jackson was certain that Dickinson would have done the same if the fortunes of fate had been reversed.

Most historians agree that Henry Clay, of Kentucky, upended Jackson's first run for President against John Quincy Adams. It is a widely accepted rumor that Clay leaked the story of Rachel to the Cincinnati Press.

Clay, who was Speaker of the House, and also a candidate for President, threw his support to John Quincy Adams after no candidate won a majority vote in the presidential election. Adams won the Presidency through an election by Congress. Adams then named Clay Secretary of State. Jackson never forgave Henry Clay.

Jackson, commonly known as "Old Hickory," lived to win his second election attempt for the office of President of the United States. Andrew Jackson took the bullet with him, along with his hatred for Henry Clay, to the White House. In fact, the wound never fully healed and he carried the bullet he acquired in Logan County to his grave.

It was this same southwestern part of Kentucky that seceded from the Union during the Civil War. Delegates from 64 Kentucky counties, over half of the total counties in the state, met at Bethel College in Russellville and voted to separate from the Union and join the Confederate States of America. The "Convention House," now known as the Clark House, still stands near the town square.

There, they voted for Kentucky to secede from the Union and become the thirteenth star in the Confederate flag.

A session of the Kentucky legislature in Frankfort, however, voted to stay in the Union and that was the vote that mattered. Kentucky, however, was divided, brothers against brothers, sons against fathers.

The whole confederate thing had little or no meaning to me growing up. I read about it and there would be the occasional comment, but there was no Klan sneaking around in the dark of night, at least not that I saw, and not that I was told about, and not in the era when I grew up, the era after World War II. The years before the war were another story altogether

Few would know the answer to the question, "Who is Woodson James?" It is not much of a clue that his father was a Baptist minister. Woodson James is better known today as Jesse James. He and his brother, Frank, first rode with the Quantrill's Guerillas. Many know them now as Quantrill's Raiders. They were never in the service of any army but were regularly associated as free agents of the Confederacy. The bunch was famous for their profitable raids on northern towns.

When the war ended, the raiders continued using the profitable bank robbery skills they had learned and perfected.

In 1868, the Old Southern Deposit Bank stood at the corner of Sixth and Main Streets in Russellville. One fateful day, the little bank in Russellville became the site of the first documented, post-war bank robbery, by the James-Younger Gang. That robbery by the James-Younger Gang is reenacted each fall during the Logan County Tobacco Festival that is now called the more acceptable name of Logan County Tobacco and Heritage Festival. To the casual observer, it might appear that bank robbery has come to be held in higher regard than tobacco.

After the robbery of the Old Southern Deposit Bank, all was quiet for a few years. The Black Patch Wars were a notable break in the peace. The Wars occurred for several years around the turn of the century. One night during the Wars, fires were lit in the tobacco warehouses in Russellville. Several businesses near the warehouses also burned.

Hopkinsville, a larger town to the west, got most of the publicity. Princeton, Kentucky still celebrates the Wars with an annual Black Patch Festival each fall. The Black Patch Wars was a battle between big tobacco and local farmers against the local farmers who refused to sell. Hooded vigilantes burned barns and terrorized residents who sold directly to tobacco barons.

Because it was a war on common ground between common people, the sides were difficult to define. Secret codes were devised to protect the identity of the vigilantes and keep infiltrators out of the inside circle.

Cryptic conversation was developed to identify fellow vigilantes.

"I see you've been there," one would ask and then wait for the correct response of, "on bended knee."

Both the man who asked and the man who answered then knew they were on the vigilante side of the war.

As in most southern towns, there is a Confederate soldier statue in the Russellville town square, now known as Carrico Park Square.

The statue faces south. Now, I confess that I have no clue of statue rules regarding the direction a stone or concrete southern soldier should face. There was once some discussion, as I recall, on whether this particular soldier was in retreat or was facing south as a sign of respect. I personally believe he fit better on that end of the park, so that's where they put him.

The Logan County Courthouse once occupied the square. It has moved twice since the olden days where its presence once dominated the center of county commerce.

Carrico Park Square is now the hosts a central fountain, a beautifully restored cannon, the Confederate statue, and several historical information markers.

Granted, the statue is adorned with symbols of the rebellion. But, it is actually only an old relic of an almost forgotten period in Kentucky history. It reminds us of the way it was.

Every town has a history and a "Historic District." It is simply a fact, however, that some places have a history that is more interesting than the history of other places. I always thought Logan County had more than its fair share of interesting "historic" history.

One thing is for sure, Logan County has had more than a little excitement over the years. With the good, not so good, but mostly good of all that was my old Kentucky home, this is the place I called home while growin' up. This is the place where I got my "raisin'." This is the place I met my friend, Rub Wells.

For a white boy to have a friend who is black, and, they both lived in the old South, well, it took some "gettin' there."

Chapter 1

"The truth is, everyone is going to hurt you. You just got to find the ones worth suffering for."

—Bob Marley

The late afternoon Birmingham, Alabama sun was starting to cast long shadows along the pool deck. It was a lovely spring day in 1970. Normally, a constant belching of red ash, from a score of Birmingham steel mills, gave the air a rusty glow. On that day, the sky had been cleared by a steady southern breeze.

The temperature was still hotter than hot. Sweat was a constant companion. Women call it a "glow." People who don't sweat much call it damp. Nathan came from a long family history of people who sweat. The day had cooled a bit from the hottest part but any exertion was going to show as plain as rain.

There were four, sweaty white college boys sitting at a table on the deck near the pool. Not a one of them was from Birmingham. Heck, none of them were from Alabama. They had pulled up a table and were playing cards. It was Spades, or maybe Hearts. No mind, it was just a way to pass the time. No real work could be done until the Birmingham Park and Recreation Department and the county commissioners made up their minds about whether the city pools would open at all that year.

Emotions ran high in the southern city. Only a few short years before, in 1963, four young Negro girls had been killed in a bombing at the 16th Street Baptist Church. The 16th Street Baptist Church was only a few blocks away from where the four boys were playing cards. Now, this mostly white neighborhood swimming pool, in Norwood Park, was being forced to allow

1

black children admission to the pool. The whole idea of black folks in the same waters with white folks was not going to happen. Not if some local white leaders had any say in the matter.

Armed police guards had been replaced by a continuous circle of patrol cars in procession around the city block that housed the park. Every few minutes, a police car would slowly roll by. Several times a day they would stop and check on the pool employees. Everyone became well acquainted. The Birmingham Police Department was all white in those days. The only time there was an interruption in the patrol was during shift changes, early morning, at lunch, and at supper time (dinner time up north).

It was at about supper time when trouble showed its ugly face. The sound of screeching tires rang out through the still, muggy, afternoon air. A car was making the sharp turn from the side street, 15th Avenue onto 28th Street in front of the park. The community pool sat close to the sidewalks that bordered the streets of this old working class Birmingham neighborhood. The sharp noise immediately caught everyone's attention.

Nathan Weaver was one of the boys playing cards. He looked up briefly at first. The sound of screaming tires is not unusual in the South. Hot tires are prone to this behavior. Events, however, evolved quickly and there was an increasing awareness of danger. Mental alarms were sounding, along with the sound of a man shouting.

The source of the shouting was riding "shotgun" in the front seat of the sedan. The car window was down. There was also someone in the back seat, or maybe two men. The man riding shotgun had his head stuck out the window. He was, in fact, halfway out of the car and he was shouting "Nigger Lover" mixed with a full buffet of common curse words. The whole commotion was loud and fast. The man had something in his hand. He threw the object towards the pool in the direction of where the card playing quartet was assembled. Eight eyes locked immediately on what appeared to be a stick of dynamite. It came flying through the air in a slow tumbling motion. A fuse clearly burned at one end. There were no screams nor was there any discussion of what move would be most wise. The only sight and sounds on deck were of chairs, Coke bottles, table and cards going airborne as four young men dove in all directions.

*

2

On the other side of the world, it was early morning. Rub Wells was crouched as low as he could get. Viet Cong regulars were zeroing in on his position with mortar fire. It was only a matter of time before his squad was hit and possibly overrun. Covered in mud, sweat, blood, and the stink of all that is war, Rub tried to stay calm and look like a man in command. 1st. Lt. Danford was dead for sure. Rub was too busy to go looking for him. He had seen the blast and heard the cries. Gunny had probably died in the same attack. If they weren't dead, they were hurt too badly to lead.

The rainy season would start soon. Both sides of the war were trying to gain as much real estate as possible before the whole world became one, big swamp. Rub didn't care why he was there. What did it matter? Some general, somewhere, was always saying how it was important to "go here" or "take that" or "hold some hill or road or whatever." If he wasn't there, he would be in some other crap-hole, somewhere else.

Rub had figured out a long time ago that his chances of getting out of that war alive were slim to none. He was black and poor and, therefore, expendable. No, Rub fought for his buddies. The men on that line had his back and he had theirs. That's the way it had always been and that's the way it was on that hellish early spring morning in 1970. He fought for the man next to him more than he fought for Uncle Sam. Hell, in Rub's view, Uncle Sam was trying to kill him, too!

The platoon was spread out across the ridge in a defensive position. They had earlier held the ridge in a bloody battle. Rub's squad was dug into the center and was flanked on the right and left by the two other squads that made up what was left of the platoon under the command of Lt. Danford. Sergeant Rub was squad leader. With Lt. Danford out of commission and no sign of Gunny, Rub had taken charge and had regrouped the troops after the initial engagement.

The enemy had attacked with mortar fire and small arms. That first push was designed to test the strength of the defensive line. The VC had pulled back and were now pelting the American line with mortars and small arms. Rub had assessed the strength of the assault and believed he was up against a force of maybe 200 or more VC Regulars. The enemy was spread out, so it was difficult to direct effective counter-fire. Rub had ordered rounds of 60mm mortars fired in hopes of pushing the VC back far enough to give some space from small arms fire and the air assault that was on the way.

3

All forward positions had been overrun in the first assault. Survivors had retreated and dug in atop the ridge.

Thump, thump, thump. Bullets were hitting the sandbags just above Rub's head. His fatigue was held at bay by the adrenaline pulsing through every cell in his body. Dirt and sweat covered his face in natural camouflage. Holding the radio close to his face, Staff Sergeant Victor (Rub) Wells, listened in as two F-4 Phantoms sped to his position. Rub knew he didn't have much time. The enemy knew it, too. He thought about his family and his home in Kentucky. He prayed a prayer without words. In less than five minutes, this battle would be over one way or the other. Only one side was going to survive, maybe. Rub had called in support so close that the rain of fire could easily wipe out both sides. He figured his chance of survival with an air strike was 50/50. His chances without an air strike were close to zero.

Two minutes until fire. Rub signaled his men to light all their flares before he pulled his helmet tight and buried himself as best he could in his shallow foxhole. He closed his eyes and prayed that his current shallow piece of a hole would not be his grave.

Suddenly, waves of thunder rolled across the ridge. The ground shook so hard that Rub's teeth rattled in his head. Forty-five thousand pounds of liquid hell and cluster bombs rained out of the sky.

It was a singular moment in time. Two very young men on opposite sides of the world. Two friends who had always been in different worlds, even while growing up in the same small southern town. It was a friendship that should never have been, but was. It had endured in spite of the odds.

But, dead is dead. At that particular moment, both young men were in a tough spot. How were the two situations connected? How did two old friends since grade school; one a white boy and the other one black, come to be friends in the first place?

Chapter 2

"I freed a thousand slaves. I could have freed a thousand more if only they knew they were slaves."

—Harriet Tubman

To understand Rub and Nathan, it is necessary to first travel back in time a few years. It is necessary to go back to rural southern Kentucky during the dark days of the depression. To the farm and to the core of the southern economy.

The burley tobacco was taller than the head of the young 14-year-old Samuel Wells. That was saying something because Samuel stood over six feet tall. He looked down at his feet. He was doing men's work now so he wore shoes. It was taking some time getting used to them. An uncle had died and Samuel got his shoes from his aunt. No socks. They had fit fine when he got them last spring but they were a tad too small now, so he cut out the big toe on both shoes. They would do fine until winter and they were better than no shoes at all. There had been times past when he couldn't get to school in the winter because he didn't have shoes.

The rawhide shoestrings were cut from cow leather off an old bull they had butchered in the winter. Mr. Bull wasn't "cuttin' the mustard" anymore so Mr. Diddle put him down. Nothing was wasted on the farm.

It was August in south Logan County. The year was 1936. Late August was when the tobacco was cut, spiked onto stakes and hung in the big tobacco barns. Samuel's father, Levi, was a regular farmhand. He worked mostly for Mr. Diddle, but during seasons, all the hands from all around came together to work the patches. Then, they would move on to the next

5

until all the tobacco from all the farms was in the barns. Everybody worked, white and black, including the younger boys big enough to pull their weight. The little ones were out in the field, too. They carried water and fetched whatever needed fetchin'. They also watched and learned. They learned how to work, and how to work with men. Soon their time would come.

Tobacco was a big cash crop in Kentucky. Almost every farm had a patch. Small patches of a couple of acres or less were usually worked by the white families who owned the land. It was about the only income they had during the depression.

The big farmers like Mr. Diddle had black tenant farmers who lived on the farm and worked the land. All were the descendants of slaves. Most worked the same land as their slave ancestors.

The relationships between white landowners and Negro farmhands varied. As in all of humanity, there was some bad and some better. By modern standards, it is strange looking back on it. In the case of Edward Diddle, his father, grandfather and great-great-grandfather had farmed this same land. Mr. Diddle grew up playing with Levi and the children of all the workers. On the surface, it was one big happy extended family.

Levi knew it was not exactly one big happy family. "White folks just don't know or maybe they don't want to know," he told Samuel. "They good people and all, but we always still be what we is. They always be what they is. And that's all there is."

Mr. Diddle allowed his tenants to have a garden and some farm animals for milk and eggs. The wages were low but the families survived, even in hard times. This looked to be a pretty good year. Edward planned to give all his colored tenants a ham after hog killin' was done. They deserved it.

Everybody in the field that day was black, except for Mr. Diddle and his two sons. His two boys were good friends with Samuel. They played all day most every day until they all started school. They still worked the fields together. Occasionally, the boys would all go fishin'. Not so much anymore. The older they got, the more the whites stayed together. The Negroes kept themselves out of sight on the farm.

Levi couldn't read much but he knew his numbers and letters. Nobody was too good to do hard work but Levi wanted something better for Samuel.

Samuel had worked tobacco many times before. There was nothing he hadn't done at one time or another. In the spring, when he was little, he had ridden a "setter" and planted little plants called slips. He rode on the setter with Mr. Diddle's daughter sittin' right up there on the other seat next to her. Everybody worked because the season waited for no man.

During the hot summer months, Samuel had hoed weeds, pulled off suckers and "topped" the tobacco. Suckers were little branches that were pulled off the plant so the nutrients would all go to the big leaves. In late summer, the plants got a sort of bloom on top. This bloom was cut off and the process was naturally called topping.

Mr. Diddle had a big patch of burley. Samuel figured it at over eight acres. Maybe closer to ten acres. There was another smaller patch of fired tobacco of maybe two acres. Fired tobacco was a smaller plant. It was hung in a separate barn. Sawdust was brought into the barn and a smoldering fire was kept burning for a couple of weeks. Fired tobacco barns were a sight to see with smoke pouring out from every crack between the doors and walls. It was a common occurrence for an excited, well intentioned Yankee to come knocking on the door and pointing at the barn thinking it had caught on fire.

Samuel didn't smoke or chew. It just didn't suit him for some reason. His mother told him it was bad and he knew his mother was smart. He always got dizzy working the tobacco when it got tall. The nicotine rubbed off the leaves and soaked directly into the skin. It was like a gum that jumped off the leaf and into his head. He had worn long-sleeved shirts, even on the hottest days, but somehow he still staggered for a few days before he got adjusted. The little ones would sometimes get sick and lose their breakfast. The old men would laugh. It was hard work and a hard life. The quicker the young ones learned that lesson, the better off they would be.

Tobacco cuttin' started early mornin', before 6:00 a.m. Everyone had been in the field since before sunup. The entire patch needed to be cut before sundown. Samuel carried a long, special blade that was sharp enough to slice through the stalk with one blow. The cut was made low to the ground, under the bottom leaves of the tobacco plant. Had to be careful not to damage any of the leaves. Every leaf was gold in the pocket of Mr. Diddle. It would be graded and the higher the grade, the better the price it brought at the auction.

*

Samuel had been bent over cutting tobacco for a couple of hours. It was starting to get some heat in the air. He was getting thirsty and his stomach was growling. Suddenly, the image of a wagon could be seen moving down the fence line from the Taylor house. Two plow mules were pulling a long tobacco wagon. Mrs. Diddle had the reins. Riding on the wagon holding several large baskets was Samuel's mother, Ruth Ann Wells, and two other black women from the next farm over. A dozen happy faces lit up at the sight of the wagon loaded with food and drink.

On the farm, breakfast isn't served before work starts. Hands go to the field and work a couple of hours. Most times, if it's only white folks, they come back to the main house where the wife has been cooking since before sunup. Because there was a field full of hands, Mrs. Diddle had brought in some help and cooked everything up as usual, except when they got done, they loaded the baskets on the wagon and brought it all to the field.

The wagon pulled up to a stop under a big, white oak shade tree at the edge of the field near the gate. The women jumped off the wagon and started spreading tablecloths and cups and food. The wonderful smell of buttermilk biscuits, sausage, hash brown potatoes, grits, gravy, onions and red tomatoes, drifted in the air and caught the noses of the field hands.

Tools dropped to the ground like hammers on a nail. All eyes turned towards the wagon. As heads turned, feet followed. It was an effort not to run as everyone quickly gathered around the wagon.

Before anyone was going to start chewing more than the usual sample morsel, a prayer was in order. One thing shared by both whites and Negroes alike was a strong Godly faith. Mr. Diddle was a deacon at the Baptist church. Levi had practically rebuilt New Pilgrim Baptist Church after the storm almost blew it down a few years back. Jesus was common ground. It was Ed Diddle who first took off his hat, wiped this brow, and gathered everyone close around the wagon. With conviction even stronger than the powerful hands raised to the heavens, he gave thanks for the food. He asked God's blessing on the crop and on all who gathered in his field that day.

Mr. Diddle and his sons, followed by the regular field hands, were first in line. After that, came the next generation of younger boys, and finally the little ones. Usually the little ones were thrown a biscuit, "quick like," to shut them up and get them out from underfoot.

Ruth Ann looked at Samuel and marveled at how he had grown.

She made sure her son and husband had all the food they wanted. Samuel saw the look of pride in her eyes when she saw him. He was on his way to becoming a man.

When people talk about "country cookin'" this would be what they are talkin' bout. No one went hungry. They all ate until they were full as ticks and there was still food left over. There was a short rest and then it was back to the field.

After all the leftover fixins' were gathered up, the wagon turned back towards the house. It would return around 2 PM with a big dinner of fried chicken, mashed potatoes, gravy, green beans and cornbread.

People in the South have "dinner" in the middle of the day. Dinner is followed in the early evening by "supper." Southerners never eat "lunch." Nobody on the farm ever ate brunch, either.

In the winter, when there was too much bad weather to do very much outside work and everybody was stuck in the house, or nearby in the barn, it was common to sneak back to the breakfast table and steal another ham and biscuit. This short meal was usually washed down with sweet milk or a little coffee. There wasn't a special name for those little meals. At least nothing ever heard of.

Samuel looked up at the sun. It was gettin' close to about noon. The hottest part of the day was ahead and he sweated in the heat. It was hard to hold onto the blade with wet hands. He wiped his face with an old rag but the rag was dripping and not much help keeping the sweat out of his eyes. His father had offered a hat early mornin' 'fore they left the house, but it was dark then and Samuel didn't think he needed a hat. "You might be thinkin' different 'bout noon," his father Levi had told him. Shore nuff, them words were ringing in his head as the sun beat down. Tomorrow, he would take that hat if it was offered again.

But tomorrow was yet to come and today had a long way to go. By sundown the entire field would be cut. By early morning tomorrow, every stalk would be spiked onto long sticks and ready to hang in the barn. By sundown tomorrow, all of the tobacco would be lofted high and starting to dry.

In late November or maybe December there will be a cold wet day. Actually it was often an evening. Mr. Diddle would have been watching the tobacco hourly. If the tobacco is too dry, the big leaves will crumble and be worthless; too damp and the tobacco is graded down at the market. No, when the tobacco "comes in order," all hands have to be ready to "strip" the leaves off of the sticks and press them into bales for transport to the auction barns in Russellville.

It was a big day when the tobacco sold. An entire year's work is paid at one time and in one check. If it brought a good price, Mr. Diddle would usually bonus his best and regular workers with a big Christmas box of groceries from M.J. Grocery and Hardware, located in the center of Schochoh. Uncle Dick and Aunt Annie owned and ran the store. They always made sure the box included some fruit and candy for the children.

All across Logan County and much of the south, it is the same. In January everybody does some maintenance work on the equipment and rests a bit. Then in February, they burn the insects and weeds out of a bed and plant tiny tobacco seeds. The new tobacco season starts again.

Chapter 3

"The Grand Ole Opry is an artist and I am proud to be one of its songs."

—Blake Shelton

The Weavers lived two counties east of Logan in Allen County, Kentucky. The Barren River wove through Allen County making it rocky and hilly. The farms were small because the good dirt lay in the valleys in what was called "bottom land."

It had been a depression for so long, some folks could hardly remember better times.

Charles Thurman Weaver fell into his feather-bed. He was sore all over after plowing all day behind two, big plow mules. His father, Lester, had also plowed all day riding on the old International tractor. It had been raining for a month and the ground had been too wet to work. Now spring was getting on and there would be no corn or tobacco if the ground wasn't broken in a hurry. Every resource that could be borrowed, shared or rented was being put into action to save the crop. The crop was all that stood between survival and not surviving. Thurman, his family always called him Thurman and not Charles, had no passion for farming. He had dropped out of school after the 8th grade to work. It was the depression years and all the boys had to work. All the boys in that part of Allen County, Kentucky anyway.

*

11

Frank L. Weaver had organized a country band. They called themselves the *Allen County Ramblers*.

It was mostly family and friends from Allen County. They had played a few times at gatherings in the area. One night over in Bowling Green, the show was being broadcasted by the local AM radio station, WBGN. The station manager liked what he heard and set up an audition for the band in Nashville, at the Grand Ole Opry.

Nobody had much money. The banks had already taken all the farms that had a mortgage. The family farms were safe, only as long as they avoided crop failures and didn't borrow money. Lester had been farming rented land until the bank took it and the family had to move from Thurman's birthplace in Settle, Kentucky.

On Sunday, it was church and then an afternoon of food and singing. Thurman's father, Lester, sang in a southern gospel quartet. Southern gospel was a mix of country and gospel. It took the music of the church out of the church to anywhere people wanted to go. Thurman Weaver's baritone voice was as smooth as butter and he, like his father, found escape in the music.

After arriving at the audition, the band played a few tunes. The Old Judge tapped his foot, stood, and clapped at the end of the audition. He seemed to like what he heard and what he saw.

The Old Judge, George Hay, himself, was seated center, front row. Thurman was amazed to see that the Old Judge didn't look much older than 40 years of age. The "radio" picture of the Judge had him white headed and with a beard at an age nearer 80 than 40. That was Thurman Weaver's first lesson in radio. "This is real showbiz," he thought to himself.

The War Memorial Auditorium was a big place. Located in downtown Nashville, in the shadow of the Tennessee State Capitol, it could seat 2,000 people. It was the home of the Grand Ole Opry from 1939 to 1943.

There were pats on the back and a promise to arrange another audition in late November or early December. They were told the band could be playing on the stage of the Grand Ole Opry very soon. Maybe by January.

Thurman played the mandolin and sang harmony on most songs. Any trip to Nashville was a very big deal to the young lad. Having just turned 18 years of age on the 12th of September, Thurman was overwhelmed as he stood on the great stage. It was the throne of Bill Monroe, Ernest Tubb, Roy Acuff and all the well-known greats in Opry circles.

The Way it Was

Thurman was a hired hand for anyone who needed a hand. He worked long and hard every day except Sunday. On Saturday nights, the family would gather and listen to the Grand Ole Opry on a 12-volt battery operated radio. It was broadcasted live from Nashville on clear channel WSM AM 650. (During World War II, the Grand Ole Opry would move to its later famous location at the Ryman Auditorium.)

*

Thurman was the oldest of four brothers. Thurman, Morris, Carlene, and Robert were the sons of Lester and Lois Weaver. They lived in a small house near Osborne Bend in the Meader community. Allen County is nothing like south Logan. There were never any big plantations in those parts of the South. There were no blacks living around there, either. Bowling Green was the closest town that had a number of "coloreds," as they were often called back then.

Walking out into the cool air that November night in 1941 and standing on the steps of a memorial to those who died in World War I, the war to end all wars, who could have known that in less than a month, the United States would be in another world war. All the dreams and all the plans and all the hopes of a nation and its young men were about to change. The attack on Pearl Harbor would throw Charles and the entire world into the theater of war; not music. Charles Thurman Weaver would soon be a United States Navy sailor on the other side of the world. The stage of the Grand Ole Opry would never hear his voice or the smooth country music of the *Allen County Ramblers*.

Thurman Weaver would soon be leaving his farm days behind him but he was part of a large and hardy group. You could always tell men of the depression era. Their hands were hard and calloused. Their skin was tough as leather. They gathered strength from their faith in God and family. They made do with what they had and found some joy, somehow, in where they were.

Chapter 4

"History will be kind to me for I intend to write it."

—Winston Churchill

"Being a young black boy in rural southern Kentucky was better than being a young black boy in some places," he reckoned. At least Samuel was getting some education. Education for Negroes in the South was never "separate but equal." It was mostly just separate.

Unfortunately, many white rural schools, in the South, were slow to develop, also. It is said that "the lack of education, just leads to *more* lack of education." Education must be a part of the value system or it will not be promoted. It will, in fact, be discouraged.

In the early to mid-20th century, most of the rural white schools and black schools were one or two-room, multi-grade institutions.

It is not wise, however, for outsiders to make broad negative assumptions about the education of southerners. There are many areas in the South where education was, and still is, a priority. Logan County had its moments but there was still work to do, especially in the rural areas. Lack of money and lack of transportation mandated that the schools be small and close to the families they served. The Negro schools lagged many steps behind whatever the white schools were doing.

Samuel had been attending a Rosenwald School near Schochoh, Kentucky.

Schochoh is one of those tiny crossroad communities you see all across America. Most consist of a general store with gas pumps and a couple of churches. There may be a school, also.

Schochoh was a small, friendly community in the southern part of Logan County near the north branch of the Red River. The neighbors knew one another and would lend support in hard times. The larger yet still small town of Adairville lies to the south southwest. The historic Red River Meeting House is just a few miles west.

In 1917, Julius Rosenwald funded what became known as the Rosenwald Schools. Rosenwald was an Illinois businessman and philanthropist. He was a large stockholder and executive of Sears, Roebuck and Company. The purpose of his philanthropy was to narrow the gap in funding for Negro schools. Kentucky was a leader in Rosenwald schools and Logan County had more Rosenwald schools than any other county in the state. There were eight Logan schools at one time.

The Schochoh Rosenwald School was on Corinth Road so Samuel could walk the distance from his house to the school in about half an hour in good weather.

The school was a small two-room building. It had a pot-belly stove for heat. The boys had to get coal and wood. Without a coal shed, the coal and wood was often wet. In the winter, the older boys would fire up that stove early in the morning. Everyone sat in a circle that got larger as the stove got hot. The students sitting near the stove would be hot all day while the older boys, who always sat in the back, would have to keep their coats on some days. Most schools did not have electricity so school couldn't start until there was good enough light inside. There was a big yard surrounding the school and two outhouses out back. At any given time, the school had eight to eighteen Negro students. The teaching staff changed over the years but you could depend on there being two teachers teaching first grade through two years of high school. The teachers were all Negroes, too. Nobody ever heard of whites teaching in a black school.

Books and teaching aids were always in short supply. Rosenwald may have narrowed the gap in funding for Negro schools but there was still a gap. It was more of a chasm.

The white school in nearby Adairville had nice blackboards, chalk, erasers, books and a big library. Books were the most critical need for Negro schools. The success of the Negro schools in Logan County had brought some attention to the problem and a small library was in the works. Meanwhile, the Logan County Board of Education loaned books to the Negro schools and allowed students to get access to books from the

15

public library in Russellville. Black students were not allowed at the library, so the students would request books through their teacher. The teacher would make the book request known to the County Board and the Board would then acquire the books from the school or public library.

Logan County was not yet ready to have black folks in the public library unless they were cleaning the place.

A person would assume that Negro teachers would be scarce as hen's teeth but, in fact, the opposite was true. Historically, there was a surplus of Negro teachers. The reason being that there were no other opportunities for educated Negroes. Not in the South anyway.

A basic knowledge of the 3 R's was plenty enough education to be a farmhand or washwoman. The few who continued their education were forced to compete for the limited teaching jobs available.

The Depression had dragged on for several years. Families were forced to move where there was hope for employment. These movements had caused a demographic shift and a temporary shortage of Negro teachers in Logan County.

*

Patricia Clay was a thin, attractive black woman, not that anyone ever noticed, or even cared. She stood 5'7" tall and she didn't weigh more than 120 lbs. Her eyes were soft, but those same eyes could stare a hole through a rock wall if she desired it. Patricia had a nice figure, too, but what struck everyone immediately was how she always carried herself like a real lady. She seemed to float across a room. Her mother had coached her endlessly to keep her head high and her back straight. She wore a hint of makeup that made her high cheekbones look even higher. Her skin was young, smooth and soft. She stood out like a sore thumb in the colored community where she lived and worked. The Negro wives of farmhands and sharecroppers were weathered and bent with the burdens of many years of hard work. The young girls were beautiful but they had not been schooled in how to be a lady. All young girls had to learn the skills necessary to survive on a farm. One day, those skills would be necessary as the wife of a sharecropper.

Patricia lowered her head down onto her arms in a moment of fatigue and self-pity. Her move to southern Kentucky from Illinois had been a culture shock. "This may be where God led me, but I never dreamed it would be this hard," she silently sobbed to herself.

Her old life in DeKalb seemed so long ago. What good was her education when she had no tools to help her teach? Her students seldom stayed in school past 8th grade anyway. She was wasting her life and she was wasting her education.

The letter she held in her hands from her lifelong friend was the source of her current blue mood. They had been roommates all through college and for several months after. Beth had written to tell Patricia that she was getting married and she had included a picture of the couple. "What kind of Christian is jealous of the happiness of others?" Patricia said silently to herself. Patricia berated herself and the whole cycle of misery repeated.

It wasn't fair. Patricia had no one to talk to. The only women she knew were the mothers who had children in school and the women at church. They were all married, except for a couple of old widows. Some had been married since they were twelve or thirteen years old. Patricia would be 19 years old in November. She was an old maid by local standards.

She was used to the finer things in life. Her mother was a professor of English at a Negro college and her father was a Methodist minister and writer.

A fateful letter from a former resident, teacher and writer from Logan County set in motion the events that led her on this journey. Alice Dunnigan had written to her father asking if he knew of any black educators who would come to Kentucky and teach. She said the need was urgent because many educated Negros had left the area because of the Depression. Alice painted a picture of hard work and low pay but also of green pastures and rolling hills and students who wanted to learn.

Patricia had chosen her life as a missionary of education to rural Kentucky. She had not anticipated the effects of the loneliness, fear and despair.

As an educated black woman, she had few peers, other than the other teachers. Thank God for May Miller. May was much older but she was smart and also a fine Christian lady. The problem with May was that she was always trying to fix her up with a man. It was the same in her church. Patricia always politely refused. Her plan was to stay for three years and then return to her home in Illinois. She had almost finished one year of her personal commitment. Hooking up with a farmhand might ease the current pain but it was not a good long-term solution.

Most men, Negro or white, had little use for a well-educated "nigger" woman. What was she good for? She couldn't cook. She had no idea how to preserve jams. She knew nothing of herbs or how to plant a garden. An education was of little use in those parts. The typical white man was not about to help a black person get any more education than it took to read a little of the Bible or count out some seed.

Her fear was rooted in the common belief that, "knowledge was a dangerous thing," that is, if the knowledge resided between the ears of a "colored" woman.

There had been lynchings for less, and it hadn't been that long ago, or that far away.

In August of 1908, in Russellville, four black men were hanged from a cedar tree. Joseph Riley, Virgil Jones, Robert Jones and Thomas Jones were lynched. Four innocent men died due to the anger following a black man shooting a white man in self-defense. The accused had been moved to Louisville for his protection. A short time after his safe departure, an angry mob stormed the Logan County Jail and took its vengeance on the only Negro inmates available that day for hanging.

A note was left behind after the lynching as a warning to all Negroes. "Stay away from white people or this will happen to you." The message of fear was clear. The KKK had success for a while all across Logan County.

Some had forgotten the incident but the elders were always there to remind them. Patricia had heard the stories so she stayed close to the small rented room she had in the home of her minister and his wife. She prayed for strength and wisdom and she kept a low profile as a school teacher.

*

An unusual local situation was, however, pushing her out of her cocoon. One of her students showed extraordinary promise. She had noticed it right away. His name was Samuel. She had encouraged him and had spoken to Brother Brown about helping Samuel get more education than was offered in Logan County. It brightened her spirits thinking that maybe her calling did have purpose beyond what she understood. Maybe God had a plan for her and her work after all.

Samuel was a bright student. His teachers had always pushed him to stay in school and work at learning all the school could offer. His parents supported him, too, and never allowed him the option to drop out. He excelled in math and geometry in particular. Although Samuel lacked the literary exposure gained in better schools, his reading skills were high. He could also structure sentences well in both speech and in writing.

He would need to finish high school before he could go to college and there was no high school within 100 miles that would take him. Negro schools in Illinois had four-year programs but Samuel had no way to get there and no way to live if he made the trip.

Patricia prayed that some way would be found to help Samuel. Samuel was a good boy. He was a fine young man, actually. Truth be told, he was only a few years younger than she. As Patricia prayed that night, she felt a strange peace about it, about everything in her life. She felt that God was in charge. She felt her life and Samuel's life were both in good hands.

Chapter 5

"The mediocre teacher tells. The good teacher explains. The superior teacher demonstrates. The great teacher inspires."

—William Arthur Ward

The halls of the school were empty and quiet. It was a nice day to paint a few rooms. The entire project would probably take him all summer to finish. He hoped he would get some help and maybe finish early. If possible, it would be nice to take a few days and go fishing before the fall term began.

Stepping down from the ladder, he took an old rag and wrapped his paintbrush so it wouldn't dry out. Reaching into a brown sack, Robert took out a baloney and cheese sandwich wrapped in wax paper and a napkin. His wife, Harry Lee had packed the sack and added some cookies, too. And a coke. He sat down on the steps at the entrance to the school to enjoy a restful moment. There was always a breeze there.

It was now late spring of 1938. Robert E. Stevenson had been principal/teacher at the Adairville school since 1937. Robert was a tall, lanky man. His long legs carried him with a certain confidence. It was not intentional. It was simply a knowing way that was obvious to the observer.

There was little tax money to keep the school in good repair, or even fair condition. In those days, the principal worked all summer doing whatever jobs needed to be done. Stevenson got no extra pay for his work, plus he had to buy many of the supplies. These supplies were in addition to his typewriter and all of his office supplies. He also taught four classes and

20

often served as janitor, bus driver and secretary. It was still hard times, but Stevenson was happy to have a job.

Robert E. Stevenson grew up on a farm in Adair County, Kentucky. He graduated high school and junior college from Lindsey Wilson Academy and Lindsey Wilson Junior College in Columbia, Kentucky. After graduation from Lindsey Wilson, Stevenson took classes at Western Kentucky Teacher's College in Bowling Green and also taught school. In those days, teachers could teach with a two-year degree.

Stevenson went on to graduate school in Bowling Green. He also studied at Peabody in Nashville, Tennessee.

Robert enjoyed teaching. He had come to Adairville after finishing his graduate work. Robert was hired initially as a teacher, basketball and baseball coach and assistant principal. In a couple of years, he was named Principal.

And so it was on that late spring day that Mr. Stevenson, as he was and would always be called, sat down on the front steps of the school to have his lunch. Harry Lee knew how to make a fine sandwich. Yes, his wife's name was Harry Lee. Her parents were positive she was going to be a boy. They picked out a good name and had no desire to change a good name due to a gender issue.

So, Mr. Robert Stevenson or Mr. R. E. Stevenson, if you will, ate his sandwich and took long draws on his Coca Cola. He looked out towards U. S. Highway 431 and took note of the occasional car or truck that passed by.

A dusty, white Chevy pickup pulled off the highway and made its way up to the front steps of the school where Stevenson was sitting. It was James Bell. James was a local farmer. He had a small farm by the standards of the area but he was well respected. James had a two-year degree from Jefferson-State Junior College in Birmingham, Alabama. He had come back to Logan County after some time in the Army and after getting his degree. His father had gotten a bit feeble, so James worked the 200 acres of family land.

James exited his truck, tucked his shirt into his overalls, and walked up to Stevenson. "How you doin', Mr. Stevenson?" James offered.

"Extremely well, James, thanks for asking. What can I do for you?" Stevenson asked.

James leaned against a ladder, "Well I'll tell ya and I hope I'm not bothering your lunch and all. But the preacher at the colored church over my way came walking right up to me at the M. J. Grocery and Hardware store the other day. Aunt Annie had just handed me an RC and I was about to take a swig when all of a sudden he was right there in front of me.

I was surprised to see him come walking up like that and all. I had been tryin' to drive a key out of an old crank shaft and he came right up like he was somebody. I looked at Uncle Dick. You know him. Well, he looked as surprised as anybody."

"This preacher, he told me about a colored boy over at the Schochoh Negro School. He says this colored boy is mighty smart. His teachers say he's smarter than any boy they ever taught over there. They say he needs more schoolin' than he can get round here. Everybody knows he can't come to this school, him being a nigger and all. Well, they wondered if there was some place else he might go and how would he go 'bout it and all. He asked me if I had any idey. I said I didn't know of such things but I told him I would try to talk to you on my next trip to town."

Robert Stevenson looked at James. Politics is as much a part of education as teaching. A principal depends on the community to get the tools to teach. If a principal wants to stay around, he has to have some skills common to elected officials.

Stevenson took a rag out of his back pocket and wiped his brow. That bought him a moment to collect his thoughts and choose his words. "What would you like for me to do, James? You must have been thinking about this. The colored folks around there must have respect for you and think of you as some kind of leader. They came to you after all."

Stevenson had played it well. He needed more information before giving a position. It was best to punt back to James and see where he was on the issue and find who else he had talked to.

James had certainly been thinking about it. He had already told the story to his neighbors. There hadn't been any trouble with the niggers in a long time. Nobody wanted a mess like they had over in Olmstead years ago. He hadn't told Stevenson that the preacher let it be known real clear that the whole black community wanted this black boy to go to college.

James looked at Stevenson. He spat into the grass. "First of all, I'm not any leader of the colored so don't start that talk. I did speak to a few members at lodge and we think it is a good idea if we make an effort to help this boy. We aren't gonna be runnin' 'round doing charity work all day for a bunch of niggers but if this boy has real talent and the whole colored community is behind him, reckon we will do what we can."

Stevenson saw the situation immediately. The big farmers were always nervous about a black revolt. The farmers would win the war but the battles could cost them a crop. They had to keep the Negro help happy enough to stay and work, without the farmers giving up too much power.

I was hard to believe that the grandparents of many of the Negroes who worked the fields of South Logan were slaves on the same land their grandchildren now worked. The time of slavery was not so far past that it was not forgotten. First hand stories were recalled and retold to the next generation. The fires of slavery were gone but the smell of the smoke still remained.

"Does he play ball?" Stevenson asked. Everyone knew that some schools might forget a student was black if he could shoot balls through the hoop like nobody's business.

"I don't know 'bout that. I don't think he is a star or anything. I reckon, from what I'm told, that he just picks up things real quick, like in school," James replied.

Mr. Stevenson wished this had happened a couple of years down the road, after he had more experience and more tenure with the superintendent and the board. But, this was the job and this is what he had signed up for. No one said it would always be easy.

Truth be told, Mr. Stevenson had often thought about segregation and the problems it created. There must have be over a dozen one or two-room black schools around the county. He believed that everyone deserved an education. He knew these small schools did not provide the same level of education required under the "Separate but Equal" Supreme Court Ruling. There were many challenges in education. He was only one man. He had other fish to fry and had not spent any effort on the problem. It wasn't one of his assigned tasks at that moment

"Tell you what," Stevenson said after taking a sip of his Coke. "What say you bring this boy by here sometime? I'm here every day. Have his teachers make up a transcript of his grades. I'll think about what might be done after I have met the boy."

James wished Mr. Stevenson would just take care of this and get him out of the middle. His wife told him this was goin' to be a mess. She told him he was gonna get his butt in a sling. This was probably the best he could expect, though.

James agreed to the plan and was saying his farewell to Mr. Stevenson as he walked in the direction of his truck. "I'll be coming back by with the boy as soon as it can all be arranged," James said a little louder now. "Say hello to the Missus"

Stevenson nodded and then turned to pick up the old rag that covered his paintbrush. It was good to simply paint and think.

Chapter 6

"The classy gangster is a Hollywood invention."

—Orson Wells

By 1940, vice was alive and well in many parts of the United States. It was also creative.

The newly elected Republican attorney general of California sat down in the big, leather chair behind his new desk in his new office in Sacramento.

No one could have expected that this unknown California politician would someday change Logan County and the entire nation. He would also one day be, both one of the best loved, and, most hated men in America.

He was about to make a name for himself in California. Later, he would hold the highest seat on the highest court in the nation.

To avoid federal and state law enforcement, gambling ships sailed outside the three-mile boundary, jurisdiction, and territory of California. After leaving port, these beautiful stately vessels were safe from all probing eyes and ears. The ship's activity menu offered gambling, plenty of good liquor, and equal portion of bad women. Yes, sir, that was the recipe of a successful ship on the high seas in those days. Sail just a few short miles off the coast of California and the wolves could eat all the sheep they could load onto the boat. The best part was that the sheep loved it. They came back again and again. Captain Levine was a seasoned seafarer and he knew the secrets of the sea. He had risen up through the ranks on the merchant ships. This was a lucky job compared to his old mates who were riding death barges and being sunk by the U-boats of Germany.

No, Captain Levine worked for men with names not spoken. He took a small, approved cut from a large pot. The liquor profits were small. Liquor was the grease that made the gambling and prostitution highly profitable. Hell, sometimes they gave the liquor away. It didn't really matter because nobody was keeping books. He would start the "cruise" with a box of money and return to shore with several boxes of money. There was some little guy in a small stateroom who counted the cash and paid the dealers, cooks and waiters. He may have had some idea about the profits, but if so, he wasn't telling anyone.

Captain Levine ran the overall prostitution operation, personally. He had a team of heavies who protected the women and the ship from trouble. The money for the cheap hookers was handled by the muscle. The high-end whores were occasionally independent contractors who managed their own financial "affairs." Sometimes the services were paid well in advance.

Three times a week, the pigeons walked up the ladders and onto the ship. Beautiful women and handsome men greeted them with wine and song. Some guests were there as a reward for a favor. Those guests never lost money. They were taken to special staterooms and were given what later became known as the VIP treatment. The bigger the favor, the better the reward.

Most of the guests were regular gamblers. They lost money 90 percent of the time. They liked to gamble and sleep with whores, or they were addicted to gambling and whores. Either way, there were plenty of "made guys" around to loan and collect. Some of Levine's best whores were the ex-wives, girlfriends, and even mothers of bad gamblers. Debts were always collected, one way or another.

It was a good life for the Captain. It was becoming difficult to find places to hide all his money. Hard to remember why he drank so much or how he had lost his family or never saw his daughter anymore. What the hell, he had plenty of whiskey and plenty of whores and plenty of time to sample the merchandise.

Captain Levine looked out across the sea as his ship plowed the gentle waves off Catalina Island. He had no idea that his ship's days were numbered. No, the Nazi U-Boats were not a threat. A new California Attorney General had recently won his election and taken office. This new Law Officer had his sights on the corruption that was centered in the Mafia's *rum/gambling ships* that operated offshore.

California's new Attorney General had ambition. He was a smart up-and-comer with his sights far beyond his current position. He would make gambling ships unprofitable by extending the state boundaries outward to twelve miles. He could not stop crime but he was able to make it so unprofitable that it died on the vine.

Attorney General, Earl Warren, would also serve three terms as Republican Governor of California. Later, he would be nominated Chief Justice of the United States Supreme Court.

Warren's liberal court would reshape America all the way down to its roots. All the way to places like Logan County, Kentucky.

Chapter 7

"Miracles, in the sense of phenomena we cannot explain, surround us on every hand;
life itself is the miracle of miracles."

—George Bernard Shaw

Sometimes there is no other explanation than to say that the hand of God must have been in a project. The week after Stevenson's encounter with James Bell, he received a letter forwarded from Logan County Superintendent of Schools, Moss Walton.

In his letter, Dr. Jackson Washington at Tennessee State College in Nashville had written to all the area superintendents. Tennessee State College was one of the two Negro colleges in Nashville. In the letter, Dr. Washington was inquiring if Mr. Walton had knowledge of any Negro students who might qualify for a work/scholastic scholarship. The goal of the program was to offer continuing education for colored students in and around the greater Nashville area.

The serendipitous nature of the letter was not lost on Mr. Stevenson. Here may have been the opportunity that everyone was praying for, but Stevenson was not sure yet. He had not met the Negro student. It would not be kind to give the boy hope if he had no possibility of meeting the qualifications. No, he would hold this letter in his pocket until he had more information. The first thing to do was to write Dr. Washington and find out the requirements for the scholarships. That would take a couple of weeks. In the meantime, Stevenson would give James Bell a ring and push him to get the boy with his transcript over for a look see.

It took three days to get James Bell on the phone. Farmers are busy during the day and there are very few hours spent near a phone in the evening. Finally, a connection was made. Bell answered the phone.

"Mr. Bell? Robert Stevenson here." …

"Yes, I'm fine. Thank you. And you?" …

"Good, good. Say, about that young Negro boy we talked about the other day, when could you get him by my office? I would like to talk to him and see his records. I would like to meet his teacher, too" …

"Yes, yes, go ahead and talk to that preacher and let me know when you find out something. I'm working on projects at the school every day, so I will be there when you get it all together." …

"Very well, then." …

"You're welcome. Have a good evening." …

"Goodbye."

*

Reverend Brown could hardly hold his excitement until Sunday. Mr. Bell told him that he had used all his influence and persuasive skills to get Samuel an interview with Mr. Stevenson. He told him he had pushed hard and it was now up to Samuel. He made no promises but said he would drive Samuel to the meeting. He said to get that school teacher to come with him and to be ready early Tuesday morning because he didn't have all day to fool with Negroes.

Sunday morning at church, Brown caught Samuel and Patricia first thing and told them about the meeting planned for Tuesday morning. Patricia assured him she would have all of his records ready to show Mr. Stevenson. Patricia and Samuel wanted to know the point of the meeting but Brown had nothing more to tell them. Mr. Bell only told Reverend Brown that Stevenson wanted to meet the boy. That was all that Mr. Bell said. Still, that was somethin' and, "somethin' is better than nothin'," they thought.

Early Tuesday morning, Reverend Brown, Patricia Clay, Samuel Wells, and James Bell all met up at the M. J. Grocery and Hardware Store in Schochoh. Patricia and Samuel were dressed in their best Sunday clothes. Everybody had scrubbed up real clean the night before. Samuel noticed that Patricia smelled like spring flowers.

Bell's pickup pulled up to the store. Patricia and Samuel climbed onto a bale of hay in the back of the truck and off they went to Adairville for their meeting with Robert Stevenson.

Mr. Stevenson had called James Bell on the previous Friday. He had agreed to meet on Tuesday morning, first thing. Dr. Washington had been prompt in his response to Mr. Stevenson's letter regarding Samuel. The procedure would be very simple. There would be an entrance exam, and if Samuel could pass and was physically able to take classes, he could be admitted. Mr. Stevenson could administer and grade the exam.

The only other formality was that Samuel's parents would have to approve because he was still underage.

*

Robert Stevenson was seated in his office. It was already a warm day. He heard the clanking sound as the heavy main school doors opened and closed. He listened to the footsteps in the hall as Samuel, Patricia and James made their way to his office door. He listened to the echo of voices, not unlike any school day. No one was there to see the Negroes enter the school. The sight would have certainly started some tongues to wagging.

Mr. Stevenson rose to greet his visitors. His first impressions were good. Everyone looked neat and clean. Samuel had a bright smile but did not look Mr. Stevenson directly in the eye.

Robert Stevenson glanced the young lad over as he ushered them in. He smiled to himself as he noticed Samuel's shoes were so worn they were almost sandals. Samuel had more foot sticking out than was confined inside his old, shoes.

The shoes didn't matter to Mr. Stevenson. It was a depression after all. What made Robert Stevenson sad was that these were the best clothes that Samuel had to wear.

"Please, everyone, come in and sit down. Do we need any extra chairs?" …"Good, good. Have a seat. It is so nice to finally meet everyone."

Stevenson offered his hand to Samuel, Patricia, and to James.

"Thank you for coming in this morning," Mr. Stevenson smiled wanting to make them all feel more comfortable.

The tone in Stevenson's voice then changed indicating a shift in purpose. "Mr. Bell, here, has been telling me about you, Samuel. I am

30

Robert Stevenson, Principal of Adairville High School. Are you Patricia Clay?" he inquired turning toward Patricia. ...

"Yes, I have heard about your skills as a teacher at Schochoh School. Your reputation precedes you. It is nice to finally meet you. Do you have Samuel's records so I can take a quick look?"

"Good. Thank you for bringing this. Please give me a moment to study these records."

Stevenson sat quietly and looked over Samuel's grades and his classes. His grades were excellent. His classes were fine as far as they went. He expected that Samuel was weak in some areas and thought he was equal to a high school freshman, at best. He would be challenged to pass an entrance exam, but he looked to be qualified to give it a shot. At worst, an effort had been made.

Mr. Stevenson then told the group about the letter and the scholarships. He asked if Samuel would be interested in taking the test. He warned him that it would be a challenge and to do his best but not to be disappointed if he failed. He further told them that he would write back to Dr. Washington and order the exam if everyone was in agreement.

"Spend the next couple of weeks in review of your math and language skills. Do well in those areas and you may make the cut," Stevenson advised.

Mr. Stevenson gave Samuel some general advice on how to prepare and take an exam. This was followed by some casual conversation about the scholarship. "Be sure to talk to your parents too," Stevenson advised. "They may not favor you going off to Nashville."

Everyone in the room finally rose. Robert escorted his guests to the front door and told them he would call James when he had received the exam and then they would set a date for Samuel to sit for it.

All was quiet until the truck started down the road. Patricia turned and looked at Samuel. His eyes were as big as silver dollars. He sported a grin from ear to ear. Both erupted in a squeal that could have been heard in Russellville. Each grabbed for the other and Samuel felt Patricia's tears of joy as her cheek touched his face.

*

The sound of gospel soul rocked the walls as voices joined in praise of the God that was their only salvation and hope. The old piano lacked some tuning but the spirit was still in it. There were no song books. Everybody knew the words. One song led into another. Many eyes were closed. Faces looked upward through the roof towards Heaven and whispered words that only God could understand. Others held up their arms and swayed in rhythm to the music, or possibly to their own private spiritual harmony.

There was both joy and tears all mixed together throughout every pew of the New Pilgrim Baptist Church that Sunday morning.

New Pilgrim was an old rock-faced church that sat back in a grove of walnut trees. It was one of the oldest African American churches in the state of Kentucky. It was one of a half-dozen of the oldest African American churches west of the Alleghenies. The oral history of the church claims that it was established shortly after the "Second Great Awakening." The epicenter of the Second Great Awakening, that occurred around 1800, was just down the road at the Red River Meeting House. Thousands of souls were added to the great book in Heaven. Preachers preached the gospel in a revival that lasted for several years. They preached to masters and slaves alike. Missionaries from the revival spread out across America.

Both white and Negro churches sprang up in the new West of a young America. New Pilgrim was one of the first. Samuel was baptized in that church. Both of his parents, Levi and Ruth Ann, were baptized in that church. Reverend Brown had been the pastor for over 30 years. The cemetery next to the church was a place of rest, first for slaves and now for the descendants of slaves. The oldest tombstone is dated 1808.

It was in the church and from his family that Samuel gathered his strength. Later that day, Reverend Brown would be driving him to Nashville to start his new life.

In an odd but welcome quirk of fate, a local funeral home had loaned Reverend Brown a hearse for the trip to Nashville. It had plenty of room and a "good engine." Good enough to make it to Nashville, Tennessee and back. There were not many automobiles in the hands of Negroes. Rarer still were cars and trucks in good enough condition and up to a trip that far. It was also not safe for Negroes to be out on the highway after dark. It was even more risky if their car broke down and they were stranded on the side of the road.

Reverend Brown had worked as a farmhand before getting a job at the sawmill. He had learned to read and figure pretty good, so he could measure lumber. He also delivered lumber in a truck owned by Mr. Simpson, who owned the sawmill. It was better work than the farm 'cuz it paid regular and it was mostly inside labor.

Reverend Brown never had to work on weekends after Saturday noon. That gave him time to pastor his small flock, visit the sick and such. The little bit of pay he received as pastor was mostly from the gardens of his parishioners.

Everybody brought a dish or two for a grand feast on the church grounds. There were tobacco wagons pulled up under the shade of big maple and walnut trees near the church. Sheets and tablecloths covered the wooden decks of the wagons. Atop the cover was all manner of vegetables, biscuits, cornbread, chicken, and even some ham. Although no white folks attended, several had contributed. All the ham and most of the chicken. The wagons, too. All were sent with best wishes for Samuel. The whole community was happy for him.

The service had gone a little longer than usual. The church had pooled its pennies and bought Samuel a few items for his new life. They presented him with a toothbrush, toothpaste, soap, and a towel and washcloth and one very special gift. Some white woman had donated an old suitcase. Patricia Clay put the church gifts in the suitcase and presented it to him.

After the invitation hymn at the end of the service, Reverend Brown asked everyone to be seated and told Samuel to come to the front. Patricia then also came forward and told the story of Samuel in the Bible and how their Samuel would also do great things. She handed him the suitcase and had a good cry with many others seated in the church that Sunday morning.

Then, they all moved out into the churchyard. A few of the women had already started uncovering food on the wagon. There were pats on the back for the proud parents, Levi and Ruth Ann. Congratulations and best wishes flowed like the spring water they drank to wash down the salty ham.

It was a bright, warm, sunny August day. Tomorrow, these same wagons would be loaded with tobacco and headed for the tobacco barns. Tomorrow, most of the men and boys eating this good food would be in the fields. For the first time in his young life, or for as long as he could remember, Samuel would not be in the tobacco patch with them.

*

A few weeks earlier, R. E. Stevenson had graded Samuel's exam.

As he sat and carefully checked the answers, Mr. Stevenson could hardly believe what he was seeing. This young black boy had an excellent grasp of high school math and English. He was weak in science, but that was expected. The Negro schools did not have the resources for science labs, and such. Still, his other skills were so strong that he had passed the exam. He had made it! According to Dr. Washington, he was exactly the kind of student they were looking for.

Mr. Stevenson called James immediately. Later that day, Mr. Stevenson could have sworn he heard a shout from over Schochoh way.

*

It was getting to be about 2 p.m. Reverend Brown wanted to be back before dark, if possible. He had a letter saying he had permission to be driving the hearse. It was signed by Mr. Wallace at the funeral home and the sheriff of Logan County. If he was stopped, it could still be trouble no matter what proof he was carrying. Reverend Brown knew it was just the way things were and a man has to go on and do what he needs to do... and pray.

Brown, Levi, Ruth Ann and Samuel piled into the hearse and rode back to the house. Samuel needed to pick up a few things and he wanted to say goodbye to his parents from home. He had no idea when he would be back. Although not far in terms of miles, he had no way to get home. It would be at least Christmas, and maybe longer, before he saw his family again.

Samuel loaded his meager belongings. There wasn't really much to pack. Samuel had only two changes of clothes and he was wearing one of them. Two of his gifts were another shirt and a pair of denim trousers. He had a couple of pairs of socks and underwear. He was really proud of a picture of his parents that his mother's Sunday School class had framed for him. Everything he owned fit easily into the suitcase.

Samuel paused and looked around the small room where he had slept his entire life. Walking through the small house, all the memories of his life flashed through his mind. A mix of sadness and the preamble to homesickness flooded him with emotion.

He picked up his pace and shot out the door onto the porch and then out into the front yard. Everyone was waiting together under the big maple tree.

Samuel pushed down the tears he felt. He didn't want anyone to see them. Pulling himself together, he shook the hand of his father and kissed his mother.

Ruth Ann didn't even try to hide it. She shed more than a few tears of both joy and sadness. He was her only child. The only child that God had given her. She was happy that he had an opportunity in life but sad that her boy was leaving home so young.

As the hearse pulled out onto the road, Samuel looked back to see both his parents still waving from the front porch. Samuel was so scared, his stomach churned, but he wasn't going to let it show. His eyes burned. He hid it all as best he could.

He looked down at his new shoes, the church's special gift. He was wearing socks for the first time in his life, too. He could almost see his face in the shine someone had put on them. Members of the church had pooled their money and bought him his first pair of new boots. He knew they had sacrificed for him and he hoped he would not disappoint them. He couldn't go back home a failure. He just couldn't. He raised his head up and stared straight ahead. The white line in the road zipped by. This was the first mile down the road that held his future.

In less than ten minutes, they crossed the state line into Tennessee. Reverend Brown asked Samuel if he had ever been to Nashville before.

"No sir, Reverend Brown, this would be my first trip to Tennessee. Truth be told, sir, this is my first trip out of Logan County."

Chapter 8

"There is no secret to success. It is the result of preparation, hard work, and learning from failure."

—Colin Powell

Samuel settled into his schedule. He had classes from 7:00 a.m. until noon every day. By 1:00 p.m., he needed to eat a bite of lunch, change clothes, and run or hitch a ride over to the railroad stockyards.

For the next six hours, Samuel pushed, poked, pulled, directed, stirred and counted livestock. Mostly cows and pigs. The operation ran 24 hours a day, 7 days a week. Trucks rolled into the Nashville yard and loaded or unloaded stock. Livestock was shipped up north or out west to big feeder lots. The trucks and the trains rolled in all day and night.

Local cattle and dairy farmers delivered livestock for sale or picked up cattle they had purchased. Buyers also shipped all over the world. Registered cattle were a valuable commodity to the development of quality herds and dairy operations.

The sales would start early and run until all the stock was sold. On weekdays, most sales were finished by noon. On Saturdays, the sales concluded around 3:00 p.m.

The work was hard but not as hard as the work Samuel was used to doing. He had the youth and the stamina to make it. His job was to move the livestock from one pen to another as required. It was a matter of opening and closing gates and prodding the animals with his cane. Hot, cold, rain or shine, there were always animals to move. Close to quitting time, he would sometimes slow down because he was getting hungry.

There wasn't much way to eat at the yard and he seldom had time to bring anything. The "eatin' places" were all white owned. There were more Negroes working the yard than white folks but nobody wanted to feed them. Samuel didn't think anything much about it though. That was just the way it was.

After he got back to his room, Mrs. Holmes always had him a good supper. He rented the room for $10 a month. The rent included a breakfast and a supper, most days. Mr. and Mrs. Holmes were a different kind of folks than he had ever known, except maybe for Miss Clay. They read newspapers, listened to the radio and talked about a whole range of interesting things. Both were teachers at the school where Samuel was taking classes.

Tennessee State Technical College was an all-Negro school. Samuel was taking additional basic classes because he was behind many students due to his lack of a high school diploma. He was also one of the youngest boys in school. Mrs. Holmes tutored him a little but he hated to ask. He continued to do well in math, English, writing and spelling but he struggled to catch up in the sciences.

All of his teachers were nice enough and they encouraged him. He studied every night until he fell asleep. Between work, study, and school, Samuel had no time for a social life or for anything else for that matter.

Some days, nights especially, Samuel would get so lonesome he wanted to cry. Only his stubborn determination kept him from quitting and going home. He could not face the failure of walking back into that tobacco patch. He could not stand the thought of letting his friends and family down. Samuel knew an education was his only hope of a better life.

Samuel was only 45 miles from his Kentucky home, but he could not find a way back for a visit and his family could never come to Nashville. It might as well have been a thousand miles. There was simply no means for him or his family to travel. Partly because they were poor and partly because it was dangerous for Negroes to move about. He wrote a letter every week telling everything he was doing and asking about them and his friends. Levi and Ruth were not very good at writing letters, but they got together with Rev. Brown and others to get him a couple of letters a month, most times. Miss Clay also wrote to him and helped Ruth if she asked.

Life was especially difficult during the holidays. Samuel thought about taking a bus home for Christmas but he had only two days off from work plus he had no way to get to the bus station downtown. He was forced to stay in Nashville and celebrate the holidays with Mr. and Mrs. Holmes.

Samuel grew in knowledge and experience during the next couple of years. His excellent grasp of math and later the sciences, led him into an interest in engineering. Teachers believed he had real potential.

Samuel earned his high school diploma. He also completed a number of college level courses in math, engineering, and physics equaling roughly two years of college credits. In total, he would have qualified as a college junior.

Then, on December 7, 1941, the world changed. It was the day the Japanese bombed the American naval base at Pearl Harbor, Hawaii.

The effect was immediate. Samuel was only 17 on the day of the attack. He stayed in school and continued his studies until he turned 18 in January of 1942. The Selective Service Act of 1940 changed the law and brought Negroes into the draft. Samuel knew his day had arrived. He couldn't swim so he joined the Army.

Chapter 9

"I hate war as only a soldier who has lived it can, only as one who has seen its brutality, the futility of its stupidity."

—General Dwight D. Eisenhower

Frank L. Weaver hopped off the LST as it came to a stop at the small dock. He had hitched a ride over from Manus Island to the even more remote Island of Ponam.

Ponam was serving as a transport operation station for LSTs or Higgins Boats. These small vessels transported troops and supplies ship to ship, from island to island and from ships to islands.

Frank had heard that his cousin, Thurman, had, at one time, been on the island and might still be there. It was worth a trip to see if he could be found or was still alive.

Frank was serving with the 1st Cavalry Division. His unit had been fighting in what became known as the Admiralty Campaign. He had been in a series of battles in the South Pacific around and near New Guinea. The campaign was drawing down and the troops were getting a well-deserved rest before moving on to the next island battle.

He had bought and saved three cartons of Lucky Strike cigarettes. He used the first carton to buy his way over to Ponam. One carton would be a gift to Thurman and he would need the third carton to get back to Manus Island.

There was a lull in the fighting. The war wasn't over but the focus, at the moment, was with the Navy and the Australian troops. Frank had a four-day pass and he was using it to find his cousin, Thurman.

It was Frank who auditioned with Thurman at the Grand Ole Opry not long before the Pearl Harbor attack. They were cousins who had grown up together back in Allen County, Kentucky. Thurman had sent a letter to his mother and mentioned the island where he was stationed. The information was old news but it was worth a try.

Sergeant Frank Weaver threw his gear out of the small skiff and made his way up the dock. A Chief was working with a crew to salvage a boat engine at the end of the ramp. Frank walked up to the Chief and asked if he could have a word with him. Frank was a First Sergeant in the Marine Corps. He was equal rank with the Chief but this was not his turf.

The Chief wondered when the damn marines had landed on his beach. He looked the marine up and down and stood staring at him without comment or answer to Frank's question.

"I am Sergeant Frank Weaver. I hitched a ride over here from Manus Island to see if I can find my cousin, Thurman Weaver. He was here a couple of months ago and I hope he is still around somewhere."

"Yeah?" the Chief grunted. "Where you from, Sergeant?"

"Allen County, Kentucky, Chief," Frank answered.

Chief knew exactly who the sailor was that Frank was looking for. It was a small island but it paid to play it safe. He figured this fella was square, so he decided to help him out.

"We got a Charles Weaver. I think he is from Kentucky or Tennessee or someplace down south. Follow this path and you should run into a bunch of tents. He will be around there nearby."

Frank threw his bag over his shoulder and started up the path. All these islands were the same. They were all thick with vegetation, hot, humid with lots of insects and surrounded by water.

Frank came to a clearing occupied by six tents. It looked to be five sleeping tents and one cooking and eating tent. There were a couple of men playing cards under the eating tent. Frank waved and answered the question on the lips of both the sailors. "I'm looking for C. T. Weaver. Anybody seen 'im?"

Pointing to an even smaller trail, one of the sailors shouted back at Frank, "Follow that path down toward the windward beach. He was down that way a short time ago."

The reality finally started to hit Frank. Thurman was on this island! Excitement built as small patches of a white sand came into view through the thick brush.

Frank finally reached the tree line. He stepped out into the bright sun. There were several men on the beach but none of them was Thurman. There was one man up in a coconut tree. He didn't look like Thurman, either.

Frank walked farther out onto the beach. The sailors all stared at him. He surveyed each face. None was his cousin Thurman. Finally, he moved towards the coconut tree so he could get a better view. Standing directly below, Frank looked up the tree. The man he saw had a faint resemblance to an emaciated version of his cousin, Thurman.

"Hello up there!" Frank shouted. The man in the tree looked down. He saw the top of the head of man in a marine uniform. "Thurman, it's Frank. Frank L. Weaver. Is that you up there, Thurman?"

Thurman shinnied down the tree in a flash. His bare feet hit the sand with a thump as he leaped off the trunk of the tree. There were a few coconuts scattered around the base of the tree that Thurman had thrown down before Frank had walked up.

At last they faced each other. Frank could not believe what he saw. Thurman left Kentucky big and strong. The man he saw now looked to be half starved. His face was hollow. His rib bones stuck out too far. While Frank was dressed in his regular uniform, Thurman wore nothing but a pair of dirty shorts with a web belt. They had once been navy pants but had been cut and hemmed. There was a knife hanging from the belt.

As was the custom of all Weaver men, they shook hands. Men of this clan did not hug or show emotion, but their eyes clearly betrayed the glee they felt in seeing each other.

Charles Thurman Weaver had not seen a familiar face in almost two years. He had been stationed on that island for four months as a Petty Officer Second Class. His main duty was to load, pilot and unload his LTV. He usually carried supplies but would often transport troops from island to island. They hadn't been doing much lately except maintenance

Thurman was first to speak, but his words came out in a spray of unconnected thoughts. Questions really. "What, how, when, did, where?" he stuttered.

41

"Aunt Lois told Mother that you were here. Mom wrote me, so I took a chance that you might still be somewhere in the area. I had a four-day pass. I heard there were women over here," Frank laughed.

"There are women on the island but you wouldn't like them. They don't wear shirts!" Thurman laughed back.

Thurman gathered up an arm load of the fallen fruit and walked with Frank up the trail towards camp. He turned with a grin, "I hope you like coconut milk. I'm afraid that is all I can offer you. We haven't been resupplied in a couple of months. We move supplies but we don't get supplies, except for what we steal." Thurman went into a nearby tent and came out with a hand drill in a box of other tools. "There's a bunch of ways to do this but we find this way is the fastest. Less waste too," Thurman said. Frank watched in amusement as his cousin sat on the ground and put the coconut between his bare feet. He first took a hammer and punch. He punched the nut so the bit would bite, then began drilling a hole. In no time, coconut milk was served!

Thurman picked up the fruit and handed it to Frank. "Aren't you gonna join me?" Frank inquired.

"Nah, you go ahead," Thurman told him. "I can't have more than a couple of those things a day. They give me the runs somethin' awful if I eat too many."

Frank had faced the horrors of combat but he had never known of any U. S. marine, soldier, airman or sailor who wasn't fed.

"So let me get this straight," Frank exclaimed. "The only food you get here is what you steal?"

Back in Kentucky, stealing food, stealing anything, would have been a foreign concept to Thurman. Now, he didn't feel anything about it. Now, it was an accepted method of survival.

"We had regular mess until about three months ago. As the battle moved, we were just forgotten, I reckon. We cut back to two meals a day for a while. Then, it was one meal until the food ran out. We catch some fish and we trade with the locals some."

Frank sat mostly dumbfounded as Thurman talked of life on the island.

"Everybody dreams of an island paradise. Trust me cousin, it's not what it's cracked up to be. But at least we aren't gettin' shot at!"

The two cousins laughed while they shared the memories and stories of their young days in Allen County. "Do you ever look up at the sky and wonder what life is like back home?" Thurman asked.

"Sure, I guess everyone does that at one time or another. I try not to dwell on it. It only makes me feel bad when I come back to earth," Frank answered.

Thurman stared off into nowhere in particular. "Do you reckon this war will ever end and life will go back to the way it was?"

"The world has changed. Nothing will ever be the same. Not the world and not us," Frank replied. "We are blessed to be alive! I will never understand why I have survived when so many good men have died. I thank Jesus every day but I still wonder 'cuz I know I ain't special."

Both men silently thought about that for a moment. Thurman and Frank had spent a lot of time on their knees in church before the war. Prayer was not a foreign concept to them. Faith brought strength during the long years of the Depression and it brought them strength and a bit of peace during war. After a long moment of silence, Thurman spoke first. "I reckon we will learn the answers one day but not in this life." Frank, and a few others who had gathered around, nodded their heads.

The visit brought a bit of Kentucky to the South Pacific. The other sailors on the island soon all came around and everyone met Frank. They heard the story of how he had hitched a ride to Ponam Island to find his cousin. Frank noticed the common signs of starvation, and even malaria, in the men he met there on the island. Just the same, it was a good moment in the midst of a horrible war.

Over the next couple of days, Frank learned how a small group of farm and city boys had put their skills together to survive. One of the men from Queens, N.Y. was the master thief. He had just lifted a case of beer that very morning. With luck, they might have fish and beer for dinner. If not, they would have beer.

*

Meanwhile, back in America, in an east Tennessee town not that far from Allen County, all the power that the Tennessee River could generate, was producing something that would end the war. Tragically, thousands more lives would be lost before the war was over.

Both Frank and Thurman would survive the war and return to Kentucky. They would never forget the hardships and the horrors they saw. But they would rarely ever talk about it.

It would be many years before Thurman Weaver wanted another coconut.

Chapter 10

"You cannot invade the United States. There would be a rifle behind every blade of grass."

—Admiral Yamamoto

Colonel Heath Twichell and his staff circled the potbellied stove trying to warm their hands and feet. They had been walking and/or driving for hours in the deep snow of the Alaskan wilderness.

"It's not bad enough that I'm stuck up here in Alaska during a real war. No, I'm stuck in Alaska, during a war, with a bunch of damn niggers," Captain Wilson said with all the frustration he harbored in his soul.

The Colonel didn't respond to the Captain. There had been enough bitching and he wasn't going to add to it. The Captain was a holdover from the previous command. A command that did not move the dirt or build the road they were sent there to build.

Colonel Twichell was the Executive Officer of the 35th Engineering Regiment. They were sent to this God-forbidden place to build what would become known as the ALCAN Highway, linking Alaska to the Pacific Northwest.

Alaska is the closest mainland American land mass to Japan. The brass in Washington feared that an invasion was possible and no road existed to supply a defense of U. S. territory. White troops in the Engineers and Quartermaster Corps. were first sent to Alaska to build the road. Soon, the white troops were joined by Negro troops.

Joined is not the perfect description. The races were not together. Fearing integration of the Negroes into the local population, the Negro

45

troops were isolated in even more remote areas and, in spite of the severe conditions, they were bunked in tents. The tents were kept far away from the white troops and far away from everything and everybody else in Alaska.

The white soldiers were barracked in regular Army housing. Their wooden walls kept out the Alaskan cold air much better than the canvas Army tents occupied by Negro troops.

Colonel Twichell already knew some of the problems. Supplies and heavy equipment had been taken from the Negro troops and given to the white troops. Half of his force was working with shovels and the other half with bulldozers. He needed both shovels and bulldozers working everywhere.

The other problem was that there was no chain of command in the Negro troops. The Army only allowed the commission of black doctors and black chaplains. White officers were not effective leaders of Negro troops. They all had the same attitude as Captain Wilson. Leadership of Negro troops was a dead-end command and all the white officers wanted to transfer out into the real fight with real (white) fighting men.

The first problem could be solved, if the second problem could be managed. Colonel Twichell's first job, therefore, was to find leadership and command potential inside the Negro troops. He would put his plan in motion that night. He would be waiting at the tent camp when they returned for mess at dusk.

*

Corporal Samuel Wells arrived in Dawson Creek, along with seven feet of snow and the coldest cold he had ever experienced. Cold was not a strong enough word to describe the frigid temperatures of Alaska. He was brought into the 95th Company for two reasons. It was mostly because he was a Negro, and Negro soldiers had very few options. A Negro with a rifle was an absurd notion to most whites in America and, therefore, also in the Army of America.

The second reason he was in Alaska was a big surprise to the NCO crowd back at Ft. Bragg. Samuel tested higher than all of the Negros and all of the white enlisted soldiers in the science of engineering and math. He was not the best in physical skills, but he didn't have to run fast to build a bridge. Samuel was fit enough alright and he had stamina.

Then, because of his obvious intelligence and education, Samuel was handed his corporal stripe and rushed through a surveying class in time to make the flight to the North. After a few months, he got another stripe.

His duties as a surveyor brought Samuel into direct contact with white civil engineers and white officers. His name was the first name Twichell heard when he asked for the names of Negro candidates for leadership. No one knew anything about Samuel's ability to lead. He was well educated and a good surveyor, however, and that was a cut above what they saw with most of the Negro troops.

*

The Colonel found Samuel at his desk and invited him outside to sit in the truck he had driven over to the Negro camp. The cab had some heat in it. There was no place else to meet in private.

Twichell got right to the point. "We have fallen behind on the road schedule. Tell me what you would need to give me five miles a day from the 95th."

Samuel was shy by nature, especially with white people. He had learned to speak up with his professors but they were all Negroes like himself. He was not sure how to respond. He was raised to speak "honest" so he went with his gut. Careful not to look directly at the white officer, Samuel began, "Colonel sir, I am nobody here. I am just a lowly sergeant in this big army, trying to survey out a road. But if you are sincere in wanting to know some answer, sir, I guess I can give you what I believe is right."

"Go ahead, Sergeant, I'm listening," Twichell responded, trying to encourage him.

Twichell was already impressed with the communication skills he was hearing from the sergeant. He hadn't expected this much from a southern Negro.

"Well sir, I'm just not accustomed to givin' advice to white folks, that's all," Samuel replied somewhat shyly.

The Colonel laughed and told Samuel, "You might be surprised to know that I am just as uncomfortable as you are. We're both in new territory here. What say we give this a try?"

47

"Okay sir. Well then, the thing is, we don't have any equipment heavy enough to move a shit bucket of snow. The mud doesn't thaw enough to shovel until midafternoon and it is starting to freeze again by late afternoon. We need bulldozers, backhoes, and dump trucks that will run in cold temperatures. We need tires that have some treads. Give us some good saws and gas and oil to run them. We need drag lines and chain to get the trees out of our way. We need what the other troops have. We get some equipment for a while but then they come take it away."

Samuel stopped and realized he had been talking too long and he was suddenly uncomfortable.

The Colonel listened in mild amusement. He had heard the talk since he was a young man. He had been told these Negroes were too stupid to do anything. Maybe some, but apparently not in every case, because this young man was smarter than the officers who led him. It was exactly as the Colonel has suspected. Any fool should have seen the facts.

"Anything else?" Twichell asked.

"Yes sir," Samuel spoke up. "We need some Quonset huts to house the men. We can set them up on sleds and move them as we move. An army cannot march on frozen feet and the wind blows right through these tents. We can't keep heat in or the cold out."

Twichell smiled to himself. "Did he say Quonset huts? What a great idea!"

"I'll see what I can do, Sergeant. Are you finished?"

"No sir." Samuel continued. "One last thing, sir."

Twichell thought he may have opened box he couldn't close. But he listened.

Samuel continued, "I'm sure you have heard of a half-track. I saw a picture of one once. A half-track could move men and equipment and supplies over snow or mud. If you get us one of those half-tracks and the other stuff we need, we will build your road in record time."

Fact was, Twichell didn't give a flying flick about changing the world. He didn't care about Negro rights or their progress in the U. S. Army. What he cared about was building this damn road and building it now. New challenges called for new direction.

"That was smart talking," the Colonel admitted. "I agree with about everything you said and here is what we are going to do. You are now Master Sergeant Samuel Wells. You will review the men under your command in the 95th and select a chain of command that will organize your unit at the most efficient level possible. I will expect your plan in 24 hours. I will speak with Captain Wilson tonight at officers' mess and give him the details of our conversation. I expect results and if you do not live up to my expectations, I will bust your ass back to corporal and find someone else to do the job. If you perform, as I have every confidence that you will perform, we will finish this road, save the freaking world and live to go do another job. Do you understand Master Sergeant Wells?"

Twichell was observing Wells out of the corner of his eye. If the sumbitch didn't jump out of the truck and run, it would be a victory. Wells didn't move.

Samuel had a frog in his throat the size of a baseball but he managed a croaking sound that was understood to be, "Yes, sir."

Opening the truck door, the Colonel said, "Follow me, Master Sergeant Wells."

A biting wind howled, freezing everything it touched. A large tent served as the mess and many of the 95th were still sitting at tables eating, drinking coffee, and trying to stay as warm as possible. Twichell walked into the tent followed by Samuel as "Ah-Ten-hut!" rang out calling everyone to stand at attention.

"At ease men. My name is Lieutenant Colonel Twichell. I am the executive officer for this unit. I regret that I have not spent more time out here with you. My duties keep me busy all up and down the line, but I have heard your concerns and tonight changes are being made. Effective immediately, your new NCO is Master Sergeant Wells here. You already know how smart he is. Master Sergeant Wells is going to help me reorganize this unit. Twichell stands up on a chair so everyone in the tent can see him clearly. Master Sergeant Wells tells me you are the best damn unit in the Engineers, is that right?" A roar goes up in the tent.

"Master Sergeant Wells tells me you can grind out five miles a day if you have some equipment."

Another roar louder than the first shakes the ground and the tent.

The Colonel got louder with every word. "Master Sergeant Wells tells me we need to get out of your freaking way and let you build a goddam road to Fairbanks freaking Alaska."

The roar was so loud, Samuel thought the tent might collapse.

That was the beginning of the remarkable story of the ALCAN Highway, later known as the Alaskan Highway.

The 95th did build five miles a day. They did so well that the project finished a year early. In fact, the 95th put down more road miles and did it faster than any outfit in Alaska. It proved the value of Negro troops and their ability to perform far above the previous expectations of the Army.

Negro contribution to the construction of the highway remained mostly secret until years after the war ended. The ALCAN Highway project is still not a well-known story.

Master Sergeant Wells' efforts did not go unnoticed. After the highway was completed, the Colonel sent most of the unit back to the states but kept Wells until he was reassigned to Europe. After the invasion at Normandy, they were reunited to rebuild the roads and bridges of France and Germany. Twichell and Wells would continue their working relationship until the end of the war.

First Sergeant Samuel Wells was discharged on May 1, 1945. On May 24, he stepped off a BG&H bus and saw his mother and father for the first time since he left home for school that hot summer day in August of 1938. He was finally back home in Logan County.

Chapter 11

"A ship in port is safe, but that's not what ships are built for."

—Grace Hopper

A line of six Higgins boats lumbered the short distance towards Manus Island. Petty Officer 2nd Class Charles T. Weaver had been stationed on Ponam Island for almost seven months. He thought his patch quilt unit had been forgotten.

Charles figured some officer somewhere must have discovered them. He didn't understand how that could have happened because he hadn't seen an officer in months. That was until two days prior. First, some lieutenant had come over to the island and was seen talking to the Chief. Next thing Charles knew; they were transferring to Manus Island. The Chief wouldn't say what was going on. He simply told them they were to motor over to the small Navy port on Manus Island and wait for orders.

Charles steered the small vessel into a high wave as the Higgins boat labored toward the docking facility in the bay. War is one paradox after another. On the island where he had been sitting for months, there was relative safety from the threat of war. They had been ignored, abandoned or possibly forgotten on a beautiful South Pacific beach inhabited by fishermen and topless native women. The downside was that most of the sailors were fighting malaria and he had been slowly starving to death.

That night, Charles would have his first decent meal in so long he couldn't remember. That night, he would have a shower, a real bed, and a pillow under his head. Unfortunately, soon he could be shipped out and become the target of some enemy shore battery.

First thing the next morning, the Chief came around with new orders. They were going to spend the day loading their Higgins boats onto the transport ships. After the boats were loaded, the men were to report to their designated ship. All hands were to be on board by 1800 hours.

The Chief had no idea where they were headed. The sailors knew that if the Chief did have an idea, he couldn't or wouldn't say. Odds were, an enemy island lay somewhere over the horizon waiting for their arrival.

Charles found himself on a Windsor attack-class troop and cargo transport ship, the *USS Griggs*. It was loaded with cargo, Charlie's Higgins boat and about 250 marines and sailors. Plus, a full crew and officers.

After mess, Charles settled into his bunk in the tight crowded quarters below deck. It was loud and cigarette smoke filled the hole. A few of the men were already seasick. Charles was never seasick. The smell of others in distress was enough to turn the stomach of most men, but Charles was somehow immune. He never, however, looked forward to the first few days at sea. Pulling the pillow over his head, Charles drifted off into a restless sleep. It had been a long war and he was tired.

Sometime after midnight, the ship slipped out to sea. Over the next thirty-six hours or so, a small convoy of troop ships and destroyer escorts motored northwest. Additional ships could be seen off to starboard and port with the same heading as the *USS Griggs*. The extra ships made the passengers feel safer. The *USS Griggs* was lightly armed with two five-inch guns and two 40mm anti-aircraft guns. The men spent their time up on deck, played cards, rolled dice or slept. At night, the men played cards, rolled dice or slept.

Charles woke up early just before sunrise the second morning at sea. By the time he slipped into his clothes and got topside, light filled the sky with a pink hue.

What Charles saw from where he stood on the main deck was a sea of ships. Every ship imaginable was anchored off the bow, the stern, to port and to starboard. To the west was what Charles learned was the Philippine Islands. The great Mayon Volcano rose from the fog inland on the distant shore. The day was August 6, 1945.

The armada was like nothing ever seen in the history of mankind. There looked to be a thousand ships. Cruisers, destroyers, battleships, all manner of transport and support vessels, and at least ten carriers off in the distance.

"What purpose under Heaven had brought such forces together in one place?" Charles wondered.

For two days the mass of ships sat rocking at anchor. The sound of metal creaking and popping could be heard as chains and ships fought for superiority against the wind and the sea. Additional ships continued to arrive while others circled.

Signal flags and lights flashed messages from ship to ship. The messages were steady but not constant. Rumors were rampant. There were enough sailors with signal corps experience to piece together a few details of the situation. The most consistent and logical rumor was that the invasion of Japan was being assembled. This was too big a force for a single island assault.

During the middle of the night after the second day at anchor, the ship's engines started, the anchor could be heard cranking and the ship was soon under-way.

Early the next morning, most of the ship's passengers were topside to the sight of an almost empty sea. The armada had scattered like the wind. The only obvious oddity was that the *USS Griggs* and her small convoy was not making much headway speed. She was capable of eighteen knots. Her constant speed was currently more in the range of eight knots. It was enough speed to keep course and make her steady in the water but it was clear that she was in no hurry.

There was no word from command. After another twelve hours, every experienced sailor knew that the ship was circling in the Philippine Sea. The men were curious why but no one was in a hurry to get into another battle, so they waited.

Charles wondered to himself why the mission was still a secret. They were miles from land. Who were they going to tell?!

On the seventh day, August 15, the captain came on the ship's loudspeaker. "Now hear this. Now hear this. The war with Japan is over. Japan has unconditionally surrendered to Allied Forces," he announced.

The apparent wind changed as the *USS Griggs* altered course and set sail for San Francisco, California by way of a refueling stop in Hawaii. Orders to the ship and to all on board were to "immediately stand down from all hostile action."

Later, it was learned that the armada was indeed amassed for an attack on the mainland of Japan. On the initial morning at anchor, the first atomic bomb was dropped on Hiroshima. It was decided to postpone the invasion due to the success of the bomb. The armada was dispersed but ordered to stay in the South China Sea awaiting orders to reassemble if necessary for an invasion.

After three days, Japan had not agreed to an unconditional surrender, so the second bomb was dropped on Nagasaki, and then Russia declared war on Japan. A third atomic bomb was in preparation for delivery but was never deployed.

Upon hearing the news that the war had ended, some of the men on the ship cheered. Some cried and a few simply stood or sat in silence.

Charles T. Weaver's first thought was to pray. He was thankful to God and the only hope he ever had for survival. His second thought was of family and home.

Suddenly his knees felt week and he needed to sit down. If there was a lump in his throat, Charles never showed it. He sat and looked across the vast Pacific Ocean towards the east and the shores of California.

Chapter 12

"Never doubt that a small group of thoughtful committed citizens can change the world. Indeed, it is the only thing that ever has."

—Margaret Mead

Samuel Wells and Charles Weaver had been very small cogs in a vast and great wheel. During the final year of the war, the military joined with the political and industrial giants to map the future of America.

On one afternoon in Detroit, Henry Ford sat listening to a presentation by Colonel Alonzo "Duck" Drake. Colonel Drake was a wiry career officer who was narrowly five feet tall even wearing his cover. Small, yet strong, he qualified to fly in the first World War with the Army Air Corps. He was smart, ambitious and politically savvy. He had moved up the ranks quickly.

Ford had his key people in the room and Colonel Drake had his staff there, also. The support staffs on both sides of the room sat, watched, and listened to the only two men in the room who mattered.

The Colonel's job in the war had been to bring together the needs of the military with the resources of American industry. The two men had worked together since just after Pearl Harbor. The Army Air Corps had taken all of Ford's production capacity not already taken by the ground war. Ford still manufactured a few civilian trucks but nobody bought cars during the war. What good was a car without tires and it took a lot of coupons to buy a single tire. Forget getting four tires.

The Russians and western Allied forces were moving towards Berlin. The end of the war in Europe would come soon. The war in the Pacific was another matter, but Drake was all Air Corps and the Air Corps was all about Europe.

Ford listened while Colonel Drake made his pitch. He asked a few questions and acted concerned here and there. The fact was, Ford had made good money in the war business. He had converted his plants, retooled and produced anything and everything the military wanted. Most of his younger employees were drafted or had joined after Pearl Harbor was bombed. His manufacturing plants were now mostly staffed with women and older men.

If he played his cards just right, Washington would pay to put his automotive and truck manufacturing business back into production and back into business.

Colonel Drake thought the brass would approve a clause in the contract that would help Ford retool and put returning soldiers, sailors and airmen back to work after the war. It was a win-win opportunity for everybody. In spite of the public outcry after the attack at Pearl Harbor, the war in Europe was given priority over the Pacific campaign. Colonel Alonzo Drake wasn't exactly given a blank check but the Army Air Corps needed planes and spare parts. Ford had stepped up but it came at a price.

Europe had been destroyed by the bombings on both sides. There was hardly a factory left standing on the entire continent. Japan would soon be destroyed, also. The war would leave the United States of America as the only undamaged industrialized nation in the world. There would be no competition until Europe and Japan rebuilt. It could take decades to fully recover. That left the door wide open for a boom in American manufacturing.

During the war, the U. S. had actually expanded its manufacturing capacity. Farming also modernized in order to first feed the fighting men, and later feed the world.

The Ford Motor Company built almost 6000 B-24 Liberators. They sent another 1,800 in parts.

Ford knew, without a doubt, that an unprecedented economic expansion was on the horizon. His aim was to position the Ford Motor Company to capitalize on that opportunity.

In the end, Colonel Drake, was going to get his new air planes. The deal insured that Ford would have his manufacturing plants ready to make automobiles after the war.

*

Ford's predictions were right on target. The world survived the long and terrible war. At the end, however, only one mighty nation stood with its industry, agriculture, and infrastructure still intact.

The United States of America was tooled up for production to supply the world with everything it needed to rebuild. What America required to be successful was a labor supply. America needed a labor supply that had survived a major depression, that understood hard work, and knew how to get the job done. That labor supply was soon on the way home by ship, plane, train and bus. To every big city and small town, they would spread across America. These fighting men and women had won a war. They were young. They could do anything. The American GI was the critical cog in the wheel that made America great. They were the "Greatest Generation."

Chapter 13

'For last year's words belong to last year's language
And next year's words await another voice
And to make an end is to make a beginning."

(Little Gidding)
—T. S. Elliot

No one knew him as Thurman Weaver. That was his Allen County family name. His name outside of Allen County was Charles or Charlie Weaver. Charles got his discharge papers and was processed out of the Navy in San Francisco, California. Charles and about a million other sailors, soldiers, and marines took buses and trains destined out across the nation. Every single one was heading to a home, or at least some place they called home.

There were twelve years of Depression and three long years of war and disease behind Charles. The worst was over now. The memories would fade but never go away. The scars would heal mostly, except for those occasional reminders that come with all wounds.

To the brave men and women who rode those buses and trains, one glaring realization was obvious. They were alive! For whatever reason, they had survived the biggest and deadliest war in world history.

There was no explanation as to why some survived while others died. Many survivors would feel guilty because they were spared. Those wounds would also need time to heal.

One advantage these men had going for themselves was their brains, experience and instinct. These men had grown up during the Depression.

58

Many knew hard times before the shooting started. Except for the dangers, some had a better life in the service than they ever had in their lives.

Among these men were both farmers and city dwellers. Men who knew how to make do with almost nothing. They were inventors and innovators by necessity. Men with confidence who stood out in the crowd. They stepped up without being asked and solved problems or simply got things done. These skills had, many times, been the difference between life and death. These skills may have been the real secret American weapon that won the war.

*

Charles slept most of the way back to Bowling Green, Kentucky. There was a change of trains in St. Louis and again in Louisville. The L&N train pulled into the Bowling Green station just after dark. Lester Weaver was there standing on the pad waiting for his eldest son. Lois sat waiting in the family's Model A Ford. It had bald tires and was held together with baling wire, but nothing could have kept them from this moment.

Charles Weaver was Thurman again as he stepped off the train, shook hands with the porter, then turned and shook hands with his father. The two men, father and son, stood for a moment shaking and locked in the grip of all four of their strong hands.

Lester and Thurman jumped off the platform and walked towards the car to hug a tearful Lois. She was shocked at how thin he was, but her worries were cast aside with the joy of his return in one piece.

It was suddenly the beginning of post-war life for Charles Thurman Weaver. He, and the world, would never be the same.

Chapter 14

"Soon after, I returned to my family, with determination to bring them as soon as possible to live in Kentucky which I esteemed a second paradise, at the risk of my life and fortune."

—Daniel Boone

1946 was the first year in a long time without war. The Dow Jones Industrial Average would peak at 212. A postage stamp cost 3 cents. A gallon of gas was 15 cents. The average home price was $1,459.

Jackie Robinson left the minor league field in Daytona Beach, Florida to debut as second baseman for the Montreal Royals. The bikini went on sale for the first time in Paris. The St. Louis Cardinals beat the Boston Red Sox 4-3 in the 43rd World Series. In its first meeting, the new United Nations Security Council vowed to end war forever. There was news of war criminals being executed in both Japan and Germany, but most warriors were trying to put the war behind them.

And so it was, that in the spring of 1946, Samuel and Charles arrived back in Kentucky.

The first thing Charles did was relax for a few weeks. He took his youngest brother, Robert, on an outing. They boarded the train in Bowling Green and rode up to Indianapolis for the 1946 running of the Indy 500. The track had been closed since 1941 because of the war. Gasoline and tires had been rationed. Everything had gone for the war effort.

Samuel had crossed the Atlantic on the Queen Mary. It was converted to a troop transport ship and docked in New York City harbor. Leaving from Union Station, Samuel rode trains for two days finally arriving in

Bowling Green, Kentucky. From Bowling Green, Samuel took a BG&H bus to Russellville. When he fell into his old feather bed at his Schochoh home, he practically slept for a week. When he finally woke up, his mother started trying to put some meat on what she called his "skinny bones."

Russellville was best known as a sleepy small town down the road from the larger city of Bowling Green. Both Charles Weaver and Victor Wells felt the town had good potential.

Charles attended the trade and technical school in Bowling Green on the GI Bill. Charles studied to become a welder and machinist. He took classes in business management, plus he completed drafting school and also studied music.

*

When Samuel's army time was close to ending, Colonel Twichell tried to convince him to make the army his career. It was tempting but Samuel knew he was not a world traveler. He missed his home and was ready to put his war days behind him.

Colonel Twichell finally gave up but he had been holding another ace in the hole for Samuel. The Colonel had been an engineer with the Army Corps of Engineers before the war. The Corps of Engineers worked with a lot of private corporations and he had connections. Those connections always needed good employees. He said he would set him up with a job because Samuel was the best damn road engineer and paper shuffler the Colonel had ever known.

The Colonel kept his word and it wasn't too long before Samuel started his new job. Samuel was a road engineer for the L&N Railroad. It was his job to patrol the rails and keep them safe and in good working order. He also worked to rebuild lines and bridges. It was a good job for a black man in those days. Truthfully, it was a great job for anyone anytime. Still, he knew he had to keep a low profile. A black man with a good job was always a target.

Samuel Wells had built a road across Alaska. He had supervised the landing of everything needed to conquer Europe and then rebuild it. Then rebuilt roads and bridges to deliver those supplies. Now, he was just another black man living in a small rural southern town.

*

Charles arrived in Russellville and rented a small building for a welding shop. It was mostly repairs at first. There was also a radiator repair section. Charles slept in a loft above the shop. On weekends, he drove his truck home to Bowling Green to wash clothes and get a good meal.

Both men, Charles and Samuel, had grown up on farms and seen hard times. Neither man had ever known anything other than hard work.

They both had other assets necessary to be successful. Charles and Samuel were intelligent men. Some of their skills came from natural ability and some were learned. They were well educated in their trades. Charles worked at learning the business side of business. Samuel worked at being the best engineer at L&N. They were good students. Each man first survived and then thrived. In short order, they had both married and started a family.

Charles went all the way to south Florida to find his bride. Athelyn was the pride of Arcadia. Yes, she was.

The unlikely union occurred because Charles and a business partner by the name of "Speed" Pedigo, decided to take a vacation trip to Florida. Charles had an aunt in Arcadia. His aunt Bess Kittrell had moved from Kentucky to Florida after she married. Aunt Bess had a daughter and her daughter had a best friend. They were both telephone operators.

It was a whirlwind romance. Athelyn and Charles met, fell in love and were engaged within a couple of weeks. But, Charles and "Speed" had to leave Florida and go back to Russellville.

The next few months involved letters and phone calls, and then Athelyn took a train to Kentucky. She stayed with Lester and Lois in Bowling Green while a small wedding was planned. They were married in April of 1949. In July of 1950, a son, Nathan Edward Weaver came along. Dr. Walter Byrne was there at the hospital to deliver Nathan. Over the years, Nathan was joined by two beautiful sisters, Martha and Janet.

*

Samuel spent every Sunday with his family. He purchased an old Ford truck to get back and forth to work. On Sundays, Samuel would drive to Schochoh in time for church, then sit for dinner at home before heading

The Way it Was

back to Bowling Green in late afternoon. The first Sunday back, he noticed his teacher, Patricia Clay. She was still teaching school and living in the same room in Reverend Brown's home.

In school, she had seemed so much older, when in fact, their age difference was less than four years. How was it he had never noticed before how beautiful she was? Samuel made his way over to her. She smelled like something from Heaven, he thought. He stuttered a hello but was mostly lost in her big brown eyes.

Later, Samuel asked about her at dinner with his parents. They told him that she felt she was needed at the school so she had stayed one year extra, then another, then another.

The next Sunday, Samuel spent a little extra time after church talking with Patricia. He asked her if she was busy later that afternoon and wondered if she might like to come over to the house. His parents had talked about making some homemade ice cream if they could find a few ripe peaches on the tree.

Patricia had resigned herself to being an old maid schoolteacher. She never dated. She had come to terms with her loneliness and started writing a journal that was working into a book. She stayed busy but there was little joy in her life. The community had quit trying to be matchmaker for her. Some believed she didn't like men. There were whispers. but she never gave anyone anything to talk about, except that she was a good teacher.

When Patricia saw Samuel, she was so happy. She had heard he was on his way home. Over the years, Patricia wondered how her prized student was doing. She had written a few letters and prayed for him and all the soldiers she knew from Logan County.

"He has turned into a man," she thought to herself. "A very handsome man too!"

When Samuel invited Patricia to come over for ice cream, she felt something she had never felt before. It made her a bit dizzy, in fact. Her legs were a little weak and there was a knot in her stomach.

Patricia picked out her very favorite dress for her afternoon with Samuel. She paid a little extra attention to her hair and makeup.

Samuel was at his parents' house pacing the floor. He walked back and forth. Samuel would churn the ice cream awhile and then get up and pace some more. The time ticked slowly by until the appointed hour of Patricia's arrival.

Samuel looked up and saw Patricia walking slowly up the path. She looked as if she was floating. Samuel thought she was the loveliest thing he had ever seen. That first afternoon was the first of many Sunday afternoons and then Saturday nights they spent together. Very soon, Samuel and Patricia were a couple. The minor age difference was not an issue to either of them. Patricia was beautiful and smart and Samuel was smitten something awful.

They were married in the summer of 1949. Samuel and Patricia soon welcomed their son, Victor Ashby Wells. Victor was delivered at home by the local midwife, Nora Sue Ashby. Negro women were not welcome to deliver their babies at the hospital in those days.

Victor would grow to be the best friend of Nathan Weaver, and much more.

Chapter 15

"Sit on the truth too long and you mash the life right out of it."

—Margaret McMullan, *Sources of Light*

As a young boy, Nathan made family trips to visit his grandparents in Arcadia, Florida. The Weaver station-wagon would pick up old U.S. Highway 41 South in Springfield, Tennessee. Highway 41 took the Weavers through Tennessee, Georgia, and most of Florida. It wove through the big towns of Nashville, Chattanooga and Atlanta. It also passed through hundreds of small towns such as Monteagle, Tennessee, Adrian, Georgia and Lake City, Florida. Along the highway, Nathan saw billboards with big letters reading, "Impeach Earl Warren."

Earl Warren led a liberal majority and used the power of the United States Supreme Court to change America in dramatic fashion. The Warren Court stands today as the "dream team" of the progressive movement of that period. Warren's leadership on the bench is legendary. Decisions seldom were even close.

To say that Warren was not popular in the South is an understatement. It was also the Warren Court that prohibited officially sanctioned prayer in public schools. The central focus of the southern firestorm against Warren, however, was the famous decision of *Brown vs. Board of Education of Topeka, Kansas.*

Brown vs. Board of Education changed the law on the education of Negro children in public schools. Previous to this decision, there was a separate but equal rule. The Warren Court changed all of that. The Court said that education for Negroes was *not* equal. It was only *separate*. The effect of the decision was the integration of all public education. Everywhere. Even in the South.

Few United States Supreme Court decisions have had the impact of *Brown vs. Board of Education*. This decision changed the entire landscape of American education. No longer was *"Separate but Equal"* good enough. The Earl Warren Court said that every child, black or white, would be educated together at the same places. Integration was the law of the land.

The decision was announced in May of 1954. Shock waves went out immediately to every state, county and city in the nation. Every school board was on the clock to integrate every class of students, everywhere.

The South did not exactly welcome the news with open arms. Some states did better than others. Governor Lawrence Wetherby of Kentucky made a public statement early. He told the people of Kentucky that he would comply with the decision of the Court. In other words, he said he would follow the law because he had no choice.

Lieutenant Governor Emerson (Doc) Beauchamp made no public statement on the matter. He supported the decision of the Governor, but he did not make news with any comments on the pros or cons regarding integration.

Kentucky had been divided during the Civil War and it was still a divided state. Louisville and the area around Louisville would integrate with few problems. The Courier-Journal would support desegregation with editorials and positive stories. The state newspaper, however, did not carry enough weight to do it alone. The southern counties near Tennessee, and the southeastern counties near Virginia and West Virginia, were potential hot spots of resistance.

Logan County sat just 40 miles north of Nashville, Tennessee. It certainly leaned in the direction that opposed integration, for sure.

*

Logan County had something going for it, however. That something was in the form of two special men: Robert E. Stevenson, Superintendent of Russellville City Schools and Robert B. Piper, Superintendent of Logan County Schools.

Robert E. Stevenson first became acutely aware of the gap in education many years ago when he was Principal at the Adairville school

66

Piper and Stevenson were friends and talked regularly. It was not long after the Supreme Court ruling on integration that they had their first conversation about the matter.

For the past several years, Negro students from the county had been bussed to the Knob City School, the Russellville Negro school. Knob City was located on the Morgantown Road, near the railroad tracks, on the edge of Russellville. At Knob City, Negroes from grades 1-12 were educated in what was supposed to be a separate but equal system.

The state paid the county an amount for each student. The county added its share and then contracted with Russellville to provide the facility, teachers and staff. Mr. McClusky, Principal at Knob City School, did the best he could, but resources were scarce for Negro education. Resources were scarce for all education in the South.

Robert Stevenson and Robert Piper had audited Knob City just before the Court ruling. The school was meeting only six of fifteen standards for full accreditation. The state would not recognize the diplomas of the graduates if Knob City could not meet the minimum requirements of all the required standards necessary to achieve full accreditation.

It wasn't that Mr. Piper or Mr. Stevenson lacked interest in Knob City. Far from it. They had pooled every possible resource to educate the Negroes from Russellville and Logan County.

Knob City School was thought to be the best option available at the time because there were not enough funds to achieve the best options possible. The Negro school in Russellville, however, like Negro schools everywhere, got the leftovers. The neglect had added up over the years.

Piper and Stevenson studied long and hard for the best approach to both the funding for Knob City and the eventual integration of both county and city schools. It would be possible to get by for a year or two if the school boards of both school systems could come up with the money to improve Knob City. A tax increase would be required, and taxes were not popular. A tax on the ballot to fund a Negro school was not going to pass in the county, and it would probably not pass in the city either.

If the money could not be found to upgrade Knob City, then immediate integration of the high schools was the only realistic option to solve the problem for grades 9-12. The elementary grades would require very little funds to upgrade and full accreditation could be achieved.

Robert Stevenson called Robert Piper early one morning and said, "I have some coffee going and my staff is out of the office today. Can you drop by and meet on this Knob City problem? I have been up half the night thinking about it."

Robert (Bob) Stevenson had been thinking about integration since his days as Principal at Adairville. As an educator first and an administrator second, he knew both the needs and the challenges of public education.

Mr. Piper had been having some trouble sleeping, also. He had intended to make the same call that morning but Stevenson beat him to it. "Sure thing, Bob. I'll be there by around nine o'clock," Piper told Stevenson.

Mr. Piper drove over to the city school offices and walked in. The two administrators often met at Felts Restaurant for coffee. Stevenson knew well how Piper liked his coffee and had it ready for him as soon as his foot hit the door.

"Good to see you, Bob." ...

"You too." ...

The two men exchanged pleasantries for a few minutes, as gentlemen always do. And make no mistake about it, these two men were gentlemen. Soon, the subject moved over to the reason for the meeting. Both superintendents restated the situation from their separate and common perspectives.

Piper was the first to say it out loud. "We have no choice, I fear, but to integrate immediately. Integration is now the law of the land. To postpone would bring harm to the Negro students who may graduate from a non-accredited high school unless we find a solution to the accreditation problem. Neither the city nor the county can afford to throw good money after bad. The choice has been made for us."

Stevenson agreed and went straight to the point. "The people will not be pushed into desegregation. They will need to be led. First, we must stick together and speak with one voice, or we will fail. Second, every move must be well planned and organized."

It was decided that they would first take their recommendation to the chairman of each board. They knew that if they could not convince the chairmen of the merits, their plan would be doomed to failure with the full board.

The second step would be a full board presentation and that would be followed by a joint-meeting, assuming both boards were in agreement.

Mr. Stevenson and Mr. Piper then set about preparing the outline for integration of all public schools in both the Logan County School System and the Russellville City School System. They set a target date for August 1956, for the integration of all of the high school grades 9-12.

The Negro elementary and middle school students would continue to segregated or bussed to Knob City. Integration of the lower grades would follow some years later.

This plan would satisfy the law and solve the immediate issues with accreditation of Knob City Schools.

The superintendents hoped that the boards would not only approve, but also give counsel and support to an action plan to gain public support.

*

The meetings with the board chairmen went very well. They both immediately understood the situation and got behind the project 100%.

Stevenson and Piper were well respected by their boards. After 30 minutes or so of presentation, the discussion in both board meetings turned quickly from "WHY?" to "HOW?"

The joint-meeting went much the same. The local newspaper, The News-Democrat, kept the news quiet until a proper announcement could be made. Duties were assigned to board members. Some went to Frankfort to the State Board of Education to get more details on the state's role in integrating Kentucky's schools. Others were assigned to make contact with local community leaders, the local bar, and church leaders.

The chairman of each board took the task of reaching out to the Negro community. Stevenson and Piper were assigned the politicians.

It was further decided that both the county and the city would each appoint a committee to study and help plan a process for integration. These two committees would hold public town meetings. These meetings would give opportunities for a full and open public discussion. A final decision on integration would not be announced until both committees made their recommendations to their perspective boards.

*

The first steps had gone smoothly. Good planning was paying dividends, but, the goal line lay far ahead. The men on both school board were well educated and understood all sides of both the legal and financial situations. The hardest part lay ahead in the public debate.

Robert Stevenson and Robert Piper left the joint-meeting together. Without any discussion of what should be done first, Stevenson simply asked Robert, "You want to call Doc or do you want me to set something up?"

"You call him, Bob. You might know him a little better than I do," Piper sighed. Both men knew that all Logan politics started with Doc Beauchamp.

Chapter 16

"The ultimate measure of a man is not where he stands in moments of comfort and convenience, but where he stands at times of challenge and controversy."

—Rev. Martin Luther King, Jr.

Logan County was starting to show some sparks of life after the war. The city and county were blessed with good leadership. Some would call it legendary leadership.

There was an amazing mix of characters that came together in one place, at one time, with common values, to shape the community.

Agriculture still formed the economic base but manufacturing was starting to take a hard look at Russellville. Small businesses were springing up, too.

If people talk about the '50s, all stories about the '50s in Logan County start with Emerson "Doc" Beauchamp.

It was early April in Logan County. The trees were just starting to green up and Frankfort was pretty much shut down for the Easter break. Doc Beachamp parked his new 1955 Buick sedan in front of his house, looked around and got out of the car. He felt conspicuous in such a nice ride.

Doc's business was politics. He did all his local business from his home in Russellville. He was a man of the people, so he did business where people lived. Of course, he had his Lieutenant Governor's office in Frankfort. But all of the local business, he did in his study at home.

He had come back to Logan County to pick up the car and rest a few days. His mind was set on a Chevy, but his longtime friend and local car dealer, Carl Page, had told him that the Buick was a perfect fit for him. No question, it was a smooth ride and a smooth ride was a nice escape from the current bumpy political scene in Frankfort.

It had been one battle after another for the better part of two years. Doc loved politics more than life itself, but some days were better than others. He was feeling old. Doc's spirit wanted to move quickly but his bones were slowing him down some. His tenure as Lieutenant Governor was coming to an end soon. Beauchamp had seriously considered running for Governor. He had support, no doubt. But, Doc knew his limitations. Others, he believed, looked better on a campaign poster. His skills were rooted more in conversation and arm twisting than giving speeches. No, Doc would not seek the nomination, but he was not going to support that SOB Happy Chandler, either. It was a political risk. But no matter how hot the fire, he wouldn't, by God, do it!

Doc Beauchamp was the undisputed Democratic Party political boss of Logan County. There were no Republican bosses in the South in those days. Whoever ruled the Democratic Party ruled the political machinery of government.

*

Doc took over after the retirement of his good friend and mentor, Tom Rhea. Tom Rhea had been close to FDR. In fact, he had been a critical southern partner who helped FDR gain southern support and secure the nomination in Chicago at the 1932 Democratic Convention.

The story is told that Senator Huey Long rolled into Chicago a couple of days early, before the convention. He took up residence at the Mayfair Hotel in a suite suitable for "entertaining." He liked the Mayfair because his room had a beautiful view of the lake.

Long had all of the Louisiana delegates in his pocket. He had been governor and now was the junior senator. There was nothing, however, junior about Long. He was looking to liberalize the platform and he was willing to make a deal. His "Share the Wealth" theme was catching on in the Depression era that currently gripped the nation.

Although there were some "Stop Roosevelt" members of the Kentucky delegation, Tom Rhea controlled half, maybe more, of the Kentucky group. He was looking for a partner in his promotion of Franklin Roosevelt.

Roosevelt had little support in the South. He was a northerner, plain and simple. To the South, he was just another Yankee carpetbagger.

Rhea saw more to the man and decided to help gather support where he could find it and maybe get enough delegates to keep Al Smith, the anointed one, from getting a majority of votes on the first ballot. Rhea figured a stalled convention might open the door for Roosevelt.

The Gorrell family was from Logan County and big in road construction. Big in road construction meant, therefore, politically connected. Tom Rhea had helped get some Kentucky road business sent their way. The Gorrells had also expanded down into Louisiana.

Now, doing business in Louisiana and doing business with Senator Huey Long was all the same thing. There was no separation between Long and state.

Tom Rhea contacted the Gorrells and asked for an introduction to Senator Long. The day and time had been prearranged, so when Rhea called the Mayfair Hotel, he reached Huey Long immediately. Rhea asked if they could talk, one southern gentleman to another. Senator Long laughed big at the notion that he might be called a southern gentleman. Long was always ready to talk politics so he agreed to meet Rhea, if he brought along some fine Kentucky bourbon whisky.

Rhea was a teetotaler, but he walked into the Mayfair that early evening with some fine sour mash Kentucky bourbon. He also carried the outline of a new Democratic Party Platform.

Very late that night, or maybe it was very early the next morning, Rhea walked out of the Mayfair Hotel with some notes to revise the Platform. If FDR would support those revisions, then the Louisiana delegation would support him for the nomination. Senator Long also agreed to work with Rhea to gather support from other southern states.

History will confirm that Al Smith did not get a majority of votes on the first ballot. FDR finally won the Democratic Party nomination in a close ballot. It was the support of the South that defeated Al Smith and nominated FDR for President.

As Tom Rhea's power and influence grew over the years, he was able to bring some patronage back home. Logan County enjoyed far more than its share of paved roads and streets.

FDR once took a detour and made a train stop in Russellville. The President wanted to show the county and the whole state of Kentucky how much he appreciated the work and the support of his good friend, Tom Rhea.

Thanks to Rhea, Russellville and Logan County benefited from all that comes with the advantages of political clout.

And so it came to pass in the land of Logan that eventually the torch was passed from Tom Rhea to Doc Beauchamp. That torch never flickered.

Chapter 17

"Nearly all men can stand adversity, but if you want to test a man's character, give him power."

—Abraham Lincoln

Doc fell into the worn leather chair behind his big oak desk. His plan for the morning was to check in with his lieutenants and put out any fires that had started while he was in Frankfort. The first person to walk into the house that day was Rayburn Smith.

Rayburn Smith had gotten the reputation as Doc's bag man for allegedly stuffing a few voting boxes over the years. Legend has it that Rayburn accidentally dropped his personal mail into one of the ballot boxes during a close election. He hadn't noticed his mail was missing until the ballot box was opened at the courthouse on election night and there was Rayburn's mail sitting on top of the ballots.

Doc trusted Rayburn. Rayburn was smart. He was also a deacon at the downtown First Baptist Church and also well known as the best poker player around those parts. The locals knew that when they talked to Rayburn, it was the same as if they were talking to Doc Beauchamp, himself. Everyone knew that Rayburn was Doc's representative in Logan County. Trust is as rare as it is valuable in politics. Doc never took Rayburn for granted.

Rayburn eased into the chair across from Doc. They exchanged the usual banter that is common with old friends. Rayburn was expecting a new grandchild in a few days. He was sure it was going to be a girl. Doc made a mental note to send a gift.

It wasn't like they hadn't talked a dozen times in the past few weeks. Doc was always on the phone. The phone was his primary tool of communication. It was easy, fast, and there was never a record. Doc would often say, "Letters are for show. The phone is for people who want to get things done." Friend or foe, it was no secret that Doc Beauchamp was a man who knew how to get things done.

"I got an interesting call the other day from Bob Stevenson," Rayburn told Doc. "He and Robert Piper requested a 'sit down' with you the next time you are in town."

"Do you have any idea what the hell they want to talk about?" Doc asked.

Doc was thinking that Stevenson and Piper were not political because of their position, but then again, everything is political in one fashion or another. "They wanted something. You can bet they wanted something," Beauchamp mumbled to himself.

Rayburn shifted in his seat just enough that Doc picked up the tell. Doc was a damn good poker player too. He was also a damn good reader of people. Doc knew before Rayburn opened his mouth that Rayburn was not comfortable with what he was about to say.

"I'm not sure," Rayburn lied. "There's a rumor goin' round that they want to integrate the two school systems because of that *Brown vs. Board of Education* thing."

"I knew it! I just knew it!" Doc thought to himself.

Doc Beauchamp was fully aware of the recent Supreme Court ruling. Governor Wetherby and half of Frankfort were running around trying to figure out how to comply with desegregation without starting another war. Or worse yet, losing elections. The Governor had stated that Kentucky would comply with the ruling by the Court. The Dixiecrats all across the South were going to fight this thing. "What is the damn rush? There is plenty of time to ease into integration." Doc wished he had more time. "That's it!" he thought. He would fight for more time!

"Tell Stevenson and Piper that I would enjoy meeting with them but that my time this trip is so tight that it is impossible to fit in any last minute meetings. Tell them I want to set aside enough time to give them a full hearing. I'll be back in a couple of months and we will all have dinner. Tell them to bring their wives and we'll eat some Bar-B-Que at my house," Doc said.

Arguing with Doc Beauchamp was not easy and it sure wasn't fun, either. The shortest path to an ass chewing was to disagree with him. Sure, he would listen. Until he made up his mind. Then, it was everyone else's time to listen. Rayburn knew the risk but he also knew his job. His job was to protect Doc in Logan County.

Rayburn started slowly. "Doc, the word on the street is that this integration thing is already being organized. A committee has been formed in the county and another committee has been formed in the city to recommend ideas to the school boards. Some informal meetings have already occurred."

Doc looked frustrated but he didn't interrupt Rayburn.

"The local bar association members are openly supporting integration of all the local city and county schools. You do what you want, but it might be a better position for you on the inside rather than on the outside. Why not meet with Stevenson and Piper and hear what is going on? You don't have to do nothin'."

Doc felt the heat in his face. He knew Rayburn was right but it angered him anyway. Rayburn didn't say it but they both knew that Doc had enemies even in his own backyard. Doc had been busy fryin' bigger fish lately and had not kept his finger on the local pulse. That was Rayburn's job and he was doing it the best he could.

"Alright dammit," Beauchamp snapped. Call the sumbitches and tell 'em I'll see 'em as soon as they can get their collective asses over here."

Rayburn just sat and stared at Doc. Suddenly, they both laughed.

"Okay, okay! Give me their numbers. I'll call 'em both and set a time when we can all get together. Now get out of here. If Fount is standing around somewhere out there, tell him to come on in."

Chapter 18

"We're fascinated by the words - but where we meet is in the silence behind them."

—Ram Dass

In the South, sweet tea is the drink of choice for just about everybody and every occasion. It was decided that Superintendents Piper and Stevenson would meet at Doc's home late afternoon for some cold sweet tea and maybe some pie.

Doc had a nice patio behind his house that was shaded in the afternoon, quiet, and private. There was a table under an umbrella with four reasonably comfortable chairs. Three would be enough. Rayburn Smith had a new granddaughter, Martha, and was busy being a new grandfather.

Doc welcomed them and led both men through the house and to the table already set with glasses, pitcher, pie, and plates.

"Have a seat, gentlemen. I sure wish you had taken me up on my offer of Bar B Que. We would have loved to have had you over one night soon for a real meal," Doc offered.

"Thank you, Doc," Stevenson said. "We would have enjoyed that very much but we are on a tight schedule. We needed to get you in the loop as soon as possible, and we need your advice and guidance on several important matters."

Doc shifted in his seat a bit and smiled to himself.

The afternoon sun was shaded by a big white oak tree. Doc was not a small man. His belly was held in by his trousers and tucked behind suspenders and a long-sleeve white shirt. His tie was pulled loose and the top button was open. Doc commanded respect because of his accomplishments and skill as a politician, not his appearance.

What Stevenson and Piper needed was Doc Beauchamp's blessing. As Lt. Governor, Beauchamp would have to support integration in principle, but he could delay the timetable if he thought it was politically wise.

"Why don't you boys tell me what's on your mind and I promise to give you the best advice I can," Doc allowed. Doc knew he was being played. This was not his first rodeo. He needed to hear the details, then he could decide his role, or his manner of exit.

Robert Stevenson began with a summary of the Supreme Court decision and the local city/county situation concerning the Knob City School. He detailed the financial challenge of accreditation and the consequences for Negro students if accreditation was not achieved.

Mr. Piper continued with a review of the Logan County perspective. Doc's strength lay in the rural areas of Logan County. He was very interested in how the citizens would react to integration.

Doc liked the idea of the two committees and the town-hall meetings. That gave him some political cover.

Doc rubbed the bridge of his nose then looked up at both men. "You say you have the support of both school boards?"

"Then we will have to do something," he said with a big smile on his face.

"Look fellows, I am Lt. Governor. I don't have any official role in local politics. But we don't have any damn choice about this integration matter. It's gonna happen sooner or later. You boys need to put together your plan."

He paused. "Do you need any help from Frankfort?" …

"Anything at all?" …

Both men smiled and shook their heads.

"Good, then you get your committees together and have your meetings. Give the people a chance to voice their opinions. I will be on the sidelines if you need help."

And so Emerson "Doc" Beauchamp agreed to *nothing* but supported *everything*. He promised nothing but offered his help every step of the way.

Doc's position would be on the sidelines while watching. If all went well, he would take some credit. If integration was a disaster, he was safely shielded from voter backlash.

The Superintendents walked away without support and without objection from Doc. That, they knew, was a clear victory. If Doc had objected, integration would not have been possible anytime soon.

Chapter 19

"Whenever I think of the past, it brings back so many memories."

—Steven Wright

The next meeting, and the next challenge for the superintendents, would be with Taylor Fuqua, Mayor of Russellville.

Mayor Fuqua was a smart businessman and a skilled politician. His one-car taxi service had evolved into a bus company linking Hopkinsville, Kentucky with Bowling Green, Kentucky. From his small bus station near the town square, people and freight moved in and out of Russellville and Logan County.

Mayor Fuqua was neither a political ally nor a political enemy of Doc Beauchamp. They simply moved in different political circles. Of course, both were staunch Democrats from Logan County and worked together to elect Democrats. They did not, however, always support the same state candidate in the primaries or the same local candidate.

The fact is that there was always a bit of friction between the county political machine and the city political faction. It was true in sports and it was sometimes the case in political battles.

The mayor knew very well what Stevenson and Piper wanted to talk about. Fuqua knew they had already been over to see Doc. He made it his business to know these things. Because the mayor was prepared, he was also ready with an answer if asked. The city had a higher percent of black voters than the county. But Taylor, like Doc Beauchamp, wanted to listen first and hold his cards close to his chest until it was necessary to play.

It was early evening by the time they arrived. Mayor and Mrs. Taylor Fuqua lived in a nice home on west 6th street. His oldest son, William, was away from home serving in the U.S. army in Germany.

The Mayor was seated in the backyard with his daughter Peggy. Peggy was home from college for a long weekend. Mr. Stevenson and Mr. Piper had ridden together in Robert's car. They pulled into the driveway, parked and came walking into the backyard together.

Taylor kissed his daughter on her forehead as she rose and greeted their guests before stepping way in the direction of the house. Both gentlemen tipped their hats and said hello to Peggy while expressing what a lovely lady she had become.

Taylor gave a rare smile as his little girl walked away. She wasn't little anymore except in his heart. He let the distraction of his daughter hold his attention a moment longer than usual, then turned to greet Stevenson and Piper.

The Mayor was more of a "get to the point" person than Doc, or most people, for that matter. Maybe it was the bottom line mentality of a businessman vs. a pure politician in the mold of Beauchamp. Either way, it would be a much shorter meeting than the earlier meeting with Doc.

It took about the same amount of time to make the presentation with both Taylor Fugue and Doc Beauchamp. However, when Mr. Piper finished his part, Taylor asked, "Is that about it?"

"Yes sir, the facts are what they are; plain and simple," Mr. Stevenson replied.

All three men sat and looked at each other for a few seconds that felt like minutes to the superintendents. The Mayor took a deep breath. "The facts in this matter are, indeed, clear," he stated without any hint of hesitation in his voice.

"The politics are God awful but I see no other option than the immediate desegregation of the city schools. I know the board members are men of good character. Smart men every one. My lawyer friends tell me that all the city lawyers support desegregation. In fact, they insist on it! The highest court in the land has spoken and we have no choice in the matter. I will not stand against your campaign to integrate the city schools. You can tell the board that they have my support in whatever plan they decide to implement."

After the meeting with Mr. Stevenson and Mr. Piper had concluded, Doc went into the house and picked up the phone. Rayburn answered on the third ring.

"Say, Rayburn, did I call at a good time?"

"Sure thing." Smith replied. "What's on your mind?"

"I just finished the meeting with Stevenson and Piper. They say they have the support of both boards of education. It looks like this horse has already left the barn. What are you hearing on the street?"

Rayburn was not comfortable but he went forward anyway. "Like I told you the other day, the local bar is supporting it. They say it is the law and that's that. There is more objection in the county than in the city but there is considerable objection in both. If it came to a vote, desegregation would fail."

Beauchamp did not comment so Smith continued. "An interesting point is that the Negroes are no happier with integration than the white people are. Their objection is mostly fear for their children. They fear they will be treated badly by the school teachers and the white students. These Town Meetings are going to be interesting!"

Beauchamp finally acknowledged what Rayburn was saying. He congratulated him once again on the birth of his granddaughter and then soon ended the telephone conversation.

It was Doc's first day back in Logan County in a while. He would take the evening to have dinner and relax. Tomorrow would bring another day and another political challenge.

On the next Tuesday, the news broke about the town meetings in both the News-Democrat and on WRUS radio. Suddenly, everyone in Logan County understood the impact of *Brown vs. Board of Education.*

Chapter 20

"Nothing in all the world is more dangerous than sincere ignorance and conscientious stupidity."

—Rev. Martin Luther King, Jr.

"You can write this down in your little note takin' book there. My children ain't goin to no school with a bunch of Goddamn niggers."

Arnold Thomas stood before the small gathering and pointed at the lady at the end of the table who was taking notes. Thomas was a Logan County native. He was also a self-identified redneck idiot, but he represented the views of many in Logan County. He was a part-time mechanic, part-time farmer and part-time pool shark victim. It was doubtful that Thomas had ever spent more than a few hours outside Logan County. Except possibly to buy beer in Bowling Green. His home was obstructed from view by high grass and old cars on blocks in the front yard. Thomas had dropped out of high school but had twin daughters in the 8th grade in the Russellville city school system. Thomas was one of the first to answer the call for comments at the first Town Hall meeting in Adairville. He planned to attend all of the meetings across the county and in Russellville.

"Niggers got no place mixin' with whites and all. I'll kill the first nigger to lay a hand on one of my daughters," Thomas shouted to the assembled group.

Arnold Thomas was the most vocal, but the meeting went on for over an hour. There were a couple of speakers in support. The vast majority however, spoke for no integration or a delay for at least a year to give more time to work out a solution.

Chairperson, Mrs. Williams Gower, closed the meeting after thanking everyone for their input and promising the full consideration of every comment. Only eight of the 14 members of the committee could be present at the Adairville School gym where the first meeting was held. The crowd left little doubt where they stood.

It was much the same with the second meeting at Olmstead.

Arnold Thomas was in attendance again, but he had more supporters than were present at the Adairville meeting. An obvious trend was developing.

After the first two town meetings, the board met informally and decided to make a more detailed presentation for the following town meetings. The people needed to understand that the decision to integrate had already been made by the Court. The committee was there for input on *how* to implement the mandate. Granville Clark was the attorney for the city and Sam Milam was the attorney for the Logan County board. It was decided that these two attorneys should attend all meetings and explain the legal issues involved.

The two boards doubted that everyone would approve integration but it was hoped that the citizens would understand why integration was not simply necessary, but mandated by law.

Thomas did not go away quietly. He and more than a few of his supporters stayed constantly in the shadows. They talked about rumors of a resurrection of the Klan. They discussed acts of terrorism they could commit to get attention, plant fear, and hopefully gain support.

Nathan Klein, Chairman of the Russellville City Schools Board of Education, drew some fire. In some of the rallies, Thomas and his friends gave the "Nigger lovin' Jew" the blame for a wide range of problems, not just in education but in all areas of local society.

The Thomas gang put on a show around town, too. They drove through the "colored" section of Russellville known as "Black Bottom" with Confederate battle flags, honking their horns and shouting threats out the windows of their pickup trucks and cars.

The town meetings in Chandlers, Auburn, Lewisburg and Russellville, however, went forward as planned. More and more people spoke in favor of moving forward with integration. The newspaper continued to run articles in support.

Much attention by the school boards and administration was given to assurances in the Negro community. Emotions ran high there also.

Board members met weekly with pastors of Negro churches and other black community leaders. Churches were a center of the black community social system, so more effort was made to connect and to communicate in that area. The primary message in all communications from the white community to the Negro community was that their children would not be mistreated in an integrated school system. Mistreatment would not be tolerated by either school board or administration.

In time, a change started to take shape. It wasn't so much a movement towards support as it was a slow drift towards acceptance.

The politicians stayed quiet. There was no political support for the opposition or comments that could stir emotions. The two Boards of Education stayed on plan and stayed unified in their message.

As an unintended consequence, the antics of Thomas and his small band of neo-rebels drew a stark contrast between those who opposed desegregation and those who supported, or, simply accepted the inevitable. The good people of Russellville and Logan County did not identify with the Thomas gang. They were considered hooligans of bad character who had briefly gained the attention of some sympathetic citizens. Arnold Thomas lost most of his support in the light of day.

The two committees made their recommendations. The county committee recommended a one-year delay if possible but did not demand it. The city committee, led by attorney Tom Noe and with strong support from noted businessman Justice Wright, gave a unified recommendation favoring immediate integration.

In March of 1956, both Boards made their individual announcements regarding their decision on integration of public schools in Logan County and in the Russellville system. The headline in the News-Democrat reported that the Logan County School system and the Russellville City School system would integrate grades 9-12 beginning at the start of school in the fall of 1956. Work would begin immediately to convert Knob City School to a primary education facility for Negro only students. Negro elementary schools in the county and in the city would remain segregated.

No date was immediately announced for the integration of the elementary and middle school grades.

(History tells us that the integration of all public schools in the Russellville City School system and the Logan County School System was completed in 1966.)

Chapter 21

"The greater danger for most of us lies not in setting our aim too high and falling short; but in setting our aim too low, and achieving our mark."

—Michelangelo

The beginning of the school year in 1956 was the first realistic opportunity for mandated integration of public schools across the nation. It would be another ten years before some schools gave up their fight against desegregation. No other school systems in Kentucky complied with the Court decision and integrated earlier than the Russellville and Logan County systems.

It was decided to start the fall school year on September 4th, the day after the long Labor Day weekend. Meetings had been held with all of administration, teachers, and staff. There would be a zero toleration of misconduct. That included staff as well as students. Everyone was warned to be on the look-out for "outsiders" making trouble. There was a story of some men driving a car with Alabama license tags. They reportedly pulled into the Russellville High School parking lot and tried to stir up some bad behavior. The incident was reported to Mr. Hunter, the Russellville High School principal, but nothing came from it.

Police officers would stay close but not too visible. It was the general consensus of education and community leaders that an environment of normalcy was the best approach. Normalcy was the goal, so why not begin with an attitude and environment that fit the picture?

Students started arriving at all of the five high schools in the county system, and at Russellville High School, well before 8:00 a.m. Negro and

88

white students entered the same doors in segregated groupings. Once inside, they all came together and proceeded to their assigned home rooms. It was as if the students were not aware that a new era had begun. The fears and emotions of many adults in the community had not transferred to the young people starting classes that September day.

*

Stevenson and Piper sat by their phones at their desks. They had arrived before sunup. Both superintendents had already been in conversations with key administrators. They went over the plan one more time to make sure everyone was prepared for the possibilities that could occur.

Harold Hunter, principal at Russellville High School, stood next to one of his teachers, Helen Carpenter, and greeted students as they entered the high school building. They were positioned near the south door and watched as the students filed by. They spoke to several, both black and white. The students responded back, but the Negro students were more shy about it.

During that entire school day and following weeks, Mr. Hunter and his staff were on patrol, inside and out. The same was happening at every county school. Mr. Stevenson and Mr. Piper were back and forth between schools and their offices. No stone was left unturned to insure both the success of the integration and the safety of the students.

It was not perfect. It would be many years before the role of Negro students evolved to a truly equal status. But overall, both sides worked to insure that this first progressive step went as smoothly as possible.

Unfortunately, this was not the case everywhere. Not in the nation and not in Kentucky. In the small western Kentucky town of Sturgis, angry mobs formed to prevent the admission of Negro students to the local school. Governor Chandler was forced to call out the Kentucky National Guard. Guard members from Russellville were sent to Sturgis and stood protecting buildings and people from angry mobs.

The situation was so tense that integration was delayed until the second semester to give the Sturgis Board of Education time to put together a better plan.

Months of planning and preparation for desegregation was the difference between success in Logan County/Russellville and the disaster of Sturgis and other communities across America. The credit goes to many people but especially to Robert E. Stevenson and Robert B. Piper. It took courage, character, and people and organizational skills to move the mountain now known as "the integration."

There was a job that needed to be done. Although the situation presented an opportunity to divide the community and possibly shift the political balance, that battle never occurred. What did occur was a lot of hard work and the commitment of leaders in key positions to focus on solving problems. Logan County overwhelmingly trusted and responded to their leadership and followed its example.

The integration of the public high schools in Russellville and Logan County did not end racism in Logan County. In fact, it ended nothing except the segregation of the high schools.

What this process did achieve was an offer for better education to black children all across Logan County. It created an opportunity for African Americans to find a path out of poverty through a better education. The integration process was a beginning in the long journey for equality. An important step.

Chapter 22

"The beginning is the most important part of the work."

—Plato

By the mid '50s, Charles Weaver and Samuel Wells had settled into post-war life. Charles had established *Weaver Welding Company* at the corner of Fifth and Morgan Street.

Samuel was doing very well with the L&N Railroad. He and Patricia had purchased a home and lived a few houses from Weaver's place of business on the corner of Fifth and Morgan Street.

One summer day, in 1957, Nathan found himself with his dad at the shop. His mom had a doctor's appointment or maybe she had gone shopping. His mother, Athelyn, would sometimes drop him off at the shop if she was going to be out for a while. It was a big treat for Nathan.

Nathan had been well instructed on the dangers always present at the welding shop. He knew better than to get close to the work inside. He knew that the light from welding would damage his eyes if he watched very long. There was also hot metal everywhere.

It had gotten loud, smoky, and boring inside, so Nathan wandered outside and was just kicking around the lot when a dog came running up to him. He liked dogs. It is risky to trust people who don't like dogs. This particular dog was a Heinz dog. That means he was, at least, 57 varieties of every breed known to man. This mutt was nothing close to a pedigree.

Nathan squatted down to pet his new acquaintance. The mutt licked his face and knocked him down in the excitement of finding a new friend. The dog's tail was beating Nathan half to death.

It was at about that moment when Nathan look up to see Victor for the very first time. Victor was standing there looking at Nathan and the big black dog. Finally, he hollered at the dog, "stop it Coal and get home." The dog apparently didn't understand English or simply ignored his command. Victor then tried grabbing the dog around the neck.

"I guess this is your dog?" Nathan questioned.

"Yeah, he ain't much about mindin' me though. I think he is too dumb to understand nothin'," Victor said lookin' at Coal and shaking his head.

They both laughed. Victor squatted down on the other side of Coal as they sat petting the happy pup. Nathan said, "My name is Nathan." Victor said, "I'm Victor Wells."

The two boys chatted about dogs for a moment and then Nathan asked him where he went to school because he had never seen him before. It never crossed Nathan's mind that he had never met a Negro child before. Neither child really noticed there was a difference. Neither child had learned to be prejudiced.

Victor told him about a school different from the school where Nathan went. Nathan had never heard of it. Victor said the name of the school was Knob City.

That made no sense to Nathan. "Was it a city or a school?" "Why would they name a school a city?"

Victor tried to explain, but Nathan did not understand.

"Why don't you go to the school where I go?" he asked Victor.

Victor said that Knob City was a Negro school for Negro children.

And so it was that on that summer day in 1957, a black second grader gave a white second grader his first lesson on segregation. Neither Victor nor Nathan knew why whites and blacks didn't mix. It was just the way it was. At least in their world in elementary school.

The bliss of youth is a beautiful thing. Two boys and a dog are about as good as it gets. There weren't many cars on the street in those days. It didn't take long until they were kicking a can back and forth in the street. Coal barked and ran in circles around the boys and the can. Soon, a few more Negro kids were out with them in the street. That was before a car smashed the can flat and that was the end of the game.

Nathan asked Victor where he lived. He said he would show him and took his hand. Nathan hesitated. He wasn't sure he should go because he

The Way it Was

didn't have permission to leave the area around his dad's shop. Victor then stood directly behind him and pointed over his shoulder.

"See that house yonder with the green porch? That's my house," he said.

"My goodness," Nathan thought to himself. Victor lived almost next door. It was only three houses down the street. There were two houses and then there was Victor's house.

"When you come back, you come to my house and we will play somethin'. Bring a glove and we will play pitch or somethin'," Victor told him.

Victor was excited and so was Nathan. He liked being at the shop with his Dad but his dad was busy and they couldn't really do anything together. A friend nearby would be great.

Soon there was a call from Victor's house. Patricia was calling Victor home to clean up and get ready for supper. She didn't like him to be gone too long. He needed to cool down and relax awhile before his dad got home from work and they sat down to eat.

Victor heard the call, turned and waved to Nathan and took off running for home. Nathan waved back and started towards the shop. The shop was shutting down for the day. Big loud welding machines were being turned off. The lack of the loud humming sound made the quiet more obvious. A welding shop is a loud place. Steel is loud. It bangs when it is dropped or when hit with a hammer. It is part of life in a welding shop that steel is always being dropped or banged with a hammer.

"Where you been son?" Charles said when he first saw Nathan.

"I've been outside, Dad. I met a new friend. His name is Victor."

"Really?" was all he said. He was busy trying to finish and get out the door and get home. It had been a long hot day. Welding is the union of steel through a melting and fusing process. It takes a lot of heat to weld. On a hot day, the whole process can drain a man. Today had been one of those days.

Nathan didn't understand any of that. He was just a kid. In short order they both piled into Charles' pickup and headed home. Nothing more was said about his afternoon or his new friend, Victor. His mother sent his dad to the shower so he could cool down. She was always concerned that he was going to have a heart attack.

93

A new friend is always something to get excited about when you are a young boy. New adventure awaits from the beyond the unknown. That night, Nathan thought about Victor before he went to sleep. He wondered if the black would wash off if he scrubbed it real hard. He was excited about playing catch. He wondered how long before his mom would take him back.

Chapter 23

"My father used to play with my brother and me in the yard. Mother would come out and say, "You're tearing up the grass"; "We're not raising grass," Dad would reply. "We're raising boys."

—*Harmon Killebrew*

Exactly one year after the integration of the public schools in Russellville and Logan County, the national focus was upon Little Rock, Arkansas.

On September 4th 1957, nine Negro students attempted to enter Central High School in Little Rock.

Gasoline was added to the "Crisis in Little Rock," when Arkansas Governor, Orval Faubus brought in the Arkansas National Guard. His objective as Governor was to stop, not enforce, the integration of Central High School.

Efforts by the school board, the mayor, and the President of the United States all failed to de-escalate the situation. The lives of all nine Negro students were in danger.

In the end, with no other local options available, the mayor of Little Rock, Mayor Woodrow Wilson Mann, asked President Dwight D. Eisenhower to send troops.

On September 24th, twenty days after the siege of Central High School began, President Eisenhower ordered elements of the Army's 101st Airborne Division from Ft. Campbell, Kentucky to Little Rock. He also federalized the entire 10,000 member Arkansas National Guard. By federalizing the National Guard, Eisenhower seized control and command of the Guard from state authority. The governor was left without troops to enforce his rebellion against integration. Soldiers from the 101st escorted the students to the school and kept them safe on the outside of the walls.

No Negro soldiers from the 101st were sent to Little Rock.

Unfortunately, the nine black students suffered terribly from physical and mental abuse by, not all, but many white students *inside* the school building itself.

The Arkansas Governor did not give up his fight against integration. He was able to delay and interfere with the integration progress for several more years. Eventually, Arkansas joined the nation in complying with the Supreme Court decision

Logan County had a small connection to the Little Rock Crisis, The Army's 101st Airborne division was located 20 miles from the Logan County Line. Logan County had always enjoyed a close relationship with the 101st.

One of the best historical accounts of the federalization of the Arkansas National Guard and the role of the 101st Airborne is written by Col. Heath Twichell Jr. Col. Twichell was a Second Lieutenant officer with the 101st and was part of the detachment sent to Little Rock.

Second Lieutenant Twichell had no command responsibilities so he was given a camera and a notebook. His orders were to record and document everything he saw.

Lt. Twichell's accounting of the moment-by-moment, day-by-day activities are still the best record available of the events surrounding the Little Rock incident.

Col. Twichell's father, Colonel Heath Twichell Sr., was Samuel Wells' commander and mentor with the 95th in Alaska and later in Europe. And it was Col. Twichell's connection and recommendation that helped get Samuel his job with the L&N Railroad.

Kentucky governor Lawrence Wetherby showed wisdom in quickly announcing that Kentucky would comply with the Supreme Court decision. Although Emerson "Doc" Beauchamp would not want to hear it. Governor "Happy" Chandler also handled desegregation very well. He supported the mandate for integration in Kentucky and saved Kentucky from the indignity and embarrassment of the kind witnessed in Little Rock and other areas of the south.

Back in Russellville, integration continued to be a community non-event. By non-event, it meant that there were racial issues, just as everywhere in the South, but school integration was not a "hot spot" of trouble.

For the next few years, Nathan would walk once or twice a week to his father's welding shop. It wasn't very far from his school. There were sidewalks most of the way. He would cut over two blocks from 7th Street to 5th Street and then walk down to Morgan Street. If it was raining or too cold, someone would always give him a ride.

Nathan liked the shop. There was stuff to do and see. His father would pay him 25 cents to sweep the office and pick up trash around the outside. With 25 cents, he could walk over to Buck Browning's Grocery and buy a Coke and a Baby Ruth candy bar and still have eight cents in change.

If Victor was around, they would share a candy bar or somethin'. Victor was usually around. He would see Nathan outside pickin' up trash or walkin' around. There weren't any other white kids in the area so it was hard to miss him.

Down a couple of blocks on 5th street was Town Creek. Maybe it had another name. It ran all over town so everybody just called it Town Creek. Nathan's dad told him there was a spring under the street down around 2nd and Main Street that fed the creek. The spring was the center of Russellville in the early days of horses and steam-engines.

The Town Creek was a good place to play. There weren't many houses down there. The area around the creek was low and it flooded often. That entire section of town was low. That's why they called it the "Bottom". Because most of the residence were Negro, the more explicit name for the area was the "Black Bottom."

Victor and Nathan would go down to the creek and throw rocks into the water. They would also throw anything in the creek that they found lying around. Catchin' frogs was big fun too. They talked about fishin' sometimes. Victor's mother said the creek was nasty and they didn't need to be around it. She said they could get a fever and die.

In 1960, the Town Creek flooded again. Water was all over the bottom and all over the lower downtown near 1st and 2nd streets. The water came up almost to Victor's house. All the houses down near the creek were flooded. It was an awful mess.

When the water finally went down, they demolished most of the houses near the creek. City officials said they would fix the creek from flooding, but it was still too risky to live nearby. That was true because the creek flooded again in 1966. City officials pledged they would fix the creek. Guess what happened?

Victor and Nathan mostly just talked about stuff. He told Nathan about his school and Nathan told him about his. He liked his teacher. She was real nice, Victor said. His teacher had him workin' on special stuff all the time.

Victor had lots of homework and sometimes he would have too much homework to come out and play. And Nathan's dad didn't want Nathan hanging around Victor's house too much. So Nathan always promised he would not stay long.

On warm days, the two would often play with some other boys. Nathan was the only white boy in the group. They were nice to him for the most part. They called him "Whitey" a few times but they were smiling when they said it.

"Why you come down here? Don't you got any white friends?" they would ask.

The Negro children never came to play in Nathan's neighborhood. In fact, Nathan had never seen any black kids near his house.

Nathan liked his friend Victor though, and they got along just fine. Nathan wanted to invite him for a visit but his mother said it "wasn't done." He didn't understand but he didn't argue. It was not wise to argue with mothers in those days.

When Nathan went to Victor's house, they had fun. His mom was nice. His dad was always working so Nathan seldom saw him, unless it was a railroad holiday or weekend. The L&N had more holidays than most workplaces so Nathan would see Samuel on occasion.

*

One afternoon, Victor and Nathan had been playing tag football in an empty lot down near the creek. It was the "hill" against the "bottom". The "hill" was the area around Knob City School. Nathan was playing on the "bottom team." The kids were gaming each other with trash talk.

It was talk like, "I'm gonna kick your nigger ass on this next play." That afternoon the n-word got a real workout. Nathan didn't say anything.

Nathan wasn't sure what it meant, but after hearing it all afternoon, he was starting to get comfortable with the n-word. When Victor and Nathan got back to Victor's house, Patricia was setting out a couple of Cokes and some cookies. Both boys were thirsty and hungry so they jumped on the snack with gusto.

Patricia sat down and asked them about their game. Nathan and Victor were excited that they had won a major victory. Both of them were laughing and talking on top of each other. At some point it got quiet. It was at that moment that a young ignorant naive white boy dropped his bomb. Nathan looked at Patricia and asked, "What's a nigger?"

Had he not been a seven-year-old child, it could have been a disaster. Patricia did not show much reaction. She had welcomed this white child into her home but always knew that white folks were just not the same as black folks.

But, Patricia's eyes betrayed her shock. Trying not to allow any emotion in her voice, she asked Nathan, "where did you hear that word?"

Now Nathan had heard that word a thousand times in a thousand places. It was his good fortune that day to link it to the reason he had asked his question. "The other boys were saying it when we played football today," he answered.

Patricia relaxed and spoke calmly. "It is an awful word." Looking at Victor she pointer her finger at him. She punctuated each word by lifting her wrist and firing her pointer finger at Victor's nose.

"I don't want to ever hear you use that word, you hear me young man?' she said.

Turning, she fired a couple of finger bullets at Nathan too.

"Either of you."

Victor and Nathan looked at each other and nodded their heads. Neither of them really knew what the word meant but they knew they better not say it around the house - ever again.

*

In 1962, Charles Weaver built a big new shop near the Bowling]Green and Franklin Road intersection. It was too far for Nathan to walk there after school. His visits with Victor stopped for a while until Nathan got his new bicycle that next Christmas.

"Home by dark," was the rule for small town kids in those days. In summer it was, "Home by lightin' bugs."

It was a time when kids rode their bikes all over town. If someone did something bad, the nearest adult would address the situation on the spot, call his or her parents if necessary and send them home for a possible whippin'. The system worked very well.

Nathan enjoyed riding his bicycle downtown and then sometimes over to the "Bottom." It was an adventure. The Herndon family owned an ice cream shop not far away on 4th Street. Victor and Nathan would often go over and get an ice cream cone for a dime.

They knew somehow that their relationship was not ordinary. No one said anything to them exactly. They were very young so they didn't attract much attention. Still, the two boys knew not to go downtown together. They stayed in or near the "Bottom."

Samuel continued to advance with his job at L&N. He was making more money than he ever dreamed he would make. Patricia and Samuel could afford to have Patricia stay home and raise their children.

Victor had a younger sister, Lili. Lili was two years younger than Victor. It seemed that Lili hated everything. Nathan felt that she especially disliked him. Nathan and Victor enjoyed returning the favor by tormenting her whenever possible. She hated it if they ignored her, and she hated it if they tried to be nice. Nathan learned over the years to make a wide circle around her.

Chapter 24

"Someday you will be old enough to start reading fairytales again."

—C. S. Lewis

Nathan enjoyed Boy Scouts. It was a great experience for young boys. He eventually became an Eagle Scout. Scouting got him out of the house. It took him away to meetings, camping and work on merit badges. Nathan did not notice there were no black Boy Scouts.

One day Nathan learned that Victor was also a Boy Scout. Henry Ashby and Davis Smith organized a Negro Boy Scout Troop. They went camping and fishing and also took trips to Kentucky Lake to work on swimming merit badges. It was another piece of the universe Nathan knew nothing about because the Negro and the white scouts never got together.

Another big part of life, both for Nathan and Victor, was church. Nathan's family attended Post Oak Baptist Church on the white side of town. Charles and Athelyn were active members.

Victor's family were members of First Baptist Church on the corner of 5th and Spring Streets. Samuel and Patricia were also active in their church

Post Oak had no Negro members and First Baptist, the First Baptist in the "bottom", had no white members.

A wise man once said that the most segregated day of the week is Sunday. That is absolutely true. Few actually believe that God makes any "never you mind" about the color of skin when he welcomes his believers into his kingdom of heaven. But on earth, throughout 60s and beyond, the body of Christ had always been divided by color. Odd isn't it? It would

101

seem that church would have been the first place to bring everyone together. Not so. It was the last place.

*

It soon became clear that Victor was very smart. His teachers realized it early and worked to push him to learn. They assigned books and extra work for him. His parents, Samuel and Patricia, worked with him and supported his quest for knowledge. Victor often started a conversation with, "Did you know that?" and then he would continue because Nathan never knew the answer. Nathan enjoyed his lectures. Victor wasn't stuck-up about anything. They discussed whatever topic had their interest at the moment. Sometimes science and sometimes something else.

Victor, however, was not the most athletic fellow around. It was painful to watch. There was something unnatural about it and it did not go unnoticed. "Victor, you stink," some Negro kids said one day. "You're so bad you smell like Vick's Vapor Rub. We're gonna call you Rub for short. From now on, your name is Rub."

And so it was. Victor Wells became Rub Wells or just Rub. Because he stunk at sports!

Then in September of 1963, everything changed. They call it high school. Both Rub and Nathan entered Russellville High School as freshmen.

That same year, in Birmingham, Alabama, an epic deed of evil shook the nation. Four little black girls died in the bombing of a Negro Baptist church.

Chapter 25

"I have learned over the years that when one's mind is made up, this diminishes fear; knowing what must be done does away with fear."

—*Rosa Parks*

Russellville High School, (RHS), had been integrated since the fall of 1956. The elementary and middle schools were, however, still segregated.

On his first day as a freshman at Russellville High School, Nathan saw a lot of people he had never seen before. There were a few Negro kids his age that he knew but some he did not know. There were also a bunch of Catholic kids he had never met. Nathan had lived a sheltered life in a small town and didn't know anybody! He discovered a parallel universe he did not know existed.

Nathan saw Rub outside before school started on the first day. He was with a group of Negro students. Nathan had ridden his bike to school and was hangin' with a few white friends when their eyes met. Nathan raised his hand giving the universal "greet" sign. Rub lowered his head and waved low as he turned and went through the school doors.

Inside, all students went to their homeroom. In homeroom and in many classes, students were usually arranged in alphabetical order. Sometimes they sat in alphabetical order rows side to side and sometimes they sat in alphabetical order front to back. Rub was in Nathan's homeroom. In fact, he sat right behind Nathan. They mostly took the same classes so he was usually beside or behind in the alphabetical order of Weaver and Wells.

That suited Nathan just fine. They knew each other and there was no get acquainted period. Inside the classroom they talked and laughed and were best friends. Outside of class, things were different.

*

On Friday nights, everyone sat together and watched the game. After the game, the races separated and walked away in different directions. Unless they met at the grocery store, the white kids did not see the Negro kids again until school Monday morning. The black students went one way and the white students went another.

Teen Town was a place of gathering for whites. Inclusion was by membership only. It was located in a building downtown. The facility was also available for Boy Scout meetings and special events. On Friday and Saturday nights, it was open for white teens to gather, play ping pong or listen to a jukebox. Occasionally there were dances. For dances, the place would be packed. It was well chaperoned but here was always opportunity for trouble outside. This was true only "if a person went lookin' for it." Teen Town was regarded as a safe place for teens.

Out on Hwy 79, but still in the city limits of Russellville, was an eatery drive-in known as the "Tastee Treet" or the "Tastee" for short. The owner, Mr. Switzer, ran a tight ship and cooked a legend of a burger-type sandwich called, you guessed it, a "Tastee!"

A typical night, if someone had a car or knew someone with a car, and there wasn't a dance at Teen Town, involved driving around town in a loop that included the Tastee. It was the town hall for teens; the village green; the place to see and be seen. And the food was good.

Negro kids could not go to Teen Town. It wasn't allowed. Negroes did not go to the Tastee. At least not that Nathan ever saw in the '60s. There was no visible barrier that limited access. It simply did not happen. That change later, along with a lot of things, but back then it was the way it was.

It was the same with downtown businesses. Negroes used back doors to enter many of shops and stores.

Never once during four years of high school did Nathan ever look around and ask himself or ask someone else, "where are all the Negro kids?" White kids lived their lives and never questioned it. The years between 1963 and 1968 were the most dramatic, violent, and history-making period in the long history of the Civil Rights movement. That same period enveloped Nathan's years in high school. He totally missed the local connection to all that was happening in the world that surrounded him.

Apparently, most of his white friends in high school missed it too. Good people thought there were no civil rights issues in Logan County because they saw Negroes every day in school. Everybody looked happy! There were some differences, sure, but that was just the way it was.

*

When the Negro students left the football or basketball games, they went down to the "Bottom." There, in the heart of "Bottom Land", was Todd's Cafe and also the KP Hall.

Todd's was a rockin' place. Mr. Todd would not allow underage drinking in his place of business. Parents knew this and allowed their children to stay out later as long as they stayed in the Bottom at Todd's Cafe. Some would hang around outside on Morgan Street and talk trash. There would be so many in the street that traffic had to detoured around the area. Especially on Friday and Saturday nights.

The KP Hall was across Morgan and around the corner on 5th Street. The main hall was upstairs but there was a side entrance up the hill at ground level. Local Negro bands would come and there would be dances for the teens. It was the Negro "Teen Town" on dance nights. The KP Hall hosted some of the best bands of the era. They actually had better music than Teen Town.

During this period, Negro teens never mixed with whites at dances. A few white girls and even fewer white boys would eventually go to the KP Hall and Todds's but Negroes never attended the white dances. There were no signs posted, but everyone knew the rules.

Rub never invited Nathan to a dance at the KP Hall but they did go to Todd's Cafe a few times. They sat in the balcony area and drank their Cokes. Everybody was very nice to Nathan. Most everybody had seen him around the "Bottom" for years. They knew he and Rub were friends.

There were always girls at Todd's. Nathan knew them very well from school. Some would wave and a few stopped by to say hello. Most were on a date or hanging with their girlfriends. Rub dated girls but never when he and Nathan were hanging together. Nathan was always friendly but he was not the same with the Negro girls that he was with white girls. He knew there were rules. Actually two rules. First, Nathan knew if he started making moves on girls, he would not be welcomed back to Todd's Cafe. Second, if a Negro girl and white boy had tried to date; they would not have been accepted in either community. They could sneak around, and a few did just that. But, never out in the open. That's just the way it was.

Chapter 26

"A school without football is in danger of deteriorating into a medieval study hall."

—Vince Lombardi

Neither Rub nor Nathan were big enough or fast enough or tall enough or had any great athletic ability. Rub was famous for being clumsy. Nathan was a too skinny for football and basketball was a challenge because he wasn't quick, he couldn't dribble, and he couldn't jump.

Both ran track and played some Junior Varsity ball but athletics, at varsity level was not in their nature.

Both boys decided independently to join the high school band. It is said that music is good for the soul. Rub took up the clarinet and Nathan got a trombone. Hazel Carver was the band director. Rub picked it up quickly. Nathan took a little longer.

Being in the band required playing at all the home football games. The band usually had a pregame and halftime performance.

In the fall of 1963, the Russellville High School Panthers were on their way to the Kentucky Class "A" state playoff game at the University of Kentucky stadium in Lexington. Only one team stood in their way.

*

The journey of Negro athletes, some say, started when Joe Louis won the heavyweight championship. The Louis victory was followed in a few years by a record four gold medals in the 1936 Olympics, by Jesse Owens.

107

Those two young men were an inspiration to Negro athletes across America. Opportunities, however, were slow to come.

It was 1947 before Jackie Robinson broke the racial barrier in major league baseball, with the Brooklyn Dodgers.

Colleges lagged behind both professional and high school sports. The South lagged behind other parts of the nation. It was 1966 before Nat Northington and Greg Page were offered scholarships to play football for the University of Kentucky.

The decision by the Warren Court integrated all aspects of American education, including athletics. Negro athletes began playing high school sports immediately after integration, but not all schools were on the same integration schedule.

In the early years, after *Brown vs. Board of Education*, some schools integrated immediately while others were slow to make the move. Those variations in the integration process occasionally brought together a clash of cultures. The clash occurred when integrated schools met segregated schools in athletic events.

This scenario became more likely during the playoff seasons. The playoffs in football and basketball brought teams together from distant places. Places where attitudes and cultures did not match.

It wasn't just the players who met at the designated gridiron or basketball gym. Each school brought busloads of fans and car-loads of families to the game. They arrived early and stayed late cheering their team.

In late November, 1963, the southwest Kentucky Russellville High School Panthers met the east Kentucky Plainsville Blue Devils. Russellville had Negro players. Plainsville did not.

RHS held the home advantage as Plainsville took the field. It was unusually cold for late November. Biting snow and a soggy field greeted the Panthers and the Blue Devils. The soggy field, however, was starting to freeze as temperatures continued to drop.

Coaches Morris and Baker had their RHS team ready to play. The Panthers quickly took command of the game with a stingy defense and an offense led by two Negro halfbacks, Gary Todd and Michael Benton.

Jerry Humble at fullback and a strong offensive line anchored by tackles Tom Ricks and Gary Silvey kept the Blue Devils on their heels the entire game.

Rub and Nathan, along with the other band members, had excellent stadium seats. They were down front and center. It was cold and the wind was blowing hard out of the north. Many of the boys wore their father's long underwear under their band uniforms. The female band members wore warm mystery clothes. Whatever the comfort level, no one was thinking of an early exit.

It was especially exciting to have the home advantage in the state semi-final game. If the Panthers could hold onto their lead, the next week they would play for the state championship.

*

Early in the fourth quarter, Russellville had the ball on the RHS 42-yard line. It was second and six. Quarterback Benny Cox was under center. On his count, Cox took the ball and pitched out to Gary Todd, a junior halfback. Todd took the pitch out and swept around the strong side. He broke into the open field on a block by Jerry Humble. A couple of stiff-arms and he was running strong down the sideline. At the fifteen-yard line, the Blue Devil free safety came across and made a good tackle on Todd. The whistle blew the play dead and there were no flags on the field. A great roar erupted from the Russellville side of the stadium. Rub and Nathan enthusiastically joined the celebration

Suddenly, from across the field, there was a commotion. Closer examination revealed that the white Blue Devil safety was on top of Gary Todd. The safety appeared to be hammering Todd with his fists. Todd was fending off the blows as best as he could but he was on his back and at a disadvantage. Two referees stood near watching the beating, but took no action to stop it.

Back at the line of scrimmage the scene began to unfold, seemingly in slow motion. All-State tackle Tom Ricks had watched the play unfold. Tom could see Gary on the ground with his arms up trying to deflect the blows. Tom's feet started moving beneath him as he exploded down field. To this day, some people still swear they felt the ground shake as he passed them by. Coaches and players looked on in shock.

The crunching sound of colliding helmets, pads, bones and flesh was clearly audible from across the icy field. Ricks had delivered a message to the safety. His teammate, Gary Todd, was not a punching bag.

Tom came in low, hard and fast. Crack! It sounded like he had taken the Blue Devil's head clean off. However you want to describe it, when the smoke cleared, Gary was back on his feet. Mr. Safety, however, was no longer among the conscious. His helmet had rolled into the end zone, twenty yards south of his ears.

Out of nowhere, red flags went flying in all directions. The referees had suddenly awoken to see a grievous infraction! The coaches from both teams ran out onto the field. The players drained their respective benches. Coaches then reversed course, turned and tried to calm the players and get control. Local physician, Dr. Dodson was on duty that night. He ran out onto the field to check on the downed player.

In the end, it was Tom Ricks who was suspended for the rest of the game and for the rest of the season. The rest of the season being only the final championship game.

Russellville won, 24-0. Fellow All-State tackle, Gary Silvey, was able to take up the slack after Ricks was forced to leave the game.

The safety for Plainsville eventually left the field somewhat under his own power.

If local sports and history buffs do not recall the story of Tom Ricks and his suspension, it is because there was no report of the incident. There was no story about the beating of Gary Todd or the melee that occurred as part of the incident. Because there was no report of the suspension, there was no report that the suspension was appealed by coaches Morris and Baker. The decision to suspend Ricks for the next game was reversed early Monday morning.

Tom Ricks played a great game in Lexington the following week. He helped lead RHS to a great victory, a state championship and another trophy in the high school trophy case. The trophy is only proof that the Panthers arrived. As with all trophies, it does not tell the complete story of the journey that was necessary to get there.

*

Although racism continued to segregate Negroes and whites in society, Negro athletes made some progress breaking racial barriers. In fact, they led the way.

Sports enthusiasts across the South gradually put aside racial resentment to passionately support their favorite teams. African American athletes were eventually welcomed on every college campus.

In athletics, if nowhere else, desegregation put the races together in a team environment where all of the players, black or white, had a common goal. Sports shifted the focus from color to performance.

A three-point shot that never touches the rim will bring the crowd to its feet every time. The color of the shooter is no longer relevant. We enjoy this reality because of the process started long ago with integration.

Chapter 27

"Elvis was the only man from Mississippi who could shake his hips and still be loved by rednecks, cops, and hippies."

—Jimmy Buffett

It was a normal high school afternoon. The air was warm but not hot. This was the time of year when it was great to be outside shaking off the recent winter.

Nathan was standing on the corner of 4th and Main Street in front of Duncan's Drugstore. The newspaper and magazine stand was located near the door in the front section of the store. High school boys would check out the latest "Mad Magazine" and watch out the window to see who was circling around the town square. Several had gathered that day at the popular after-school hangout, and several, including Nathan, had eventually drifted outside. This was after they had put away a few cherry Cokes and frozen Reese Cups.

Buzz Colburn pulled up to the curb and hollered out the window at Nathan to get in the car. Nathan had known Buzz forever. They were childhood friends, growing up in the same neighborhood. As older boys, they had been in scouting together. Nathan didn't hesitate to hop into Buzz's car. Nathan knew it must be something important.

"What's up Buzz?" he inquired shortly after his butt hit the seat. Buzz's foot pressed down on the accelerator and they headed west before Buzz said a word.

"I just saw Rub out on the Hopkinsville Road. Officer Hodge was there too. Rub was standing near his car with the hood up. Something didn't look

112

right. I had just seen you standing up here so I looped back to pick you up. I think Rub is in a pickle."

Buzz was serious. It was obvious he was worried. "I know you are close with Rub," Buzz said. "I didn't really want to stop by myself. I thought you would be good to go along."

Nathan had mixed feelings about the adventure. He wanted to help his friend but he didn't want a confrontation with the police. If this went badly, there would be a price to pay at home. His parents would kill him! It was too awful to think about so he put it out of his mind.

As they pulled up behind Rub's car, they could see Rub and Officer Hodge. There was loud conversation going on but they could not make out the words over the engine noise. Rub was still standing beside his car. He had a Coke bottle in his hand and the hood was up.

*

The Russellville police department was typical of other departments in small southern towns. The police were always white and male. The secretary was always white and female. That was the way it was.

Being a cop was the best thing that ever happened to Peter Hodge. He had grown up dirt poor and mostly just dirty. His family lived out the Morgantown Road past Knob City School. It wasn't the "Bottoms" or "the hill" but there were several Negro families who lived nearby in Peter's neighborhood.

The Hodge house was the worst kept house on his street. The house needed paint and the yard was a combination of trash, junk, dirt and weeds. A screen door leaned up against the wall, near the door, on the front porch. It was easy to see that the house had looked nice at one time but had been neglected in recent years.

Peter Hodge had few friends. He never invited friends to his house. He was ashamed that they would have to walk or ride past "nigger houses" to reach his place.

His dad was usually home. He had been wounded in the war and returned home with injuries that could be seen and many that were hidden. Peter never knew when or why his dad would start drinking. Sometimes it was because of the cold and sometimes it was the heat. He drank when he was happy and he drank when he was sad. Unfortunately, no matter where he started, he always ended up angry.

Peter's mother took the brunt of the punishment. She walked around with bruises. She told the neighbors she was clumsy. They, of course, knew better. Many times they had heard her crying and begging him to stop beating her. The whole street could hear them quarrel. Peter pretended it was a family secret.

Peter developed various coping skills. Mostly, he learned to disappear. His daily mission around the house was to maintain peace by limited contact. If that failed, Peter tried to carefully negotiate his way over and around each hurdle. Peter's primary goal was to protect his mother.

No, he couldn't risk bringing friends over to the house. The secrets were safe for now. Friends could come later.

Peter did daydream however. He dreamed of a life in a nice little house. "Man, would that be cool," he thought as he lay in bed at night.

Another "cool" idea in Peter's head was of being a policeman. He had seen the respect that people gave to a police officer. Even his dad would not give the police any shit.

Peter had seen it firsthand a couple of times. The police had been called to the house more than once. A neighbor had probably called when it got too loud or they heard his mom screaming.

It was "yes sir" and "no sir" and "thank you, sir," when his dad talked to the police. Boy oh boy, that impressed Peter.

After graduation from high school, Peter made his dream a reality. He would never forget those first moments in his new uniform. The shirt was starched crisp as you please. His black leather shoes had a shine so bright he could almost see his face in them. The leather belt and holster had that great leather smell and they crackled when he wrapped them around his waist.

The first person to see him in his police uniform was his mother. She sat in the living room of his new little rental house off Nashville Street. She had spent all day cleaning and decorating. It wasn't much but it was on the other side of town from Knob City. She was so excited for Peter.

Peter's mother looked up from her chair when Peter walked into the room. She stood up, hugged her son and cried with joy and pride. Maybe her son could finally have the life she had always wanted him to have.

Peter looked in the mirror and saw a new man. He saw a new man in a new uniform. He was starting a new life. This man in the mirror would demand respect.

Peter had always known he was better than those niggers he had been forced to be around as a child. Now he had "proof."

Truth was, Peter didn't have a problem with most niggers. That is as long as they knew their place and didn't act out. "Most niggers was good people," he thought. But nothin' pissed him off like an "uppity nigger.' No sir, that would just about make him go blind and lose his supper.

He had seen them around town. They were easy to spot if a person had an eye for it. Hodge hoped he could make a difference. Everybody knew where the threat of crime came from. If he could put the "fear of God" into the Negroes, he would be the town hero.

He had to keep a low profile about it though. The police had to appear neutral about such things. He had to keep a "public face" for show, but everybody knew the real truth about it all. His job was to keep the peace, and keeping the peace meant keeping all them darkies in line.

Peter's most obvious problem was his anger. He was known to occasionally become violent with women. Peter always blamed it on the women or the beer. But word got around. Russellville was a small town after all.

*

It started off innocently enough when Officer Hodge stopped a vehicle for a speeding violation. The driver was a young girl and she was cute as a button.

Hodge saw the fear in her eyes as she begged him to please not give her a ticket.

"I will be in so much trouble with my daddy," she cried. "He will beat me and ground me and take away my car." "I can't go home." "Can't we find a way to just forget that this ever happened?" she said as she batted her teary eyes.

Hodge barely graduated from high school but he was smart enough to see his good fortune.

"This girl is coming on to me!" Hodge said to himself. "*She* was begging *him!*"

The rush of power made his knees weak. Maybe it was the lust or maybe it was the excitement. Whatever it was, Hodge liked it. He liked it a lot! It was a real "turn-on."

After that night, Hodge was on the prowl as much as he was on patrol.

*

Officer Peter Hodge had watched Rub pass the courthouse earlier. Seeing Rub stranded on the side of the road made the officer smile.

Hodge thought that Rub had an "attitude" and that he was just the man to set him straight. Rub had his nigger nose stuck up in the air. Maybe a few thumps on his noggin with a nightstick would adjust that high-horse nigger attitude of his.

Hodge was a fast learner and a hard worker. He had gained the confidence that comes with experience. He knew when he could use his power and this was one of those moments.

The officer first pulled alongside of Rub and stopped for a moment to let him know he was boxed in. He hit the lights and punched the siren to add emphasis. Hodge then rolled in front of Rub's car and slid onto the shoulder. His tires made a crunching sound in the gravel and skidded as he stopped abruptly.

Officer Hodge kept the red and blue lights going as he got out of the squad car and walked back towards Rub. Rub turned and faced him.

The lights behind Officer Hodge blinded Rub but Hodge could see clearly. This was the advantage Hodge was looking to have when he parked in front of Rub.

Hodge made no bones about the situation. He marched up close to Rub. He stood inches from his face and poked him in the chest with his finger. His finger marked time to the beat of every word. "Say boy. What are you doin out here in that car?"

"Did you steal that car, boy?"

"You lookin at me, boy?"

"No sir, "Rub said. Rub knew the routine.

Careful not to look at the officer Rub responded, "I've been havin' some problem with the thermostat stickin'." I stopped to add a little water, that's all."

Hodge was enjoying his game. "I say you stole that car, boy."

116

"No sir officer." Rub was getting uneasy.

"Are you callin' me a liar, boy?"

"Maybe you need an ass whippin' to teach you a little respect."

Rub now knew he was in big trouble. It was late afternoon. There were no witnesses. Whatever happened would be his word against a police officer.

Still, Rub was tired of being harassed. He decided right then and there that he was not going to take a whippin' layin' down. He was going to try to keep talkin', and try to think his way out of the situation. He would try to keep explainin' for as long as he could. But, if necessary, he would stand his ground; whatever that meant.

From his power position, Hodge enjoyed watching Rub sweat. He was playing with him like a cat plays with a mouse. The officer listened to Rub's story of how he had bought the car from his boss, Mr. Parrish. Hodge pretended to look under the hood and examine the problem. All the while, he constantly slapped his black nightstick into the palm of his hand. It made a popping sound every time the leather stick struck his leather glove.

Officer Hodge stood looking at Rub while Rub jabbered. Hodge though that Rub was starting to tire from the stress. He hoped that very soon Rub was going to give him the excuse he needed to take the boy down. Hodge kept a big shit eatin' grin on his face. Always playing with his nightstick.

Then suddenly there was a distraction and Hodge took a step backward.

*

The sun was setting but some light was still visible in the southwestern sky. As Buzz and Nathan got out of the car, Hodge's voice cut through the silent air.

Buzz had pulled in behind Rub's car. Rub had not yet heard or seen Buzz and Nathan approaching. His total focus on officer Hodge had blocked out everything around him.

Rub had grown tired of the game. He'd had enough. Rub was thinking to himself that he was not going to take a beating. He said he was just trying to put some water in his radiator. Although Rub still couldn't see his friends because they were walking up behind him, Hodge had spotted them immediately.

Before anyone had time to say anything, Buzz just blurted out a string of questions. "Hey Rub? What's happenin', man? You need some help? Something wrong with your car?"

Rub turned around and finally saw his rescue team. "Officer Hodge here was just saying how he was about to whip my ass," Rub explained.

Hodge hiked his pants up and put on his authority face. "Now wait a minute here. I was just kidding about that and besides this ain't nobody's business." Looking at Buzz and Nathan he waved his hand. "You boys need to run along now."

"Sure thing officer," Buzz replied as if they were all best friends. "I thought we would help Rub get his car rolling and get this problem out of your hair. Is it overheating Rub?"

"Smooth move, Buzz!" Nathan thought to himself. He was impressed at how Buzz was shifting the conversation, avoiding conflict and keeping the duly appointed officer on his heels.

"Thank ya, Buzz. Yeah I think so. It overheated and I was just trying to add some water and let it cool when this officer arrived. I told him I didn't want no trouble. I just needed to put some water in the radiator so I can get to work, that's all."

Nathan stepped forward a little but mostly hid behind Buzz.

"Do you mind if we help Rub out and take it from here. Our dads can come and help if we need major repairs," Buzz stated frankly.

Russellville was small enough that everyone knew everyone. The police knew Buzz's dad, Calvin and Nathan's dad, Charlie.

Officer Hodge thought to himself that "tonight's fun had gone far enough and it was time to retreat to play another day."

"Yeah sure, you boys do your thing," Hodge said as he touched his hat in mock salute then hiked up his pants again.

Looking back over his shoulder as he walked away, Peter Hodge turned back to Rub. He put that grin back on his face. "Rub, you watch your mouth and you better watch your back too cuz I'm sure enough watchin' your smart ass."

With that, Officer Hodge returned to his squad car and threw a little gravel as he pulled out onto the road.

"What the hell was that all about?" Buzz almost shouted at Rub.

"He was about to whip my ass. Least that's what he said."

Rub's voice was higher than normal and it cracked a bit.

Rub continued to explain, "My car heated up. I was on the way to work so I pulled over on the side of the road here and thought I could cool her down a little. That thermostat I put in was used and it ain't no count. She has been getting hot some lately so I had some water with me just in case. I poured it into this Coke bottle here and I had just raised the hood when officer "Barney Fife" pulled up. He asked me what I was doin' and I tried to tell him just like I just told you but he was like mad or somethin."

He got all puffy and said, "What you doin' out here - BOY?"

"He's been ridin' my ass now for months. I'm startin' to get tired of it. I said that I wasn't doin' nothin' but putting water in my car. He said it was time I got my ass whipped. I said I wasn't gonna take an ass whippin', just cuz I was puttin' water in my car and that was about the time you fellas pulled up."

Rub was acting cool but a close examination would show that his hands were shaking. Buzz may have saved the day, that day, but Hodge made a statement. The statement, or perhaps it was more of an announcement, was not lost on Rub or the black community.

*

Rub had a job at Parish Texaco down the road a mile or two. The car had cooled down. The extra water took care of the overheating for the time being. Enough to get Rub to work anyway.

"Sure glad you fellas came by. I would probably be in jail with a busted head if you hadn't arrived in the nick of time!"

They all shook hands and went their separate ways. Buzz took Nathan home because it was after dark by then and Nathan didn't have a ride. Rub got to work a few minutes late but no harm was done.

Buzz never mentioned why he went to Rub's rescue. He didn't know Rub well enough to go sticking his neck out like that. Nathan didn't ask him why he did it, but, he had to admit he admired him for it.

This was the sort of thing that was, and still is the paradox of the South. White people who may shy away from the bigger picture of Civil Rights, will go to great lengths to defend, or help, a particular black person.

Years later, Rub saw Buzz in town and went over to thank him for what he had done that night. Buzz said he didn't remember anything about it.

*

Before that episode, Nathan had no idea that the police were hostile to his black friends from school. They never talked about it. Nathan didn't know that they were all getting traffic tickets and were being stopped and searched on a regular basis. Several had been arrested and a few had been roughed up by the police.

Nathan doubted he would have believed those stories about the police without his personal experience that night on the Hopkinsville Road. Until he saw it with his own eyes, he did not understand the way it was.

*

As for Officer Hodge, he eventually disappeared from Russellville. It is odd when a person is there one day and gone the next and no one knows where. His mother said that she had no idea where he went.

Some say he got a better job at another police department. Some say his attitude towards the Negro community was finally "resolved" by "outsiders."

Others say that he took advantage of the wrong "young lady" and her daddy took care of the problem.

To this day, no one seems to know, for sure, the fate of Officer Peter Hodge. He just vanished and was missed by no one.

Chapter 28

"And he writhed inside at what seemed the cruelty and unfairness of the demand. He had not yet learned that if you do one good deed, your reward usually is to do another and harder and better one."

—C. S. Lewis

Most days, it was just regular stuff between Rub and Nathan. Nathan did notice that a few of his white friends were not as friendly when he was kicking around with Rub. No one ever got in his face about it, but he noticed. It was the same with Rub's black friends.

For the most part, Rub and Nathan blended into the background of both cultures. People got used to seeing them together and no one cared much. Besides, except for rare high school sporting events, theirs was a Monday through Friday relationship. On the occasions when they did hang on weekends, they would always hang in the "Bottom."

"Rub wouldn't be comfortable at the Tastee," thought Nathan. But in reality, it was probably the other way around. Nathan would not have been comfortable taking Rub to the Tastee.

*

After school one day, Rub disappeared. Rub and Nathan had 6th period English together and they usually did a "see ya" as they parted ways. But on this day, Nathan turned around and there was no Rub to be found.

Next morning, Rub was at band practice same as usual. "Missed ya yesterday," Nathan greeted with a questioning smile.

121

"Hey man! I didn't want you in on no part of it, so I split," Rub said grinning from ear to ear.

"Part of what?" Nathan questioned back.

"Oh shit! It was unreal! You should have seen it."

"What already?" Nathan was getting annoyed.

"You are a friend and all but, you know, some things are just a black thing. I didn't want you in the middle of it in case it went badly."

You ever hear of the Greensboro Sit-in at Woolworth?" Rub asked Nathan.

Nathan shook his head.

"It was before the Civil Rights Act. Four black guys walked into an all-white lunch counter and sat down. It was a big deal back then."

"We, a bunch of us, been talkin'. We go down to Perry's Cafe for somethin' to eat now and again and we go in the back door. There is a place back there where we order and sit without goin' into the main room where all the white folks sit and all."

"We were thinkin' and talkin' and we say, "Like damn, you know, we got some rights now!"

So, we decided that we would walk in the front door at Perry's Cafe, sit down in the white section and see what happened."

"No shit! Really?" Nathan said. "I didn't know Perry's had a "white" section."

"It's not marked or anything but yeah! It was Leonard Vick's idea. I didn't know he had it in him but that is one bad cat. It was me and Leonard Vick and Larry Bell and Preacher Hollins. We walked in the front door, proud as you please and we all sat down on stools at the counter."

"You know what happened?"

Nathan shook his head.

"Nothin'! Absolutely nothin'!"

"Joyce came over and asked us what we wanted. We all ordered a hamburgers and Coke. Nobody said a damn thing. We couldn't freakin' believe it. We ate our hamburger and drank our Coke, paid and walked out. We kept sorta' lookin' around ya know. I thought any minute the door was going to bust open and "the man" was going to rush in and start poundin' the livin' crap out of us or somethin', but nope! It didn't happen. I think that was the best damn burger I ever tasted."

Nathan was worried about the consequences.

"Was anybody else in there?" Nathan wanted to know.

Rub was still excited. "Yeah, hell, there were two white couples eatin' in a couple of booths. I saw them lookin' once but they didn't say anything or freak out."

Rub couldn't get the grin off his face all day. There was a lot of action at the black tables during lunch break. None of the white kids knew what was going on, except Nathan.

The Perry's Cafe incident is a popular story in the local Russellville African American community. There is no official written record of it. The story has been handed down. The fact that it happened and didn't cause any notice was memorable in itself. That is why it is so important. It was a small step, but a step, nonetheless. Everyone knows the Perry's Cafe story. It is legendary.

Things, however, didn't change much after the Perry's Cafe incident. Not even at Perry's! Few blacks wanted to push the envelope for push's sake. Old black men were not comfortable sittin' up front in the "white section'. That work, and other heavy lifting would be left for the next generation.

*

Nathan worked as a lifeguard at the local swimming pool, Spring Acres Park. He told Rub many times to come out and he would get him in free. Rub would have none of it.

"Number one, I never earned my swimming merit badge. Hell, I can't swim a lick: and number two, the last thing I need is a suntan," he told Nathan.

Very few blacks came to the pool. It was way out of town and swimming pools had traditionally been an all-white activity. Nathan didn't think Rub was comfortable with the idea of being out there.

Nathan really wanted to teach Rub to swim though. One warm summer night he finally talked him into going out to the pool for a swim lesson. Rub was less than enthusiastic about the idea. Nathan always prided himself in his ability to teach anybody to swim. Rub was one of his rare failures. He swam like a rock.

Spring Acres Park's water came from a cold spring that was also the mouth of the Muddy River. The swimming pool was famous for its water temperature. Even on the hottest dog days of summer, Spring Acres was a cool place to be. Rub, however, did not appreciate the cool nature of the water.

In fact, his teeth were chattering so loud they sounded like dice rolling off a tin roof. His lips turned a dark purple color.

Nathan adjusted quickly to the water but poor Rub was not enjoying the adventure one little bit. Nathan tried every teaching trick in his book. Rub couldn't float. He couldn't kick and his glide looked like a diving submarine. It was nearly hopeless. And anyone who saw him that night would swear he was gradually turning an odd shade of blue under goosebumps the size of golf balls.

The best Nathan could accomplish was some basic survival skills that would get Rub to shore if he fell in relatively shallow water.

Eventually Rub became foul. It was the first time Nathan had ever heard Rub cuss with total abandonment. Nathan laughed but Rub was mad as a hornet at Nathan for dragging him out there into that dark, cold, water.

Rub did try for a while, but there wasn't enough success to reinforce his effort. The water temperature; the water up his nose; the burn of the water chemicals in his eyes, and the exhaustion of muscles never used before, soon took their toll.

Rub bobbed over to the pool ladder, using his newly learned survival technique. He climbed the ladder and lumbered over to his bag on his tired, numb, knocking, knees. As he angrily grabbed his towel, he let it fly in Nathan's direction. "Damn you Weaver. You white folks are crazy; you know that? We are supposed to have evolved out of the water. We are not supposed to be in there, dammit. I ain't no goddamn fish! It's August and I'm freezing! I'm done!"

"Lesson over huh?" Nathan smirked.

Rub pointed his finger at Nathan. "You're gonna get yours soon, asshole!"

Rub would have said more but his lips were quivering, his teeth were chattering, and he was shaking all over. He knew he didn't look like much of a threat.

It was a quiet ride back to town after the swimming lesson. Rub's teeth were still chattering as they pulled onto 5th Street and came to a stop a half block up the street from Todd's. The warm town air started to thaw Rub's blood and his lips were the right color by then.

They laughed about it an hour later but when Nathan thought back on it, he thought he had noticed a subtle change in Rub. Rub had never used that language before. They were both churchgoers. They never said the "GD" word. They just didn't!

When they got back to town, Rub bragged to his friends about his skills in the water. The events of that night eventually became just another good story.

Chapter 29

True terror is to wake up one morning and discover that your high school class is running the country."

—Kurt Vonnegut

Their senior year at RHS was upon them. Both had taken all of the necessary college preparation classes. Rub sat beside Nathan in Mrs. Ruth Carpenter's college English and literature class.

Mrs. Ruth, at that time, was senior chair legend at RHS. She was one of several outstanding teachers in residence during, some say, the greatest days of education at Russellville High School, or anywhere, for that matter.

Mrs. Ruth was kind to Nathan when she read his writings. Getting praise from Mrs. Ruth was like manna from heaven. Rub, however, was the star of the class. He was the star of every class.

Rub was also becoming quite the class "man of the hour." People were beginning to respect his brains and warm to him. He could be a funny guy! His popularity was really put on display when he was tagged with a starring role in the Senior Class Play.

Every junior and senior class, in those days, would put on a play. It was always done. Mrs. Brodie Simmons was tapped that year to direct the senior's effort.

Rub didn't know her because he was still at Knob City, but Mrs. Simmons had been one of Nathan's 8th grade teachers during middle school. Nathan liked her well enough. The first story that Nathan remembered writing was for Mrs. Simmons. She liked the story giving Nathan an "A." Rub had checked the spelling for Nathan.

126

Years later, and as director of the senior play, Mrs. Brodie Simmons was absolutely charming!

The play was a musical comedy. Rub would have gotten the lead role but there was a problem. The script called for the leading man to kiss the leading lady. The leading lady was white. Therefore, the leading man could not be black. No Way; No How! No one even questioned it. Logan County was far from ready for - *that kiss*! That was just the way it was.

By his senior year, Victor (Rub) Wells had developed into a handsome young man. He was six feet tall with a strong chin and, according to the girls, he had "nice features."

Nathan got the leading part instead of Rub. Both Nathan and Rub had solo musical performances in the play. Rub seemed totally at ease on stage. His rich deep baritone voice rang through the auditorium. All of those years singing in church must have prepared him for his debut "on south Broadway!"

Play performance night arrived and Nathan watched and listened to Rub on stage. He started to regret having to follow his friend. The more he watched, the more nervous Nathan became.

Then suddenly it was time. Nathan heard his que. He stepped onto the stage with weak knees. The lights blinded his view of the audience, but he could see his classmate, Carol Guion, at the piano. The piano was center and just below the stage.

Carol looked up, smiled at him and replayed the introduction to his big on-stage number.

It would be interesting to see a brain scan of a brain, when the brain is in total lock-down. It is that moment in time and space when half of the brain is knocking and the other half refuses to answer the door. Nathan's eyes widened as he realized that he had entered that place known as... "the stage fright paralysis zone."

Nathan knew the music, but the words would not come. He fought the urge to run. The urge to run ended when Nathan realized his legs would not run. His options were then limited. So, Nathan started moving around the stage as directed. Instead of singing the scripted musical dialog, he improvised a series of la la's where the words should have been! When Nathan got to the chorus, the words started to break out of their cerebral lock-down. Nathan was finally able to finish the song as scripted. No one in the audience ever knew the difference. Backstage however, laughter went on for several minutes.

After the Senior Play was over, Nathan moved on to the next event. The "senior trip" was one of the last "hurrahs" of high school. The seniors had been saving for the trip since their freshman year. Money was collected every six weeks on the day when report cards were returned. The money was collected by the class treasurer during "homeroom period."

The "senior trip" included a day trip to Washington D. C. followed by two days in New York City.

For the first time in Russellville High School history, the class would travel by plane. Previous trips were by train. This was the first commercial airplane trip for most of the seniors.

Nathan and Rub had never really discussed the trip. When time was getting close to the big departure date, Nathan asked Rub if he was getting excited.

Rub brushed him off.

Sensing a problem, Nathan probed. "Rub, I've known you too long, so cut the BS. What's goin' on?"

Rub showed his annoyance at Nathan, "All these years and you never noticed. When you were paying your money every six weeks, you never looked over and saw that I wasn't paying into the "kitty?"

The wheels were now turning in Nathan's head. "You never paid into trip did you?"

"Why not? Why? Didn't you want to go? I don't get it."

Rub waited until Nathan finished, then he spoke deliberately. "When we were freshmen, no black had ever gone on the trip. Did you know that?"

Nathan was silent.

"I sure as hell wasn't going to be the first Negro on the "bus," if you know what I mean."

"You never said anything! Blacks are now going, aren't they?" Nathan said. He was still somewhere between surprised and annoyed.

"The girls have started to go but the black guys haven't signed up yet. Some of the younger guys are paying in so I guess the male racial barrier will be broken soon but not on this trip."

Nathan was uncomfortable with the conversation. He thought that he and Rub were on the same wave length and suddenly it felt weird. He didn't understand exactly what Rub was saying.

Nathan almost spit the words. "Are you saying that you never wanted to go on the trip or that you didn't feel like you were invited. I don't remember anyone ever saying you couldn't go."

The truth be known, Rub wished he had signed up for the trip.

Now it was too late and he was feeling a little sorry for himself. He was also angry that the world in general, and that his high school in particular, had put him in this situation.

But Rub wasn't going to let Nathan off the hook. Rub turned to Nathan and let out some emotions that he had never shown.

"You sat beside me for four years in home room, Nathan. You never once noticed that I wasn't paying? Hell, you were class treasurer our freshmen year."

"If I had gone on the trip, who would be my roommates? You maybe, but who else? How many of your white buddies would have signed up to bunk with a Negro? Are you getting it yet, Nathan? I don't think so, because I don't think white people ever *really* get it!"

It was one of those moments when Nathan didn't know what to say or do. The problem was too big. He couldn't help his friend or "fix it" so he just stood there a moment and finally looked down and said that he was sorry.

Rub laughed. It was time to ease the tension. These thoughts were nothing new for Rub, but he had never gone off on Nathan like that before.

*

In years past, the senior trip had been a sore spot for many Negro students. There were two major problems. The first was the cost. The black families were more likely to be poor and could not easily afford the trip. Many blacks thought the system was not fair. Second, the whites were not comfortable with interracial social functions of any sort, outside of sports, that is. Therefore, black students were not encouraged to participate in the senior trip.

The following year and the following class showed signs of change. It involved the story of a young black student and his quest to make the senior trip with his fellow seniors. It is a story of small transitions. It was an example of the journey from the "way it was" to the "way it could be." And it illustrated that sometimes white folks do stuff that, as Rub often says. "don't make no damn sense."

Phillip West was one class year behind Nathan and Rub. His father ran the funeral home on Morgan Street. It was a half block from Nathan's dad's old welding shop.

Phillip lived next door to Rub so he was part of the "gang" right from the beginning. Phillip would see them outside and join in the street games or whatever Nathan and Rub were doing. Phillip was a nice guy. Everybody liked him.

Many black people didn't have much money to pay for a funeral. And, "white people wouldn't be caught dead in a black funeral home." All of the family's funeral home business, therefore, came from the black community.

More often than he wanted, Phillip's father made little or nothing on a funeral. He might even lose money or have to borrow supplies or a casket from one of the other funeral homes. The indigent cases were supposed to be split between all of the area funeral homes but West got much more than his share. The other businesses were not going to take Negro bodies so it was easier to just subsidize Mr. West and his operation. On occasion, other funeral homes would bring supplies down to Morgan Street and help Mr. West embalm.

Unlike Rub, Phillip didn't care if he was the first Negro on the bus. He figured that he would pay his money and let somebody else figure out who his roommate would be. Phillip ignored racism and went about life as if it wasn't there.

Due to the uneven cash flow at the funeral home, Phillip got behind on his contributions to the senior trip. Phillip never said anything. He paid when he could. However, when it came time to settle the account near the end of his senior year, Phillip was almost a year short in his payments.

Phillip always had a smile on his face. He was not real tall but he was strong as a bull. He was easy-going unless he was provoked to fight. Phillip did not like to be touched or pushed. When not being tormented, he was a pussycat. But get too rough or tap him the wrong way and he would be on you like a duck on a June bug.

Showing no fear, Phillip would jump anybody who crossed him, regardless of their size. Phillip, therefore, spent some time in suspension. Sometimes the suspension was off campus but often he was banished to study hall.

He played football his freshman year but didn't go out again. Just wasn't his thing plus he was tired of being broke. He worked at a grocery store after school. He couldn't both work and play football so he quit football.

Many of the high school football players lived in the "Bottom." They teased Phillip and called him a chicken for quitting the team. Coach Clarence "Stumpy" Baker, the football coach, also playfully taunted him on occasion. Everyone knew Phillip had real athletic potential, was tough as nails, and would have contributed to the team.

"March Madness" was in full swing across Kentucky. It is in March every year when basketball dominates the landscape of the Bluegrass state. The State High School Basketball Tournament was so important that school spring break was always scheduled so the coaches and administration could go to Lexington and watch the event. If a school was good enough or lucky enough to make it to "State," the entire community might make the trip.

Spring Break was scheduled for the next week so Phillip was looking forward to a few days away from classes. He had totally forgotten about the senior trip. He had moved on. He was busy with an active social life and working part-time. He was trying to stay out of trouble so he could graduate.

During Mr. Robert Armstrong's fifth period drafting class, Leonard Vick and Phillip West were sitting at their drafting tables drawing a six-sided object tilted at a 30-degree angle.

There was a knock at the classroom door. Mr. Armstrong answered the knock, stepped outside for a moment and then returned to the room. Mr. Armstrong then walked directly over to Phillip's table.

"Mr. Reynolds wants to see you as soon as you can get by his office," Mr. Armstrong told Phillip.

"Now?" Phillip asked. His voice was high showing the exact amount of alarm he felt at that moment.

Robert Armstrong shook his head. "No, not now. He wants you to go to his office at your earliest convenience but between classes or after school. He doesn't intend for you to miss class."

"Phillip thanked Mr., Armstrong and the teacher quietly moved over to another student who was waving his hand and indicating he needed some help.

Phillip spoke to no one in particular when he said, "Shit, damn, what have I done now?"

"Phillip looked over at Leonard and his eyes pleaded for an answer. He repeated the question. "What have I done?"

Leonard, of course, had no earthly idea what was going on so he asked, "Are you asking the question because you are feeling bad for what you did, or are you asking because you truly don't know?"

"And, I find it hard to believe you don't know what you've done. I mean, no one gets called to the principal's office and doesn't know why. Or maybe R. D. wants to give you an award!" Leonard said sarcastically.

R. D. Reynolds was the Russellville High School principal. He was already a legend for his balance of popularity with the students and staff while maintaining control and discipline. Mr. Reynolds had handed out a basket full of various suspensions and other disciplinary actions to Phillip during his high school career at RHS. Phillip had been working hard to improve and couldn't afford another major infraction this late in the year.

The sixth period bell rang. Phillip and Leonard walked in the direction of their next class. They were also moving closer to the principal's office.

"I gotta' stop at the restroom," Phillip said.

Leonard followed along behind him as they both made their way through the door. "You can level with me. I'm your best friend, man. So spill it. What's R. D. got on you?"

Phillip was getting worked up. What if he was about to get expelled? How could he tell his parents? What if he couldn't graduate? With his record, who would believe he was innocent?

"The man's got nothin' on me," Phillip blurted out at Leonard.

"I ain't done nothin'!"

"Okay if you say so, Phillip," Leonard mumbled over his shoulder as he washed his hands.

Leonard kept pushing, "Want me to go with you to see Mr. Reynolds?"

The question startled Phillip for a moment. He realized that he was dragging his feet and stalling his trip to face Mr. Reynolds.

Phillip decided he wasn't going to the principal's office until after school. He needed another hour to think about it and maybe figure out why he had been called.

Phillip and Leonard walked down the hall to Mr. John McCarley's general science class. On the way, he bumped unto a half dozen people because he wasn't paying any attention to where he was going.

For the next hour, Phillip sat and tried to concentrate on two things at once. While Mr. McCarley explained why hydrogen did not have a neutron, Phillip was searching his brain for unknown "infractions."

He pondered the obvious paradox: He was totally innocent. But he must be guilty. Why else would Mr. Reynolds be calling him to his office?

Thankfully, Mr. McCarley, also known as Coach McCarley, or simply, "Coach," never asked Phillip a direct question. Phillip was able to skate through the hour with his mental absence unnoticed.

Sixth period was over too quickly. Phillip searched for an excuse to postpone his appointment with "death." His time had finally run out. He had to face the music.

Phillip marched down the long hall toward the administrative offices where his destiny lay waiting. This was not his first trip down this scholastic hall of justice. That fact, did not make it any easier.

In the past though, he knew why he was called. There had always been an obvious fight with another student, or an argument with a teacher when his anger got the best of him. He would always apologize to the teacher but one thing Mr. Reynolds had taught him. "There are always consequences for actions." He had learned the hard way, but after four years, the message was finally starting to stick.

Today was a different time. Phillip was working hard to graduate. He had walked away from several altercations without throwing a punch. He thought he was getting somewhere. Until now!

R. D. Reynolds was outside his office standing by Miss Mary Ewing Hart's desk. Mary Ewing was the assistant to the Principal and the heart and soul of RHS. They were discussing some matter when Phillip walked in.

Mr. Reynolds looked up and saw Phillip. Mr. Reynolds wore glasses that slid down his nose and hid his eyes just enough that Phillip could not see exactly where he was looking. It was something that R. D. liked and found useful about his glasses. He had no intention of changing.

"Would you like me to wait here?" Phillip asked meekly.

"No, please go into my office and wait for me, Phillip. I will be there in just a moment," R. D. spoke with no indication of any "what or why" in the matter.

"He doesn't seem angry," Phillip thought to himself. But, Mr. Reynolds never looked angry.

Phillip walked into Mr. Reynold's private office. He had been invited into his private office only once before. That was when R. D. had given him a "choice." He could continue the direction he was on and be a burden to society, or he could adjust his attitude, apply another 10% of effort and self-control and be a contribution to society.

It wasn't so much the speech as it was the fact that someone at Mr. Reynold's level would take the time to help him. Phillip took the challenge. He had finally realized what was at stake. All had gone well until today. Today his world was crashing down on him and he had no idea why.

It was only a few minutes but it seemed like an hour. Phillip had read every wall plaque on the wall. He had noted how the desk was clean and organized. He wondered, as he did during his last visit, how someone like him could ever rise to the level of someone like Mr. Reynolds.

Finally, R. D. walked into his office, closed the door, and swept past Phillip to the chair behind his desk.

Phillip sat stiff in his chair like a statue, waiting for a big hammer to bust it to pieces.

Mr. Reynolds leaned forward and smiled. It was a quick smile that was unique only to him. He looked straight at Phillip. "I wanted to speak to you privately, Phillip. I wanted you to come here today so I could tell you that your shortfall has been paid and you are now fully funded to go on this year's senior trip to Washington D. C. and New York City."

Reynolds sat silently while watching Phillip. It took a moment for Phillip to absorb the information. He wasn't sure he had heard correctly.

"Are you joking with me Mr. Reynolds. Cuz if you are joking with me, I have never seen you joke before and I don't know what to do or say. I thought I was in some sort of trouble and now you are telling me I am going on the senior trip. And, I'm afraid I don't know how to act."

Phillip's ramblings did not go unnoticed. R. D. had been looking forward to this moment all day. Phillip had been a four-year project. Every student is important and somewhat of a project, but Phillip had captured R. D.'s heart more than most. Phillip somehow did that to people.

Mr. Reynolds continued. "Your progress has not gone unnoticed Phillip. Doing the right thing is not always rewarded. You shouldn't expect it, but, today your efforts have brought you good fortune."

Finally coming to the realization of the moment, Phillip asked the big question, "Who did this for me? Who paid my fees? Why would someone do this?"

"I probably shouldn't tell you, Phillip. This has never happened before. There are other deserving students who are not going on the trip. No one has stepped up to pay their way. This was a personal donation that was made especially for you."

"I promise I will keep it quiet or do whatever is best but I would like to know who it was so I can thank them," Phillip pleaded.

"Okay, they didn't ask for anonymity, so I suppose they don't mind if I tell you."

"It was Coach Stumpy Baker and Coach John McCarley who brought your account up-to-date. All of your fees have been paid-in-full."

"My God!" Phillip thought, He had just left McCarley, science class!

"Why would they do this act of kindness?" Phillip wondered. Phillip's eyes grew moist but he kept himself together.

Mr. Reynolds stood up, reached down, and opened his center desk drawer. He pulled an envelope out of the drawer and extended the envelope towards Phillip. "In addition, some of the other teachers heard what Coach Baker and Coach McCarley did for you. They got together and added extra money for you to get a few things for the trip and maybe have a little spending money."

Mr. Reynolds pushed the envelope into Phillip's hand and smiled. "Can you see that the list of people grows? I'm talking about the people in this school who are pulling for your success in life? I know you are not going to disappoint them." He paused. "Are you?"

Phillip laughed. "No sir. No sir. You can count on me, Mr. Reynolds. I will work hard to prove I was worth everyone's trust in me."

It was a long walk home for Phillip. He had missed the bus and everyone who could give him a lift was already gone. It didn't matter. He was so engrossed in his thoughts that he never noticed the distance or the time it took to get there.

He sat that very afternoon in Coach McCarley's classroom. Coach gave no indication of what he had done. Phillip didn't even look at him when he left the room because he was so deep in thought about why Mr. Reynolds had summoned him to the office.

Coach Baker was an even bigger puzzle. Phillip thought Coach Baker hated him for not playing football.

Then there was the envelope. *"The envelope!"* he suddenly remembered. Phillip pulled it from his pocket and opened it. He quickly counted the bills. "One hundred dollars!" Phillip screamed silently to himself.

In one short afternoon, Phillip's world was turned upside down. No, it was more of a full rotation. The things he thought he knew about life, and the people in it, had all changed. But, it was a good change, he surmised.

A breeze of anxiety swept over him as he suddenly felt the pressure. He didn't want to disappoint these people. Tonight he would write thank you notes to Coach Baker and Coach McCarley. Or maybe one of his teachers could help him write the notes. Phillip wanted the letters to be perfect. He would ask Mr. Reynolds if he would post a thank you letter in the teacher's lounge or somewhere where teachers could find it and read it. Yeah, he had some work to do.

Phillip had not been a regular churchgoer the past few years. Today was too much of a miracle to ignore. Maybe he should make his mother happy and go to church with her next Sunday. The thought made him smile and his step picked up as he crossed Main at the corner of 9th Street. The journey was an easy downhill trip from there. Life was lookin' up!

*

The focus for many seniors shifted towards the future. Nathan knew that he was off to the University of Alabama. He and his parents had visited the campus over Christmas break. He was easily accepted but there would be no scholarship.

Alabama had a beautiful campus with ivy and all the southern charm a person could stand. There was coach "Bear" Bryant and the great Joe Namath walking around the "Quad." Alabama was a small school. Smaller than Western Kentucky University down the road 25 miles from Russellville. Overall, it suited Nathan very well.

Nathan felt he needed to explore the world outside of his local circle but still inside his comfort zone. The University of Alabama was something new yet it provided the environment he was seeking to find.

136

Rub, in contrast, was getting all kinds of awards. He looked great on paper. Several schools were interested in him. A scholarship was certain. He could have probably gone anywhere he wanted.

It was Vanderbilt who got the nod. Located in Nashville, Tennessee, it was relatively close to home. Vandy was also one of the better universities in the nation. Rub had a full four-year scholarship for tuition, fees and books. His only expenses would be for his room and board. His parents told him they would cover the extras if he kept his grades up. He planned to work on a work-study program to earn pocket money.

On graduation night, it was Rub who spoke to the graduating class, parents, friends and family, faculty and board members as class valedictorian. He spoke of life, liberty, and the American way. He spoke of the bright future ahead for all who strive for excellence.

Samuel watched his son with a big smile on his face and a pride in his heart that only a parent can know and understand. Patricia could not stop crying.

Samuel and Patricia tightly gripped each other's hand. This moment could not have been imagined those many years ago in the tobacco fields of south Logan, and in the tiny cold Negro schoolhouse where they had both started their journey together. They had fought their way through poverty, racism, and a world war. They had worked hard to give Victor an opportunity to be successful. He had taken the opportunity and run with it.

It was the first time a Negro student had stood at the top of a RHS class. Martin Luther King, Jr. had been shot only seven weeks earlier but Rub never mentioned King in his speech. The Civil Rights Movement was not that far away but it had not yet reached Rub or Logan County. It was the spring of 1968 and that was the way it was. It would be a year to remember.

Later that evening, a band played and the Class of 1968 danced in the main lobby of RHS. The room mothers had worked with the school administration to decorate the lobby and help make it a special night. Everyone attended. Everybody! It was the first time in the history of Logan County and the first time since the integration in 1956, that the school, or any in the city, had hosted a mixed race dance —No one noticed

Schochoh Rosenwald School now on display at Logan County High School

Russellville High School about the time of integration

The Confederate Memorial in Russellville, Kentucky

From left: Kentucky governors Albert "Happy" Chandler, Sr. and Lawrence
Wetherby, Kentucky native and Vice President Alben Barkley Lt. Governor
Emerson "Doc" Beauchamp.

Russellville Independent School System Superintendent, Robert E. Stevenson, on the right with Asst. Superintendent, Jim Young

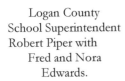

Logan County School Superintendent Robert Piper with Fred and Nora Edwards.

Bethel College at around 1900 in Russellville, Ky.

Bethel College in Russellville, shown in the picture above, represented the
higher education possible to white male students in the early 1900s
The picture below is the actual Schochoh Rosenwald School. The Schochoh
 School closed in 1950.

Schochoh School the way it was.

The Russellville Graduation Class of 1957 deserves to be recognized. They, along with all those graduating from Logan County Schools, were pioneers and heroes. Their role in the process and progress of integration cannot be understated

Graduating from RHS: * Denotes first RHS graduating African Americans

George Allison*
James Buckner*
Beverley Burchett
Patsy Byrd
Naomi Chapman
Spencer Cornelius
Martha DeShazer
James Henry Duncan
Marguerite Dyche
Shirley Fennell
Bobby Gilliam
Alma Head
Thetus Herndon
Gayle Higgins
Alpheus Hinton
Bill Major
Harvey Markham
Delmar McCarley*

Jack McLean
Gay Page
Phyllis Pillow
Walter Reed
Vivian Riley
Diana Shanklin
Barbara Simpson
Eva Smith
Kenneth Smith
Betty Smith
John Stratton
Fredia Taylor
Sue Taylor
Dorothy Tillet*
Judith Upton
Wanda Washer
Jerry White
Marilyn Williams

Chapter 30

"If you do not expect the unexpected, you will not find it. For it is not to be reached by search or trial."

—Heraclitus

That summer after graduation, Nathan worked again as a lifeguard at Spring Acres Park. His father, Charles, told him to take the summer and have fun. Charles could have employed Nathan at Weaver Welding Company but he knew that was Nathan's last "summer of youth." He wanted Nathan to enjoy himself. Plus, Nathan was not a very good welder.

Rub still worked at Parrish Texaco. He pumped gas, did oil changes and fixed tires. The owner, Billy Ray Parrish trusted Rub. He was often the only person working at the station, especially late evenings and weekends.

Officer Hodge was no longer around and Rub had his car running and in good shape. Life was looking up.

Both Nathan and Rub were working seven days a week. They were trying to save as much as they could before school started. Nathan didn't see Rub much. They made an effort to get together a few times but something always got in the way.

Knowing they would soon leave the nest for college, their parents were planning more family activities, and that kept them close to home.

*

It was a Thursday night about 7:30 p.m. in late July. The air was hot and humid. Sundown was approaching with the promise of some relief from the heat.

Nathan's birthday was the next day. Rub had called and they met after work at a little place they called the "Hoodeo." It was a drive-in on the opposite side of town from the Tastee Treet. Some kids called it the "Hoodeo" because they thought it wasn't as cool a place to hang out.

Rub and Nathan were standing beside their cars when another car pulled up alongside. It was Rub's neighbor, Phillip West. West leaned out the window and said, "Rub, you gotta get home. Your daddy is sick."

Rub jumped in his car and practically flew to his house. When he got there, his mother and dad were not home. Phillip's mother was waiting for him in the front yard. She told him they had taken his daddy to the hospital. She said they thought he was having a heart attack.

Rub hopped back in his car, popped the clutch and raced up to the hospital. It wasn't but a few blocks away. Rub ran through the front door of the small Logan County Hospital. His heart was pounding. He had trouble getting enough air. Rub looked around wildly. He had never been there before. Finally, he saw and then rushed over to the front desk. He asked where they took his daddy. The volunteer directed him to the emergency room.

Rub was running down the hall to the emergency room when he saw his mother and sister walking back up the same hall in his direction. Patricia saw Rub and immediately stopped. Her shoulders were slumped. She looked to have no life in her and Rub knew immediately that his father was gone. They all fell together in a standing pile of pain and sorrow.

*

Samuel Wells was laid to rest on Saturday. The 5th Street First Baptist Church was full up and out both doors that hot Saturday afternoon. On every pew sat someone who grieved the loss of Samuel Wells. He had worked hard for his family during the week but he had always saved Sundays for church. He was one of those people who loved to share the gospel and was not embarrassed to publicly praise God. He was generous to his church and a truly beloved leader of the congregation.

The thing Nathan would remember most about Samuel's service was the music. Oh lord, it was incredible. Voices rang out from all sides and every corner. It may have been choreographed but it seemed spontaneous. A voice started here, then another jumped in over there, and then the choir would answer. Sometimes it sounded soulful and sad and the next moment it would be rockin' wild. The emotions were so deep and strong that they filled the church like a mournful smoke.

Nathan sat up front. Rub asked Nathan to sit with the family. He was honored but still moved over to the end of the pew. That put him on the outside aisle. Rub and his sister, Lili, sat on either side of their mother. The pastor and some others Nathan did not know, gathered near Patricia and tried to give her comfort.

Then out of nowhere, a parade of singers came walking down all three aisles singing and clapping. They were dressed in purple and yellow robes. They had their hands raised and they were almost jumping and clapping to the rhythm of the music. A piano banged out an old gospel tune of "Shall We Gather at the River" in fast time. Nathan had never heard it sung like that in a white church. His feet wanted to move with the music but his Baptist upbringing kept him still and in place.

Then the head deacon took the podium and spoke lovingly of Samuel and the work Samuel had done for Jesus and for the church. There were numerous shouts of praise from the congregation. His talk was followed by a quartet and a song by the choir. After more speakers and music, the preacher finally made his way to the pulpit.

Out of nowhere, Sister Bernie jumped up and started singing and clapping. Her voice rang out with a verse of *Shall We Gather at the River*. The choir joined in and added more voices and clapping. The entire church was rocking and swaying as the spirit moved through the crowded pews.

Shall We Gather at the River morphed into *When the Saints Go Marching In.* Finally, at some point, due in large part to exhaustion, the music died down. The pastor, Brother Collins, resumed his position at the podium and preached for about a half-hour.

There was no air conditioning in those days. By then Nathan had sweated through his white shirt and sports jacket. Nathan had a West Funeral Home hand-fan going as fast as his wrist could wave the thing. When one arm got tired, he quickly shifted hands never missing a wave. Unfortunately, all he was doing was stirring hot air. In the humidity of the

South, the heat likes to stick to a person. If you have ever been inside a hot church on a hot summer day in the humid South, you know the feeling.

Truth be told, Nathan was about ready for the service to end so he could sample new air. He sensed that the crowd was wearing down too. It was starting to get quiet as the preacher said his final prayer. The soft sobs of the family were now only occasionally interrupted by an "Amen" here and there. Maybe the odd "praise the lord" from a deacon could be heard punching through the sobbing sounds.

At long last, Brother Collins gave the signal and people started to leave the church. The back of the church emptied first and that was followed, pew by pew, until the first pew, pastor and funeral home staff were the only people left in the church.

Mr. West walked over and opened the casket one final time. It was open before the service but was closed when the service began. Earlier, Patricia, Rub and Lili had stood and greeted each person as a long line passed by to view the body and say farewell to Samuel. Each person stopped and paid their respects to the family. The casket sat up front center between the two aisles allowing Patricia, Rub and Lili standing room over to the side.

With the church empty and deathly quiet, it was finally time for the family to say their final goodbye to the father and husband they loved. Nathan could easily see everything from his seat at the end of the pew.

Samuel was too young to die. He looked like he was just asleep. Rub's mother, Patricia, stood up and shuffled over to the casket. Flanked and being partially steadied by her two children, she leaned over the shell that once held the spirit of the only man she had ever loved. Her entire body shook with the agony of her sorrow. Nathan could see Rub trying to contain a quivering lip and be strong for his mother. It was too painful to watch his friend and his family suffering that way. He decided it was time for him to leave them alone. Or maybe he needed to escape. Regardless, Nathan quietly stood, backed into the aisle and turned towards the entrance.

Waiting outside in the relatively cooler hot afternoon shade of a big poplar tree, it wasn't long before Nathan saw the family follow Samuel's casket out of the church. Samuel's body was loaded for his final ride in a hearse. His initial ride being long ago when he rode with Brother Brown to Nashville on his first trip out of Logan County.

*

Nathan joined a procession of cars that made its way to the Negro cemetery outside of town on the Morgantown Road. He stood near the family but not with the family. Nathan was the only white person at the cemetery.

Family members gathered near the casket under a green canvas tent. The pastor quoted a scripture and said a prayer and it was over. Patricia and the children each took a rose and laid it on the casket. They then turned and walked away before the casket was lowered into the grave.

Mr. West, the funeral home director, gave the family a ride back to the house where neighbors had already gathered with food. Rub had told Nathan earlier that he was invited to the house afterward but Nathan decided to go home. He was hot and tired but mostly sad.

Grief had always been a solemn, quietly controlled event in Nathan's world. He had never witnessed anything like the outpouring grief and emotions that he had experienced at Mr. Well's funeral service.

Nathan didn't feel like eating or socializing. He felt oddly numb. Nathan simply wanted to be alone with his feelings. He had nothing left, at that moment, to give to his friend.

Chapter 31

"If we will be quiet and ready enough, we shall find compensation in every disappointment."

—Henry David Thoreau

It was the following Tuesday before Nathan saw Rub again. Nathan stopped by the Parrish Texaco to check on him. He was working and seemed to look OK.

Nathan decided to stay off subject and ask him when he needed to be in Nashville for freshman orientation. He didn't look up from the tire he was putting on a wheel. "Never!" he said. "I ain't goin anymore. Can't afford it now that Dad is gone."

The words hit Nathan square in the chest. "What? Why not? Can't they do something?"

He knew what this meant to Rub. It was a double punch. First the loss of his father and then the loss of his scholarship.

Rub looked up. "Mom and I talked about it for two long nights. She wants me to go. She says she will find the money, somewhere, but I can't do that to her. Dad had a small pension from the railroad but it is not enough to take care of Mom and Lili, and, also pay my school expenses."

"I have to take a full load to keep my scholarship so I can only work part-time. We did the numbers. It doesn't balance."

Rub looked back at the tire. His voice trailed off.

"What about Western?" Nathan asked looking for options. Nathan was speaking of Western Kentucky University in Bowling Green.

"It's too late to get another scholarship before fall semester. Thank you Jesus ...again! What a freakin' week!" The words spewed like vomit from Rub's mouth. Nathan could see the anger in his body language and the anguish on his face.

Suddenly Rub's jaw locked. He leaned back and threw the tire iron he had been holding in his hand. It whirled through the air across the garage and bounced off a couple of used tires. Then it hit the floor and tumbled or slid a few feet.

Rub looked down at the tire iron. They both looked at it. The piece of steel had come to rest just a few inches from Nathan's toe. When Nathan finally turned back toward Rub, he had his hands over his eyes and he was shaking all over. The emotions of it all had finally consumed him. He had lost his father and his dreams, and the load was suddenly too much to carry.

Nathan moved over and put his hand on Rub's shoulder. Real men didn't hug in those days. Rub would have none of it. He pushed Nathan's hand away. "Don't freaking' touch me. Just leave me alone," Rub sobbed.

Billy Ray Parrish heard the commotion and came around to see what was going on.

Nathan looked at Billy Ray and shrugged his shoulders in an "I don't know what to do now?" gesture. Walking forward, Billy Ray waved Nathan off. Being more of a father figure might allow Billy Ray to get in close enough to offer some comfort. Nathan left hoping something would ease Rub's pain.

Later that night, Rub gave Nathan a call. Without any preamble he said, "You aren't going to mention that incident today to nobody are you? I was doing fine until you showed up. Thanks for nothin'!" He hung up. Nathan felt like crap.

Nathan told his parents about it. They both said the obvious. Rub was hurting and when people hurt, they sometimes get angry and hurt others. They said to give him some time to heal.

*

It was a week before Rub called back. He told Nathan to stop by the garage after work. He had some beers and said they could have a brew if Nathan wanted to hang for a while.

Although their parents would not have approved, Rub and Nathan had shared a few beers in the past. The legal drinking age in Kentucky was 21. Many Bowling Green liquor stores would sell to anyone who brought cash to their drive-up-window. Impulsive urges could be satisfied by a trip to the "Bottom." in Russellville. In fact, bootlegging was one of the best and most prosperous businesses in the "Bottom." On Friday and Saturday nights, there was sometimes a traffic jam with autos lined up to buy liquor. It was curb service on 5th Street, 6th Street and on Bean Row.

When Nathan arrived at the Texaco, Rub had already started drinking. "Man, I'm sorry about that shit the other day," he said.

"What shit? Done and over," Nathan shot back.

Nathan could tell he had a big jump on him with the beer. His mouth wasn't working so well. "It's just all this freaking shit that has hit me so goddamned fast man," Rub slurred.

Rub opened the side door, unzipped his pants and started peeing out the door in full view of the Hopkinsville Road, God, and all of west Russellville.

"This is not going well," Nathan thought to himself. "I'm his friend but I don't know what to say — *again*!" Nathan was happy that no one had apparently called the cops.

"Do you have anybody you can talk to, to help you?" Nathan tried to ask tentatively.

Rub jumped up and interrupted him. His eyes were bloodshot but they still burned a hole in Nathan.

"What you can do is drink your beer, sit there, and shut the hell up while I drink my beer. That would be nice. That would be just perfect, freakin', wonderful. That's what I need, please!" he spat.

Nathan could take a hint! He took a seat and fell in line with the program. They sat in that dimly lit dirty garage and drank their PBRs and looked out the window waiting for dark. After dark, they drank more beers and listened to clear channel WLS on the AM radio until it was time for Nathan to get home.

There was nothing to say that hadn't been said. Nathan rose from his chair, shuffled across the dirty floor and offered his hand to Rub. Rub rose and took Nathan's hand pulling him forward into something just short of a hug.

The two young men stood silent for a short moment before they awkwardly broke the embrace. Nathan gave Rub's arm a couple of pats, smiled, turned and walked into the darkness.

When Nathan got to the car he turned around. He sensed this was the end of something. Nathan paused for a long last look at his friend through the open door. Rub was sitting on his stool drinking his beer. His shoulders were hunched. His head was bent forward. The fine details of his features were hidden in the semi-darkness of the dimly lit garage. All that remained visible was the silhouette of a broken young man.

Nathan left for Alabama the next week. They talked on the phone briefly the day before his parents drove him down to Tuscaloosa. Nathan and Rub would not see each other again for a while. It would, in fact, be over four years.

Chapter 32

"Growing up is losing some illusions, in order to acquire others."

—Virginia Woolf

Nathan's first semester at the University of Alabama was a growing-up process with negative academic consequences. He was a bit out of his element for a while.

"Nathan, you have a phone call!" There was a central phone at the Theta Xi fraternity house. Whoever was closest to the phone would answer. Mike Soppet had just announced the latest call was for Nathan.

It was late November when he got the call from Rub. Tuscaloosa didn't have much of a winter and fall was hardly noticed. It had cooled down a bit and Nathan was just saying that he needed to get a jacket on before dark. He wondered who would be calling him mid-week in the middle of the afternoon. Nathan got regular calls from his mom and dad, but never on a weekday.

Nathan picked up the phone. "Hello."

"Guess where I'm going?" came a voice that was clearly Rub.

Nathan played along, "I don't know! Where? Beach Bend?"

It was a joke! Beach Bend was an amusement park in Bowling Green, Kentucky.

"No, you hippy college asshole, I'm going to South freakin' Carolina."

"Really? What's in South Carolina?" Nathan asked.

"Boot camp," Rub wildly explained. "I joined the freakin' Marines!"

As they say in the South, "Y'all kudda knocked Nathan over with a feather!"

"Are you kidding me? Are you insane? What are you doing?" That was about all Nathan could say. Vietnam was cooking hot at that time. The marines were on the front lines in much of the heavy action.

Rub's voice became lower and his tone turned more calm and serious.

"I got called for my physical. They were getting ready to draft me.

I was not in school and not married so I was ripe for the pickin'. I was hoping they would leave me alone until I could get registered at Western in January. I had all my papers in but time just ran out on me. Jesus, this has been one shitty year. So, I decided to become a hawk and joined the Marines. The Navy wouldn't have me 'cuz I can't freakin' swim!" He laughed and Nathan laughed too.

"When do you leave?" It was all Nathan could think of to say. He wanted to ask if he felt better about the loss of his father or about the loss of college or about the loss of all his dreams. He wanted to ask, but he didn't know how.

Rub didn't know how to talk about it either so they both ignored all the reasons Rub had up and joined the freakin' Marine Corps.

"I bug out of here next Monday, Rub said. "I get a short break around Christmas then back for more training. I will be a Marine Corps Private by mid-January."

"I don't guess I will see you then," Nathan said. "My parents are picking me up at Christmas break on their way to Florida. We will spend Christmas down in Arcadia."

Rub didn't show any emotion about anything being discussed. "Well I guess this is goodbye for a spell, good buddy. I'll go kill some V - C while you get your D-GREE. Actually, the Marine Corps is going to send me to college when I get done killing commie midgets in funny hats for them. They crossed their hearts and hoped I don't die promised me."

"For God's sake Rub, keep your head down and take care of yourself. Come back safe," Nathan told him.

Rub was quiet for a moment, "Well friend, I don't know where the hell God is. He sure freakin hasn't been anywhere near me lately, but I do dig what you're sayin'. I will try to keep it all in mind. I'm not sweatin' it though 'cuz they are going to turn me into a lean mean killin' machine. Maybe the workout will do me some good."

"Study hard and stay in touch, ya hear."

"Yeah, I hear ya, Rub", Nathan responded weakly. "I mean it. Don't try to be any kind of damn hero over there. Do your thing and come on back home, okay?"

"Sure thing, see ya, Bye."

Click, the phone went dead and Rub was gone.

Chapter 33

"Anyone who isn't confused really doesn't understand the situation."

—Edward R. Murrow (reporting on the Vietnam War)

Nathan received the following letter from Rub:

"Dear Nathan,

I got your last stupid letter. No really, forget the "stupid" comment. Thanks man. Letters are what we live for over here. A little slice of home. We are not feeling a lot of love from the folks back there in the U.S. of A.

I am having a really good time! You know, man, how much I love walkin' in the rain. We freakin' walk in the rain every freakin' day. If we are not walking in the freakin' rain, we are eating or sleeping in the freakin' rain.

They want us to walk around in plain sight so every freakin' VC in the country will have an opportunity to shoot us. It is some kind of goddamn government strategy.

I will make E-5 soon. I will get a little more money but I have nowhere to spend it. I have to take less shit from fewer assholes, but I have more responsibility.

My promotions came easy. Everybody above me was either a freakin' moron or got shot or both. I am getting to where I can tell how long a guy is going to live as soon as I meet him. Some shit-for-brains replacement comes into the platoon and I meet him. I know right away that he's dead. I study him so maybe I can identify his body parts when they go flying by.

155

It takes some common sense and a certain attitude to survive in Nam. It's no guarantee but some jerk-off with no common sense and a bad attitude will not make it very freakin' long, for damn sure!

Same damn thing with the officers. We get these wet behind the ears, empty between the ears, wanna make general, second lieutenants over here. The gunny will usually sit them down, first thing, and brief them on the situation in which they have found themselves. If the gunny's words of wisdom do not sink in; if that second lieutenant keeps risking lives for the sake of his hope for personal recognition or glory; if he is too eager to volunteer his men for risky jobs; if he doesn't get with the freakin' program, and quick, he will find himself in a body bag. Some day out on patrol, somebody is going pop a cap and blow his head clean off his shoulders! Not me you understand. I am a loyal U. S. Marine serving my country in the fight against Communism. But I hear stories, if you know what I'm saying.

Open the enclosed package carefully. Please accept this little gift as a token of our friendship. Your buddies at the fraternity are going to freakin' shit when you show them.

Keep your powder dry.

Rub

The letter from Rub came in a box along with another smaller box and a note that said "Read the letter first." Nathan had read the letter and then began to disassemble the smaller box. Inside the smaller box was a small brown paper sack. It was a sack of the kind that might hold candy or small hardware items. Inside the small paper sack was a black and wrinkled object. There was also another note. It read, "The last thing this ear heard before my bullet went between the eyes of its previous owner were the Vietnamese words for "Oh shit."

Nathan dropped the ear and jumped back. The hair on his neck stood up.

"Shit, shit, shit! My God! Holy freakin' crap! Rub has gone and mailed the ear of some VC he shot over in Nam. I can't believe he did that!" Nathan thought while slapping his hands against his pants legs to get possible "ear remains' off his hands.

Nathan had heard stories about this sort of thing but he didn't believe regular people did that crap. He wasn't going to show that ear to anybody!

Nathan was afraid that Rub might go to jail or something bad would happen. Or, the FBI might go see Nathan's mom and dad or put them on some enemy list.

Nathan put the ear back in the bag and the bag back in the box and that box back in the bigger box. He took a grocery sack and covered the bigger box and wrapped tape around it. Nathan then took the big box and hid it in his sock drawer.

Chapter 34

"The first time you quit, it's hard. The second time, it gets easier. The third time, you don't even have to think about it."

—University of Alabama coach Paul "Bear" Bryant

The "era" of the 60s was finally over. The previous decade had witnessed the murder death of President John Kennedy and his brother, Robert.

The bombing of a small black church in Birmingham so touched the nation that it helped spur the Civil Rights Act of 1964.

Laws changed but the nation stayed much the same. Martin Luther King Jr. carried the message of civil rights but did not realize his dream before he was gunned down in Memphis in 1968.

The anti-war movement, the Civil Rights movement and all manner of counter-culture movements, mixed together during the '60s. It produced some of the best music of all time. It also was a period of chaos.

In 1970, Birmingham, Alabama was still a hotbed of racial tension.

It was against this background that Nathan decided to go to Birmingham for the summer, take a summer class or two, and find a job.

As Nathan's life got busy, his letters to Rub became less frequent. It was difficult to find the time to write. Most often, Nathan simply forgot about Rub.

Nathan applied and was quickly hired by the Birmingham Park and Recreation Department. The process was too easy. Later, Nathan would understand why!

Nathan was assigned to manage a small swimming pool on the north side of Birmingham known as Norwood Park.

Norwood Park was located a couple of blocks east of U. S. Highway 31. That section of Birmingham had been a working class white neighborhood in previous years. Lately, black families had started moving into the area. The integration had sparked panic selling by white residents. As a result of the panic selling, real estate prices tumbled. This led to tension and fear. Tension and fear are always a dangerous mix.

Additionally, and adding fuel to the fire, was the construction of two large black housing projects in the neighborhoods surrounding Norwood Park. Why were they considered "black" housing projects? Because in Birmingham, in 1970, the races did not mix, especially in housing. In other words, *some black*, meant *all black*.

Tension and fear were fertile ground for those who thrive on tension and fear. The Klu Klux Klan was alive and well and actually gaining support in neighborhoods like Norwood. It thrived because hate is a natural remedy for mass hysteria. History demonstrates that hate can also be a unifying force.

All of the Birmingham pools were scheduled to open Memorial Day weekend but the openings remained tentative. Public meetings on the subject had been heated. There was genuine fear for the safety of the children. The objections, however, were mostly racially driven. Critics had some credibility because a security guard had been killed at a Birmingham swimming pool the previous year.

While the lifeguards and other pool employees cooled their heels at the park, waiting for a decision by the city, the surrounding neighborhood also watched and waited.

It didn't take long for things to start popping. As a hot Birmingham sun heated the water in the pool, tempers also rose on the streets and in the houses around the park. To the white community, a simple swimming pool demonstrated everything wrong in their lives and in the world. The community evolved into an estuary of discontent.

*

Nathan walked out of the pump room holding a bottle of ammonia he used to test for chlorine gas leaks. The smell of chlorine was always stronger near where the chlorine tanks were located. They were pressurized to push gas into the water lines that fed the filtering system. The policy was to check for leaks every four hours but Nathan's nose told him the fittings were not tight enough. His nose had been correct.

The bright sun blinded his eyes before they adjusted to the light and he saw a small group of white adult men standing outside the fence.

Nathan noticed one of the men talking to a lifeguard who was inside the fence. The other thing that Nathan noticed was that each man was paired with a German Shepherd dog held tightly on a leash. There were six white men with six dogs. When the man finished talking to the lifeguard, all six men and their dogs circled the fence surrounding the pool and then left. They walked west towards the underpass and disappeared over the hill.

Nathan scanned the street. Most every house had someone on the front porch. Every eye was on the pool. Every face was scowled. They knew exactly what was happening. There were only two possibilities. Either the neighborhood had been tipped off, or, they were part of the plan. One thing was certain however, the visitation had been well organized.

The '70s was also the age of the CB radio fad. Most of the homeowners on the street had CB radios in their vehicle and in their homes. They stayed in regular communication. They also monitored the police and fire radio communication. During the long hot summer that followed, local residents would be opening their front doors to see the action, before park personnel finished their call to the police.

*

After the men and the dogs were long gone, Nathan called out to Bob. Bob was the lifeguard who had been talking to the visitors.

"Bob," Nathan called out. "Come here for a moment, will you? I have a quick question."

Once Bob arrived at the pump room Nathan asked him, "What the heck was that all about? Who were those men? What did they want?"

"They wanted our names and they wanted to know where we were from," Bob replied.

"You didn't tell them anything did you?" Nathan inquired, somewhat alarmed.

Bob was not the sharpest tack in the box. He looked down and quickly collected his thoughts. "Well, yeah, I told them a little. I couldn't think of any reason not to tell them. I didn't want to look like a chicken."

Nathan could feel his face getting hot and it wasn't the sun. He took a deep breath.

Nathan continued, "Do you remember what we were told about giving out information?"

"No, I forgot about not talkin'. But we didn't talk that long. They said they would be back soon though."

Bob could tell that Nathan was upset with him. "I'm sorry Nathan," Bob said meekly. "I didn't really know what to do. I was over by the fence when they came up. I couldn't just run off, could I?"

Nathan thought about it a moment. What Bob was saying made some sense. There is a certain vulnerability when confronted while standing barefoot and wearing nothing but a swimsuit. Even when separated by a fence.

"We aren't goin' to fold and be evicted by the local white trash," Nathan argued. "If that sorry delegation of redneck inbreeds were capable of anything more than intimidation, we wouldn't be standing here."

His words demonstrated that Nathan was naive at a level bordering stupidity. Ignorance was bliss, but more danger surrounded him than the young man could have imagined.

In spite of it all, the name stuck.

The "delegation" as it came to be known, were grown men. Most were old enough to be the fathers of Nathan and his crew.

It was a challenge to focus on the faces of the men because of those damn dogs. The dogs were large physical animals. Their roaming eyes and big heads were in constant motion following the movements around them. They paced as best as they could at the end of their leashes. Those were not sweet puppy dogs. They had the look of hungry wolves.

Nathan was angry. Earlier, as he watched the "delegation" disappeared over the small hill, his impulse was to chase after them, confront them and demonstrate that they and their dogs did not intimidate him; no sir!

But Nathan didn't make any moves. He didn't go after the men for several reasons. First, there had been meeting after meeting with city administrators, park and recreation administration, and the police. Nathan's instructions were clear. "Avoid confrontation at all cost." Any major incident would likely result in the closing of all public pools for the summer, possibly forever.

For their safety, the police instructed Nathan and his staff to stay inside the fence during working hours. Arrival and departure times were coordinated with the police. A personal encounter would only set a bad example and lead to an incident that would likely end badly.

Second, the action that day was pure and simple intimidation. The "delegation" had not yet issued a direct or specific threat. Their dual mission was for fact-finding plus a show of force. Too much reaction, it was felt, might encourage more aggressive behavior.

Finally, the fear of being mauled by dogs, or even killed, could not be ignored. Although he did not yet fully appreciate the level of danger, he sensed that he was "not in Kansas anymore." The police circled the park about every ten minutes but a lot can happen in ten minutes. Nathan had no friends in the neighborhood. There would be no rescue. In fact, many would cheer an attack.

Nathan decided that he would hold his fire and save his ammunition for a real fight on another day.

What Nathan did not know was that one or more members of the "delegation" had killed before, and would not hesitate to kill again.

*

After the initial contact with the "delegation," several days passed without incident. The pool was ready for the public when and if a decision was made by the city to open. There was little more to do except run training exercises, keep everything inside the fence clean, and wait.

The lifeguards and staff were beginning to relax a little as they sat around a card table playing spades.

It was near quitting time when the sound of screeching tires punched through the quiet air of the late afternoon. Rising out of the tire noise came the sound of a man's voice. His mouth spewed vile hatred.

"Goddamn nigger lovers," he called out from the car window.

The ugly phrase was repeated a number of times as a red and white Ford Fairlane completed the turn and moved south in front of the swimming pool.

A casual observer might assume that a parade was about to pass by the park. The front yards, sidewalks, porches and windows were crowded with men, women and even a few children. Most appeared to be thoroughly entertained by events unfolding on the street.

"Why hadn't I noticed the crowd in the street earlier?" Nathan thought to himself. But, the thought was only a sliver of a thought in a quick string of thoughts and reactions.

Stretching out of the front passenger side window, the "mouth of the south" revealed himself. He held a cylinder in his hand. A long burning fuse could be clearly seen protruding from the cylinder.

When directly in front of the pool, the man hurled the cylinder outward and upward. It tumbled gracefully end-over-end towards the fence where Nathan and his three companions were seated playing cards.

Then there was another scream from the car's spinning hot tires. Rubber clawed at the pavement seeking traction as smoke bellowed from the rear wheels. The Ford finally grabbed some asphalt and sped away, honking its horn in celebration.

The pool deck cleared as four young men dove for cover. Cards sprayed in every direction. Everyone braced for the expected blast and carnage to follow.

The stick of "dynamite" did not make it over the fence. It landed in the grass just short and near the front gate entrance.

Nathan and Bob had rolled into the shallow end of the pool. They kept their heads down and waited. The other two lifeguards ran into the bath house. Everyone braced for the explosion.

A minute passed. There was a phone in the bathhouse. "Call the police!" Nathan shouted.

After a few more minutes, Nathan and Bob slowly raised their heads. They could see the stick lying near the fence. The fuse appeared to be out. Nobody moved.

The first police car to arrive carried two officers just coming on duty. They hopped out of the car and walked up to the fence.

Not seeing anyone they called out, Hello, what's going on? We got some report about a bomb?"

Bob was the first to answer. He hooked his arm over the pool gutter while pointing his finger towards the stick. "On the ground near the fence," he said.

The officers turned and looked down. They saw the cylinder and jumped back. Then they looked more closely. It was too fat to be dynamite. The cylinder was cardboard. It looked like a tube that might be inside a roll of paper towels.

There were no bomb squads in those days. The officers went back to their car and radioed for some help. A couple more cars showed up. They had a long pole with a gripper on the end. They picked up the cylinder and some stuff fell out with the fuse. It looked like modeling clay. Nathan thought he heard laughter from the crowd on the street.

Over the next few days, the park hosted several visitors from state and local police and city administration. They also had their first meetings with the FBI. Everyone wanted more information on the men and the car. No one at the pool could tell them much. Amazingly, no one on the street saw anything at all.

It was decided that the best option was to keep the whole episode quiet. After all, nobody got hurt did they? It was important to open the pools, right?

The police promised to keep a closer patrol around the park. They rounded up the usual suspects, did a short investigation, and dropped the matter.

The message, however, was clear. Everyone heard it. Lines had been drawn on both sides of the battle.

In spite of the risks, the city finally made a decision. The pools would open the Saturday before Memorial Day.

*

The day arrived to open. The rule, mandated by the city, was that Norwood pool be restricted. It was open only to children sixteen years old and younger. That was fine with Nathan. He was issued mace and told to use it if trouble started. Nathan couldn't believe it. He couldn't believe that a lifeguard would be expected to carry mace.

Opening day at Norwood Park was beyond anything that anyone, in Birmingham, had ever witnessed.

Behind the pool was a dual railroad track that ran north and south. Hidden in and amongst the weeds and bushes and trees around the track, was a tactical police unit. It was something like a swat team. They wore military uniforms.

A helicopter flew around overhead. There was a marked police car parked in front of the pool. Two Birmingham Police officers sat in the car but never made an appearance outside of the vehicle. Additional police cars rolled by the park every couple of minutes.

In the parking lot next to the park were riot police sitting in four Bell Telephone trucks.

And, the Alabama National Guard unit down the street was on alert and ready to move at moment's notice.

In a near comical vein, along the front street facing the pool were maybe six or so black automobiles. It looked like a funeral procession getting ready to leave for the cemetery. The mix included the FBI, the Alabama Bureau of Investigation, (ABI), the NAACP, and who knows what else. What was so amusing? No one knew who was who! They were all walking up and down the street writing down one another's license numbers trying to figure it out.

Early in the year, the police had met with Nathan and the entire pool staff. The staff was informed of the efforts being made to ensure the safety of the employees and the children in the park.

Only later were they told that there had been specific threats of violence that were credible enough to take every precaution necessary. No one at City Hall or in Montgomery wanted another Birmingham bombing incident that killed children.

Nathan thought to himself, "What about lifeguards? We bleed too!"

*

The children did come to the pool. Hundreds of black children. Many of the same black children came every day. The white kids? Not so much. Maybe a dozen white children showed up all summer.

The local white neighborhood residents kept watching from their porches. They drove by slowly to catch everything going on plus, they sent the "delegation" to visit regularly.

It was always late in the afternoon when the "delegation" would show up and stand outside around the fence. Each man was always accompanied by a German Shepherd dog on a leash. They never tried to enter the pool

165

area. They would move around the perimeter of the fence with their dogs. They circled slowly. Occasionally they would say something to one another about "them nigger lovers" or about "them niggers in the pool." There were other comments directed toward the black children that were too disgusting to repeat.

The purpose of the "delegation" visits never changed. The dogs were obviously trained attack animals. They would charge the fence and bark if a child or anyone got too close. That was a real thrill for "delegation" members. As the summer progressed, members of the "delegation" began more aggressive taunting. They knew everyone's name.

A designated spokesman got in close to the wire, "Nathan! Hey boy. I'm talkin' to you!"

Nathan turned his back and walked away.

"Look at me, you nigger lovin' sumbitch. Why you want to be hangin' with a bunch of niggers all day? You got a thang for little nigger girls or somthin'?"

The lifeguards mostly ignored them but it was stressful.

*

As the lifeguards were leaving one afternoon, they noticed a "hippie-looking" type hanging around the parking lot. He appeared to be a little older, with long dark hair, Mutton chops sideburns and a mustache. He was dressed in worn bell bottom blue jeans, a green tee shirt, and sandals. He carried a backpack on his shoulder. They had to walk past him to get to their cars. There was no sign of police anywhere.

"Hey man, you got a smoke I could bum, man?" he asked as they got closer.

Nathan got a whiff of more than tobacco as he got closer to the old hippie.

"No man, I never took up the habit but my friend here may have a Camel to share," Nathan answered while pointing to his chain-smoking workmate.

The hippie smiled, casually took the cigarette, popped a Zippo out of his jeans pocket and lit his smoke. He took a long hard drag, tilted back his head and blew white smoke straight up into the air. The smoke stale air and low sun on the horizon behind him, formed the illusion of a halo around his head. Slowly he turned and looked at the young men. They were all standing there looking back at him. The hippie noticed that all three were cut out of the same preppy mold and wrapped in preppy shorts, button down shirts and Bass Weejuns.

"Jesus H. Christ," he thought to himself. "I am so totally screwed here."

Hippie man quickly pulled himself together and spoke confidently, "My name is James Green. I am an undercover officer with the Alabama Bureau of Investigation and I would appreciate your help."

The lifeguards stood in silence with their mouths gaping open.

"Listen to me. Put your eyes back in their sockets, close your stupid mouths and follow my lead. We need to put on a little show for the audience," Green said referring to the people who were probably looking through their windows and watching every movement on the street.

James dropped his backpack off his shoulder and untied the flap. He opened the pack and took out a bag containing beaded leather wrist, ankle, and arm bracelets. There was also a dozen or more beaded leather necklaces.

James handed each of the boys a few items of jewelry then handed the small bag to Nathan. Considering the situation, Green was encouraged that no one had run off yet.

"Here is the deal gentlemen," Green began.

"The great state of Alabama is putting you boys into the jewelry business. I am your wholesaler."

"Your job is to wear this stuff and sell some of it. Give it away for all I care. You are not paying for it and neither am I. We will meet regularly and I will resupply you."

James looked at each boy. They were children really. He knew that they had no idea where he was going, so he continued.

"All you have to do is keep your eyes and ears open. When I come to visit and resupply your inventory, you will tell me everything you have learned and everything you have seen since our previous meeting. We want you to start chewin' the fat with your friendly dog walkers. We want you to make buddies with the locals and keep your eyes and ears open for any information that sounds interesting."

James looked each boy in the eyes and walked it down the line, "Got it? Got it? Got it?"

Each one nodded his head.

"One final thing boys, this little operation needs to stay just between you fellas and me and the people on my end who are cleared know. If you want to stay healthy and grow old, keep this operation to yourselves. Don't tell your girlfriend. Don't even tell your mamma. Got that?"

Green got three nods. He then flashed them all a peace sign and turned to walk away. Suddenly, his fatherly instincts got the best of him. Officer Green stopped, frowned and gave the boys a long cold stare. "By the way college boys," he said sarcastically, "in the future, if anyone ever walks up to anyone of you dumb asses and talks to you the way I have just talked to you, for God's sake, ask for some freakin' identification! My card is in the small bag. Keep it someplace safe."

"That's it then," he said. "I'll see you in a couple of weeks. Keep it real and thanks for the smoke, man."

The three lifeguards watched him walk away. He never looked back. The three of them stood there thinking and wondering what had just happened.

The jewelry was popular. It sold very well. The jewelry also opened doors for conversation with some of the older neighborhood kids who stopped by.

The "delegation" was happy that they had broken down the resistance of the lifeguards. Soon, everybody was talkin' up a storm.

*

Next to the pool was a carve-out property with a red brick ranch style house sitting on the lot. It sat in the middle of the park but had street frontage. One morning, one of the lifeguards was taking his turn on the lifeguard stand when he caught a movement out of the corner of his eye. He looked over toward the house to his right and he saw a man standing in the backyard. He held a hunting rifle with a big scope. The rifle looked to be aimed directly at the lifeguard.

Immediately, the lifeguard dove off the tower and swam over to the shallow end of the pool. From there, a view of the backyard was blocked by the bath house. More importantly, a view of the lifeguard was blocked by the bath house.

Nathan looked at the lifeguard with a puzzled expression on his face.

"That guy next door is pointin' his rifle at me," the lifeguard shouted at Nathan!

Without a guard on the tower, the pool was cleared and then closed. The police were called and the neighbors broke out onto their porches to await the outcome.

The Birmingham City Police promptly informed Nathan that there was no law against pointing a rifle at someone. Illegality would not occur until someone actually fired their weapon. The severity of the offense would depend on the *why* and then the *what* or *who* was shot. Consideration was also given to the resulting damage or injuries.

The police made it clear that they were not going to do anything. No, they would not go next door and talk to him. It was his property and he could display a weapon any way he chose as long as he stayed on his property and didn't fire the weapon recklessly.

For obvious reasons, Nathan and his crew spent a lot of time watching the house next door. By observation and by listening to gossip, they learned that he had a woman who lived with him. The woman had two children. There was a young girl who appeared to be about nine years old. An older boy also lived in the house. He appeared to be a young teenager.

And so it went for much of the summer. The "rifleman," as he came to be known, would appear out the back door of his house around 4 PM and stand on his little back stoop. He would aim over toward the pool or the lifeguard, stand for a while, and then go back inside. It was unnerving for a long time before it finally lost its impact.

*

Regular drama continued with the "delegation" and the "rifleman." Officer Green's visits were memorable; however, most days were uneventful at the park. Twice a week, Nathan ran drills in the morning before the pool opened. Some drills involved the police and fire department. It was always exciting to hear the sirens and see the fire trucks pull into the park. The firemen took drills seriously. They would always run from their trucks carrying rescue equipment.

One particular morning was busy because of a cooperative drill that included both the fire and police departments. The street had been congested with emergency vehicles, sirens and flashing lights.

The summer sun was hot. The red Birmingham air was filled with the smell of chlorine and suntan lotion. The music of Simon and Garfunkel blasted from a centrally located 8-track player.

Over in the park, children waited for the pool to open. They played on the swings and other park equipment adding laughter as background to the music.

When ten o'clock arrived, the gate opened and the children entered the pool area. A line formed to pay the admission price of 25 cents.

Nathan kept an eye on the process. He was scanning the crowd when something caught his attention. Lifeguards develop a skill of noticing what is out of place. He did a double take and was shocked to see the teenage boy from next door standing near the gate entrance.

Nathan moved in his direction. "If you would like to come in and swim, it's my treat today. No charge," Nathan said smiling.

The lad didn't move. He wore boots, jeans and a western short sleeve shirt. He looked out of place amongst the crowd of black children. Nathan continued to stare awkwardly, trying to determine if the boy was truly the boy from the house next door. Nathan encouraged him further, "Come on in, you don't have to swim. Just visit awhile." After several weight shifts, the boy tentatively slid through the gate and into the pool area.

"What's your name?" Nathan asked.

"Jeremy," he replied.

Nathan held out his hand. "Jeremy, my name is Nathan. Welcome. To what do we owe this honor?"

Jeremy shook Nathan's hand and cracked a smile. Nathan noticed that Jeremy looked taller and thinner up close.

"My mom and stepfather are at work. I live next door over there," he said pointing over at "the rifleman's" house.

Jeremy started to open up a bit. "I seen all the commotion this mornin' with the police and fire trucks and I wanted to come over. I been thinkin' that I would like to be a lifeguard someday."

Nathan winked at Bob. "That sounds like a fine idea, Jeremy. Bob, why don't you give Jeremy here a tour of the place. I'll catch up shortly."

Bob took Jeremy around, showed him the equipment and explained it all in detail. Bob was just smart enough to figure out what

Nathan was thinking. Bob knew exactly who this lad was and how he might help their "jewelry" business.

170

Nathan slid into the bathhouse. He sent all of the support staff outside of hearing range and reached inside his wallet. He carefully removed the card that James Green had given him and reached for the wall phone. Nathan had never called Green before. Today, he thought, was important enough to give the system a test.

Nathan got lucky. Green was at his desk and answered on the second ring.

"Officer Special Agent Green speaking."

Nathan told Green the story about how the "stepson" of "the rifleman" had walked over to the pool that morning. He explained to Green how the boy was enthralled by lifeguards and his dream of being a lifeguard one day.

The officer listened with interest while inserting short phrases of encouragement into the conversation such as "Yes" and "I see."

Nathan then asked Officer Green if he could clear it with the city to give Jeremy a few dollars a week to hang around and do odd jobs. "Maybe we could learn something," Nathan said.

Officer Green liked the idea. He had already done a background check on the neighbor. "The rifleman" was an associate of the suspects with dogs but was not a part of the inner circle. Still, he might know something and it was worth some effort.

Special agent officer James Green was part of a team in the state bureau assigned to solving the bombings in the recent history of Birmingham, including the famous church bombing in 1963. No one had been arrested for the crime. There was a separate federal investigation, but the Alabama bureau hoped to get the jump on the Feds and finally break the case.

Officer Green was certain that the "delegation" and the men who threw the fake bomb, were local Klan members. He was also certain that the church bombers were part of the same local Klan. Given that the church was only a few blocks from the pool; the Norwood Park situation was a rare opportunity to observe the Klan in action.

He thought it was possible, or even likely, that the faces at the park every day were the faces of cold-blooded murderers. The eyes that watched innocent children laugh and play were the same eyes that would gladly snuff out their young lives.

James Green theorized that the integration of the Birmingham swimming pools offered a recruiting opportunity for the Klan. It was for recruiting purposes that the Klan had exposed itself and shown its face in support of local residents who opposed the "black invasion" of their community."

The officer had no plan to tell the lifeguards the complete story.

They were all clean-cut naive young men who were clearly out of their league. The truth would scare them to death and could also jeopardize the operation.

Green thought back to a time long ago when he was like those boys. War either changes a man or kills him. James had changed. Change was necessary for survival. The skills he learned in war provided him with the knowledge and experience to do his police work today. It was basically the same job he did in the Army. Take down the bad guys!

As far as Nathan and the lifeguards were concerned, why clutter their simple existence. The ugly side of the world was best kept out-of-sight where it can be hidden to the public as they go about their daily routines. It takes a special person to live with evil and not be absorbed by it.

"It was a great idea to get this young boy on the payroll," Green surmised. He knew better than to go through city channels. Klan members were embedded in every corner of city government. State government was also thick with Klan members and sympathizers. It was one of the reasons that the Birmingham church bombing had never been solved.

Green certainly had enough budget to cover this small potato operation. He was grateful for the opportunity to praise Nathan. And, Green knew he needed to protect these boys from the wrath of the Klan. If knowledge of this operation ever leaked out; he didn't want to think about the consequences.

"Good job, Nathan! I will come over tomorrow to resupply your inventory. While there, I will give you some cash to pay this boy. Let's keep this little piece of the operation between the two of us, whatcha' say? What's his name again?"

"Jeremy," Nathan said.

"Oh yeah, Jeremy, whatever, man. Offer him some work around the pool and park area. Get close to him and pick his brain. Buy him a few things and find out what you can. Give me details when we get together, or call me if it's urgent."

"See you tomorrow," Green said as he hung up the phone.

Officer Green opened the bottom right drawer of his desk. He pulled out a metal box. Fishing a key from the center drawer, he looked around the room before opening the box. Inside was a little less than $10,000 in cash.

The cash had come from pimps and hustlers over the past couple of years. He had confiscated more than this, but the cash in the box was his "working" capital.

James Green counted out $500. He would give the cash to Nathan tomorrow. This should be plenty enough to pay Jeremy and purchase a few items. Nathan could keep what he didn't spend. James didn't care about the money. There was plenty more where this came from.

*

Officer Green arrived at the pool in his usual garb. He always appeared out of nowhere and disappeared the same way. Green signaled to Nathan. He and Nathan walked outside the fence to insure a moment of private conversation.

Green pulled out another sack stuffed with some jewelry and cash. He went over the details again to make sure Nathan was on the same page.

Their meeting had the look of a drug deal. That was fine with Officer Green. If some of the neighbors came to that conclusion, it actually added some credibility to the project.

Over the next two weeks, Jeremy started to look the part of a pool employee. Nathan bought him two pairs of swim trunks and some flip-flops. The first time he wore shorts, his legs were so white they almost glowed. It was a couple of weeks before a semblance of a tan started to appear. Gradually he added some beads here and there and a subtle change started to appear. He walked with a little more confidence and he spoke with more authority.

Nathan and the other lifeguards gave Jeremy swimming lessons. He had limited swimming experience. His muscles were not developed and his technique needed work before he could even think of moving forward with his dream of being a lifeguard. But, he was enthusiastic and he worked hard. Everyone liked him. Taking into consideration that Jeremy was raised by a white supremacist, he was making real progress.

It turned out that Jeremy had a wealth of information to share. He loved to listen to gossip and enjoyed telling others what he heard. He had good information that included his stepfather's contacts with the "delegation."

Nathan reported what he learned to Officer Green.

Jeremy explained that one of the "delegation" members was a man named Thomas Blanton. Everyone on the street knew Blanton. It was common knowledge that Blanton took part in the bombing of the 16th Street Baptist Church. That bombing injured a dozen people and killed four young black girls. (Many years later, Blanton would be tried and convicted of the church bombing.)

One afternoon the lifeguards were cleaning up at the end of the day. Jeremy had been practicing his American Crawl swimming stroke when he swam over to the ladder near where Nathan was standing. Jeremy climbed the ladder and caught Nathan's attention by clearing his throat.

"You know my step-dad wouldn't never shoot you, don't you? He was just tryin' to scare you a little and maybe run you off so they would close the pool."

Nathan looked at Jeremy but didn't know what to say so he simply stared at him.

Jeremy broke the silence.

"He told me so. He told me that he would never shoot any of you. Most days, he said, he didn't even have a bullet in the chamber."

A voice screamed in Nathan's head, "This conversation is surreal!"

Nathan finally spoke to Jeremy. He tried to speak calmly. "I started hunting with my father when I was five or six years old. I owned my first shotgun when I was eight. Would you believe that my father spanked me once for pointing a *toy* gun at him? A *toy* gun!"

Nathan's face was red. "Where I come from, we don't point a gun at anything we don't intend to shoot. I'm sorry to tell you this but your stepfather stepped way over the line. *Way* far over the line!"

Nathan took a deep breath. "We all like you Jeremy," Nathan told him. "But don't defend what your stepfather has been doing with his hunting rifle. It's bad stuff and it ain't cool, man."

Jeremy stood silent with his head down.

Nathan got a grip. He patted Jeremy on the shoulder and moved away. Looking over his shoulder Nathan told Jeremy, "You be sure to be here tomorrow. We have a lot of work to do and we need your help." Nathan hoped he hadn't run Jeremy off but, ... damn!

*

Another section of the recreational park located near the pool contained swings and other playground structures common to any city park. Children would often go to that area of the park and wait for parents or friends or just to play before and after going to the pool.

The pool was thinning out one afternoon when the "delegation" arrived right on schedule. There was nothing particular or unusual about that afternoon. The players were all the same. It was a normal summer day. The only exception was the addition of Jeremy inside the fence.

Nathan was circling the pool for the millionth time that summer. He was walking toward the back fence and noticed one member of the "delegation" and his dog looking past the pool area and out toward the playground. Nathan looked in the direction of where the dog and the man were focused and saw a single young black girl on the swings. She was six, seven or maybe eight years old. She was wearing a yellow flower print sundress and flip-flops.

Some things really do seem to happen in slow motion. Nathan saw the man drop the leash. He saw the dog start to run toward the playground. Time stood still. That is, time stood still for everyone except the dog and the little girl.

Nathan had his mace clipped to his swim trunks. He didn't always have it on him but, for a reason he could not remember, he had it that afternoon.

The lifeguards and pool staff had trained for every emergency in the book. Twice a week they ran drills. They had a procedure and a policy on any crazy water related emergency, or heart attack, or broken bone, busted head, cut, or spinal injury. They were prepared for every disaster that any rational person could imagine happening at or near a swimming pool. Their objective was to be so well trained that the team would function as a machine.

This situation unfolding with the dog and little girl was not in the training manual!

Breaking for the gate, Nathan temporarily lost eye contact with the girl, the dog and the "delegation." Pulling the mace canister off of his waistband, Nathan shouted for the staff to call the police and an ambulance.

Unaware of the problem, no one understood why Nathan was running *away* from the pool. He quickly darted out the entrance and toward the girl and the dog. Another guard followed behind. A third guard stayed to clear the pool.

The dog attacked the child at a full run and drove her backwards off the swing. It had her down on the ground and was attacking her small body the way a shark attacks a piece of raw meat. The child's screams only encouraged the predatory instincts of the animal.

Nathan had the mace ready and sprayed the dog in the face. He had never used mace before, had never been trained, and had no idea what he was doing. Nathan pointed and pushed down on the button. The stuff sprayed in all directions until he finally locked in on target. It was effective and the attack stopped immediately. The dog was yelping, whining and rolling in the dirt. Meanwhile, the pool staff divided into two groups. One group cleared the pool area and the other brought first-aid supplies and equipment to the attack scene.

The police arrived almost immediately. One officer took control of the dog and others rounded up the "delegation" and the other witnesses.

By the time the ambulance arrived, Nathan and his staff had already stopped most of the bleeding and started cleaning and covering the smaller wounds. She had also been exposed to a heavy dose of the spray. They treated her for shock and tried to keep her calm. Her little brother ran home to tell her mother to meet them at the hospital.

The city ambulance service was new. In the past, funeral homes were the only option for medical transportation. In recent years, Birmingham and other cities had started ambulance services but the drivers were not well trained. In 1970, lifeguards in Birmingham had more medical emergency training than ambulance personnel.

While the lifeguards treated the young girl and prepared her for transport, the police were talking to the "delegation." The owner of the dog stated that the dog broke loose from his leash.

"It was an accident," he said. All of his friends supported his statement.

Thomas Blanton and the entire "delegation" were taken to the police station. No charges were ever filed.

It was ordered by the court that the dog be quarantined for 30 days. It was ordered that the dog be tied up or placed in a pen for observation to insure it did not have rabies.

The owner of the dog accepted the verdict and complied with the order of the court. The dog was tied to a post 100 yards from the pool at the home of "the rifleman."

For the remainder of the summer, the same dog that had sent the little girl to the hospital, barked and pulled on his chain. All in full view and earshot of every child in the pool and at the park.

*

The all-white Birmingham City Police Department was a real mixed bag. They represented a true sample of the white public at large. The police, park management and all the lifeguards were white. There were two black workers on the support staff, but the police only talked to Nathan, or to one of the other white staff members.

The police were called often to the park. Staff relationships were good with most of the officers. An agreement was struck between the pool staff and the police that minor offenders would be driven a few blocks in the direction of their homes and freed. The police didn't want to waste the time or do the paperwork required to arrest 13-year-old half-naked children.

The final big event of the summer was an act of vandalism. One night, heavy oil was sprayed over the outside walls and into the dressing rooms. Jeremy said it was Blanton who did it. No one was ever arrested but the pool was closed for a couple of days while a city crew came in to clean up the environmental hazard.

Jeremy was so embarrassed about the German Shepherd in his backyard that he quit hanging out at the pool. Information dried up.

Jeremy did come by one day and apologized but didn't stay long. Nathan told him that everyone knew it wasn't his fault.

Jeremy said the dog was keeping the whole house up at night and his mom was ready to leave his stepfather if something didn't change.

Despite every effort, Jeremy slowly slipped out of view.

Officer Green made up three bags and left a "little something extra" in each package. The officer knew the season would end soon and it was time to "terminate all contact." He had gotten some good information and added it to his book of knowledge. The project had been worthwhile. Best of all, no one got hurt. Call it a success. Call it done!

On his final visit to Norwood Park, Officer Green shook hands with his lifeguards, turned and walked in the same direction he always walked before he disappeared. Then he was gone forever.

*

The summer of 1970 was a life-changing experience for Nathan. Before coming to Norwood Park, he had no idea that people could hate with so much intensity. Blanton and his "delegation" had a look in their eyes he had never seen before. It was the look of pure evil itself. Nathan thought it might be a sign that the "delegation" was possessed by some kind of demon. Whatever the cause, their hatred had consumed every fiber of their being.

Nathan had seen racism in its rawest form. Rather than look inward however, the contrast he made between himself and the members of the "delegation" made him feel morally superior. He congratulated himself on his open mindedness. Nathan saw little need for improvement in his own personal attitude. Like many middle-class whites, Nathan had identified racism, and it wasn't him. He returned to Tuscaloosa with a good story and little else. The events of that summer did not motivate him to action, or to strive for more change from within.

Nathan, like most of the Old South would progress, but it would take time. Too much time, in the mind of many critics. In Nathan's case, it would also require the mentoring of a good friend.

Chapter 35

"Some people spend an entire lifetime wondering if they made a difference in the world. But, the Marines don't have that problem."

—Ronald Reagan

It didn't take the Marine Corps very long to figure out that Rub was a cut above the average soldier. Just as it was with his father, Samuel, Rub picked up things quickly. Even in a rifle company, brains were important.

Sergeant Victor Wells had moved up in rank rapidly. The men in his squad respected him because they knew he wanted to keep them alive.

*

It wasn't apparent to the casual observer. The change was not physical or even emotional. Rub had experienced an internal spiritual revolution. The death of his father and the loss of his scholarship added to the momentum. Although Rub had attended church at least three times a week from the day he was born, Rub had lost his faith. He simply didn't feel it anymore.

Rub was slow to admit his doubts to himself and even slower to confess them to others. Nathan had noticed the change but didn't understand its context. Rub never told Nathan exactly what he was thinking and Nathan never pushed it.

Rub finally discussed his loss of faith to Nathan in a letter. He told him that it was a lie that there are no atheists in foxholes. He said that the foxholes were full of atheist who do not believe in a God who would allow

179

war. They exchanged long letters debating the subject but Rub stayed firm in his non-belief.

So Sergeant Wells became the tough, hard fightin', hard drinkin' weapon that the Marine Corps was looking for. He wasn't afraid to die but he wanted to live. Rub also learned to kill. In fact, he was good at it and had a reputation for doing the kind of dirty work usually reserved for special forces.

First Lieutenant Danford, Rub's platoon leader, was a damn good platoon leader. He had the potential to be a damn good company commander someday. Danford depended on Gunny and Wells to be his eyes and ears in the field. They were his "go to guys" for personnel issues also. Danford tried to meet with them every day. When on patrol, he *did* meet with them every day.

The current operation was designed to probe for an encounter with the enemy and then destroy it. The ultimate goal was to push the enemy lines back to a point where the area would be reasonably secure during the long rainy season.

*

The Vietnamese had similar goals. They had moved troops and equipment into place at night to avoid being spotted from the air. VC regulars were waiting in ambush in anticipation of the American advance through the valley. American forward spotters had detected some enemy movement but they had misread the strength of the force. Danford estimated his platoon was up against a similar platoon strength unit of well-armed enemy regulars.

Rub's platoon made camp the previous night on the same ridge where Rub was currently dug in. Scouts had gone out well before sunup and reported back to Danford that the valley was occupied. Danford then sent one squad down to test the level of strength. The second squad laid back behind the probing force and a hundred yards short of the dense vegetation. A deep wet-weather ditch provided some cover. The remaining squads were dug in and set up to support the advance squad should they come under attack and need fire support. Rub's squad was positioned on the ridge along with the machine gun squads and command squad. His duty was to help monitor, add fire support and direct fire where it was needed.

The first hint of dawn was peeking over the eastern horizon when the sky exploded with light. Heavy mortars rained down on the forward line. The true size of the enemy was immediately apparent.

Gunny barked into the box ordering first squad to lay down smoke and fall back. Second squad was instructed to open fire with mortars as soon as first squad cleared the jungle. Gunny hoped to pin down the enemy and provide cover for a retreat by first squad.

Thankfully, dense green jungle foliage, fog and thick smoke limited visibility. There was enough cover to suppress target-specific action from the VC. The enemy, however, continued to blanket the valley with random small arms fire. Most of the first squad was able to retreat safely to the fallback position.

When the first squad reached the ditch, Rub's squad launched mortars into the tree line. They also launched additional smoke grenades along the south ridge to give cover as both squads continued to fall back up the hill.

The morning campaign had so far left three men dead and two wounded. One of the wounded men was in serious condition with a head injury.

Gunny split the machine-gun squads, setting up cross-fire positions on each flank. Rub and his squad took the center of the line and the two other rifle squads spread out between the machine guns along the ridge. During the night everyone had gotten busy digging holes and filling sandbags in anticipation of an attack. Danford had decided last night that the ridge would serve well as a defensive position if needed.

In short order, bullets started spitting at the sandbags and dirt short of the small bunkers. Mortars rained down as the spotters zeroed in on the platoon's defensive position. The Americans did not yet have targets in sight.

A short rock ledge below the ridge gave a small buffer to the thick vegetation line another three hundred yards down the hill. Moments after the mortar attack began, VC troops erupted from the jungle growth with rifles and automatic weapons. They crossed the short distance to the ditch and gathered there for the run up the hill toward the American lines. Danford and Gunny gave strict orders to hold fire until the enemy crossed into the M-16 "kill zone." Gunny led from the left flank and Danford took command on the right near the machine guns.

When the VC came out of the ditch, Danford waited until they crossed a line at about the 100-meters range, then he ordered all three rifle squads to open fire. At 75 meters, the machine guns lit up with a deafening barrage.

The VC started to set up mortar launchers from the ditch. Gunny saw what was happening and ordered mortar counter-fire on the enemy mortar placements. Meanwhile, Vietnamese troops continued to pour out of the jungle.

Rub kept shooting and hollering, "Drive 'em back" he barked. "Stay focused on the bastards in your sights." He could hear screams and swearing as some of the enemy mortars found their mark.

The VC had flanked the Americans and both machine gun positions were under heavy assault. The original center of the line was now the flank of two separate assaults. Rub read the situation. He called out for the other two rifle squads to re-direct fire on the flanks. He directed his squad to focus fire and expect another attack on the center of the line.

Exposed as they were, the enemy took heavy losses. They eventually retreated to the tree line and disappeared into the bush. The battlefield suddenly fell silent except for the faint moans of the wounded.

From his position, Rub could not completely assess the situation. Sixty or more VC lay dead in the field. It was impossible to assess the number of wounded.

Rub wasn't sure of the casualties on his side. He called down the line for a report. There was no response from the flanks. Enemy snipers were certain to be in position by then. Rub shouted for his men to "stay down."

As best as he could, Rub tried to figure out the strength of the platoon. A couple of men from the other squads had been picked off by snipers ' fire. He figured the platoon was at maybe, 50 percent.

Rub collected his thoughts. He knew that the last attack was either an underestimation by the enemy or a probe to test the American strength. Either way, the second attack would be an all-out assault, at company strength, or greater, with possible artillery support.

Rub needed a plan or a miracle or both.

The Major commanding the Vietnamese regulars was also trying to figure out the size and power of his enemy. He knew they were less than company strength because they did not have artillery.

He had set up the ambush in the valley between the ridges and above the river in hopes of engaging an American company or even a larger force. With his troops and artillery in perfect position, an easy victory would have been his. Major Dinh shrugged his shoulders. "Small victories are victories, just the same," he thought to himself.

Such are the fortunes of war. This little platoon has stumbled onto his plan and now he needed to clean up the mess and fall back to fight another day. As soon as he collected intel on the initial attack, he would pour the appropriate resources into a battle to end the misery that awaited his adversary on the ridge.

*

The lack of direction from command told Rub that there *was* no command. Rub was senior if Lt. Danford and Gunny were dead, or critically injured.

Rub called down the line for someone to find the radio and bring it to him.

It took a few minutes before Rub saw corporal Emory crawling up the line in his direction. Emory had no word on the Lieutenant. He said they were briefly overrun but had fought them back. Emory had taken his radio and ducked under some sand bags. When he came out, there was no sign of anybody. He didn't see the Lieutenant.

Rub told him to shut up, hand him the radio and start digging a freakin' hole big enough to bury his ass.

In less time than expected, Rub had Colonel Polanski on the horn. Rub gave his position and summarized the situation. He told the Colonel that he expected a new attack against his forces within the hour. He estimated his strength at 40 men. They were getting low on mortars and did not have enough ammunition to repel a lengthy attack. Rub estimated the enemy strength at 200 or more. He believed the main force was in the valley at the moment. Mortar fire had originally come from the valley but could have moved by now.

The Colonel spoke calmly. "I've got the map here in front of me, Sergeant. your position looks to be about three clicks from the river on the south ridge above the valley. Is that what you read, Sergeant?"

"Roger that, sir," Rub replied.

The Colonel continued. "We have options but you and your men are in a goddamn tough spot up there, son."

"Yes sir we are," Rub replied, "But I believe we can take out the enemy or bring them down to a level we can fight if we could get an airdrop on that valley, sir."

"That is not advisable, Sergeant," the Colonel answered. "You are too close to the valley. I have seen this kind of situation many times. Those sky boys are liable to wipe you out along with the enemy. No, your best bet is to hold on till we can get some reinforcements in there and resupply you. I can get a dozen copters over your ridge by eleven hundred hours."

Rub was respectful but firm. "Yes sir, I hear what you are saying, sir, but we will all be dead by then. We have the will but we do not have a line deep enough to defend an all-out assault from a superior force. The consensus on the ground, sir, is to send immediate air support, followed by copters. We have wounded who need immediate medical evac. If you have air resources in place, I will direct the strike from my position on the ridge. We will mark our position with red flares. The bombs need to drop three hundred meters south of the origin of the red smoke."

"Roger that Sergeant. What's your name again soldier? Did you say Victor Wells?"

"That's affirmative, sir."

"Well Sergeant Wells, you are the man in the best position to make the call. I don't like sending air cover that close but I will do whatever it takes to save 40 brave goddamn leathernecks."

"Thank you, sir. The men on this hill have fought bravely and, with your help sir, maybe we will live to fight again." Rub was laying it on a bit thick but he needed help in a hurry.

"Shut up sergeant!" The Colonel said. "That kind of talk gives me a hard-on.

You bastards need to dig in and hold on. The wrath of God almighty is on its way to your position."

"Roger that, sir. Sergeant Wells signing off."

Colonel Polaski turned to his EO and ordered him to get a pair of F-4s on that goddamned valley within the hour.

"We have marines dying up there and we are going to start doing something around here besides pushing paper and filling out goddamn reports."

The Colonel then turned to a staff member and ordered him to, "get the names of every goddamn Marine on that ridge".

"That platoon is going to get a commendation. Oh yeah, and make sure that Sergeant Wells gets some kind of goddamn medal; even if he's dead."

*

The ground shook with the force of an earthquake. The air rumbled with deafening thunder. Rub feared that the Colonel wasn't lying when he said he was sending down the wrath of God.

Rub had his face buried in the dirt but the destruction was so close that he could feel the heat and smell the napalm. Rub knew those were Marine pilots flying those F-4s. Marine pilots came in low. They would blacken their own tails to get the bombs on target and save Marine lives.

Fire was everywhere. The dry vegetation around them ignited as sparks drifted to the ground.

Less than a minute earlier there was no warning in the sky. The VC were breaking out of the jungle when the first plane crested in the distance above the trees. The enemy soldiers didn't make it to the ditch before bombs fell into the jungle edge. Most of the first and second assault waves, still in the jungle, were killed instantly. The concussion leveled everything and everyone in the clearing. In the instant before Rub hit the dirt, he saw the landscape rolling as the shock waves traveled along the ground.

Those not killed were bleeding from their eyes and ears. The shock wave toppled the few trees that once stood near the ditch.

The second plane brought napalm into the battle. Black smoke surrounded a rolling sea of fire and heat. Explosions could be heard inside the inferno as enemy munitions joined the chorus of destruction. No living thing survived the rain brought down that day by the air assault from hell.

Slowly Rub raised up and peered over the dirt and sandbags above his head. The sight in the valley was something out of a science fiction movie. The valley he remembered from moments before was no longer imaginable. What once was green and lush was now black and barren.

There was no enemy, no trees, no nothin'! Smoke, the stench of oily gasoline, and burning flesh was all that remained.

Rub quickly pulled himself together and assigned rifle details to set up watches on the parameters. He did that in the unlikely event that some part of the enemy still wanted to fight.

Medics treated the wounded while the dead were identified and gathered together for transport when the copters arrived. First Lt. Danford and Gunny were both found dead with pistols in their hands, a sign of close-in combat.

*

The debrief concluded that there were breaches on both flanks and both machine guns' placements were taken out by grenades and AK-47s. The breach came at a great cost of human life by the enemy. It was further determined that Sergeant Well's redirection of fire stalled the advance and forced the Vietnamese forces to pull back and regroup.

Ninety-seven Vietnamese soldiers lay dead in the open area between the jungle and the American's defensive line. Six Vietnamese soldiers were found wounded, were treated in the field, and later evacuated to a hospital. Two hundred or more Vietnamese soldiers were killed instantly by the air assault. Their bodies were never recovered.

The platoon lost 13 men and another 24 were wounded. Three of the wounded later died in surgery bringing the total deaths to 16 brave American Marines.

As Rub thought back on the battle, he couldn't believe that only two F-4's could have done all that damage. He was right. A Navy pilot, flying back to the carrier with bombs still loaded, heard the call and joined in the fight. Rub later laughed and thought to himself how he might have to rethink his opinion of Navy pilots.

The recently deceased Major Dinh had heard the roar of jet engines but, because of the thick cover, he never saw the planes. His position was 150 meters above the valley on the far rise. First he felt the concussions as twelve 500lb. dumb bombs dropped into the valley. Seconds later he heard the explosions and felt the heat from the napalm run by the second F-4 Phantom. Then there was a flash of light a millisecond before his life ended. The Navy pilot, flying off the same ship as the other planes, the USS Saratoga, had dropped his load of deadly napalm parallel to the first two runs.

That day, Major Dinh, and over 250 men under his command, died in a battle with no name; in a valley with no name. Major Dinh would not, as he planned, live to fight another day. The Americans had won the battle but they had not won the war.

Chapter 36

"To be heroic is to be courageous enough to die for something; to be inspirational is to be crazy enough to live a little."

—Criss Jami, *Venus in Arms*

Nathan's mother sent him the newspaper clipping about Rub. The clipping included a story about the battle. It told of Rub's great courage. The story detailed how, by keeping his head, he had saved the platoon from certain defeat and probably death.

Nathan was proud of Rub and sent him a letter telling him so. Nathan never got a reply from his letter. In fact, he didn't hear from Rub or see him for over two years. They would not speak again until after Rub returned home from service.

*

Meanwhile, Nathan finally got into the college groove. He remembered why he was in college and understood the sacrifice his parents made to get him there. He studied, worked hard, and good grades followed.

The nation decided to hold a draft lottery. Nathan's lucky draft lottery number was 286. He would only be drafted if a world war broke out. Nathan would have served in the military if he had been asked to serve. He was not, however, going to volunteer.

The Culverhouse College of Commerce and Business Administration, at the University of Alabama, was the focus of Nathan's academic energy. Between classes and work, there wasn't much time for anything else.

The Way it Was

Nathan was able to get a part-time job at the new Tuscaloosa Yacht Club on Lake Tuscaloosa. In those days, it was just a log cabin but the place was scripted to be the greatest Alabama yacht club north of Gulf Shores. He had gotten the work-scholarship by way of the swim coach and actually interviewed with the famous football coach, Paul "Bear" Bryant. Those special scholarships were usually reserved for football players but the yacht club job required special skills and training. Coach Bryant took "a likin" to Nathan, and signed off on giving him the working scholarship.

The yacht club offered Nathan the opportunity to be a lifeguard, waiter, ski instructor, swimming instructor, bartender, chauffeur, boat tender and boat pilot. The experience was incredible. He felt he acquired a Ph.D. in human behavioral science through his work and observations at the club.

Because the "club" had become the "place to be" in Tuscaloosa, Nathan was exposed to university deans and local business professionals. He was able to get job interviews through contacts and through channels not available to most students.

Nathan's work and study routine continued without change until graduation. Nathan developed an interest in medical business management after he interviewed with a large medical group in Birmingham. He was offered a job and joined the group following graduation.

Birmingham is only an hour northeast of Tuscaloosa. The move was a simple transition because Nathan already had friends there.

Nathan had dated in college and even had a couple of serious girlfriends. At some point, however, he always found a reason why every girl wasn't right for him.

People were constantly setting him up with their friends. When the Crimson Tide had a home game, he was usually there. Some weekends, however, he made the four-hour trip to Kentucky.

When Rub finally got his discharge papers he also headed home to Russellville. Nathan heard he was back in town, and on his next trip, he went looking for Rub.

Nathan found Rub standing in front of Todd's Cafe. He was with several other black men. Nathan had called Rub's house. Patricia told him that Rub was somewhere outside. Rub didn't have a car yet. She said he was on foot so Nathan knew he must be close.

When Nathan saw him, Rub had a beer in his hand and a cigarette. He thought it was a cigarette until Nathan got close enough to see otherwise.

Rub was taking a long drag on his joint when the alarms went off. "Narc at two o'clock," someone warned.

"Be cool, I know him," Rub said loud enough for everyone to hear.

Nathan had parked down the street a half block and walked to Todd's.

After taking a long drag, Rub passed his joint down the line. He slowly walked to the sidewalk. "You got wheels?" Rub asked Nathan.

"Sure do," Nathan shot back.

"Let's roll," Rub replied.

They hopped into Nathan's Jeep and were off. It was like the old days in high school. They swung around to Bean Row and picked up a couple of six packs, then drove around awhile. They eventually pulled into the old school parking lot.

Nathan had been doing most of the talking while Rub did the drinking. Nathan had gone on and on about all that had happened in the years since they had last talked. He talked about the fraternity house and the yacht club and the football games and the pretty girls. He even mentioned a few classes he took.

Rub was not engaged as much as Nathan. He was mostly non-conversational but would grunt, "yeah" and "no" when Nathan asked a question.

Seeing that Rub was not going to engage, Nathan shifted directions and started asking questions. He asked about Rub's health and how he was doing. Did he have any plans about life? He asked about Rub's mother, Patricia.

The more Rub drank, the quieter he got. The mood was tense.

Nathan focused his thoughts around all that Rub had been through. He thought back to the last time they had been together before Nathan went to college and Rub went to Vietnam. That moment seemed a lifetime ago. Life had flushed away all of their innocence and all of their illusions.

Nathan was momentarily lost in his thoughts and had fallen silent.

He sat with a blank look on his face when Rub broke the silence.

"What are you lookin' at?" Rub loudly demanded.

Nathan jumped. He hadn't realized he had been staring at Rub.

Before Nathan could answer, Rub fired again.

"How 'bout we go hang with your whitey yacht club friends?"

The words came out of nowhere and they stung. They burned into Nathan's psyche, rolled around and popped out into his heart and head. The burn in his heart was painful. The burn in his head made him angry.

Nathan was not yet ready to give up on Rub but was moving in that direction.

"What is wrong with you, Rub? Somethin' you want to get off your chest?" Nathan fired back.

"Okay, for starters, before we go hang with your yacht club buddies, what say we hop over to your house and have tea with dear ole mommy and daddy?" Rub barked.

"What?" Nathan asked.

"You heard me," answered Rub. "Goin' to your house would be a "first" wouldn't it? Growin' up we were always at *my* house. Why was that, Nathan?"

Rub kept it up. "You were welcome in the "Bottom." Did it ever occur to you that I have never stepped foot in your house? Why not? You were in my black life but I was never in your white life. I don't remember ever hanging with you and your whitey friends at school. Why is that, my man?" Rub finished sarcastically.

Nathan sat speechless as he tried to find an answer. He was always aware of the gap but he never wanted to broach the topic and talk about it with Rub.

As Nathan tried to bat down his emotions, his mind was in overdrive.

The thoughts fired in his brain. "Wait a minute! This isn't fair! Didn't Rub understand that he had made more effort than most white people?"

Nathan thought he should be getting some credit and "by God" gratitude. Or at least, some recognition of the fact that Nathan had *tried* to be a friend to Rub. Doesn't effort count for somethin'? The limitations weren't Nathan's fault! It was just the way it was.

Rub could see that Nathan was struggling. He enjoyed watching it.

Deep down in his gut, Rub knew Nathan wasn't too bad for a "white" guy. And, he was almost family.

Bingo, that was the problem! Rub wanted to be part of Nathan's family but the road was blocked. Rub was very tired; no, he was weary of blocked roads.

"Don't take your anger out on me?" Nathan eventually blasted back at Rub as he turned the key to the ignition and slammed the stick into 1st gear.

"You think life is supposed to be fair?"

The jeep roared out of the parking lot.

"Yeah," Nathan thought. He had been warned about being a friend to a Negro. "They'll turn on you," he was told. "You can't trust those people!"

And it wasn't like he hadn't taken grief for his "friendship" with Rub.

As these thoughts percolated in his brain. The steam fueled his self-righteous anger.

"Who does he think he is? He can't talk to me like that!"

"So what if I'm not perfect," Nathan finally concluded to himself.

Rub was also fuming in his seat. He had seen plenty of college white boys in Nam. They were usually ignorant "schoolbook" soldiers. The kind of officers who got people killed. It was common knowledge amongst the "brothers" that the "white man" couldn't be trusted. "It wasn't fair," Rub thought. "I invited him into my home and I had his back with the brothers. None of the other brothers wanted him included, but I still hauled his white ass around like a puppy."

Rub could feel the heat in his face. "Who does he think he is, treating me this way?"

With the Jeep moving, the air helped cool everything down a little. The picture of Rub in the newspaper popped into Nathan's mind.

Rub remembered that Nathan was there when his father died.

"Where can I drop you?" Nathan grunted metaphorically.

"Back at Todd's is fine," Rub answered.

The Jeep rolled up to Todd's Cafe and Rub opened the door and jumped out. No one said goodbye.

As Nathan drove back to his parents' house and Rub walked to his home, they both silently reflected back on the last couple of hours. Both felt some guilt. The good news was that, although it was close, neither had crossed a line that could not be mended.

*

It was over a year before Nathan saw Rub again. It was Rub who broke the silence calling Nathan on his birthday.

"Congratulations on another year of death evasion," Rub laughed.

Rub didn't' give Nathan an opportunity to respond. He leaped boldly into the conversation by telling Nathan that he had started college at

Tennessee State University in Nashville. "I like it," Rub said. "It is a mostly Negro school and it is where my dad attended. Nashville is a happenin' place for brothers, ya know."

Rub stayed in control of the conversation. "What is happenin' in your world?"

Nathan told him that he was learning the business side of healthcare.

Rub smiled to himself and asked, "What is the business side of healthcare?"

Nathan was ready with an answer. "The short version is that doctors don't care much about costs and hospital administration don't care much about patients. That's not totally fair, but it's not totally false either."

It felt as if they had never been apart. They talked like old friends for almost an hour and they vowed to stay in touch.

By Christmas, communications had been restored enough to schedule a visit at the Colonial Inn Restaurant in Russellville. Both were in town for the holidays.

Woody Carter ran a tight ship at his restaurant. Rub and Nathan had been there many times before. Two sweet teas were on the table before their seats were warm.

Nathan hardly recognized Rub. He was wearing some mangled threads from his Marine Corps days. A comb was sticking out of a big Afro haircut; or lack of haircut!

"Yo, man," was the first thing out of Rub's mouth. "What's up?"

Nathan shot a "Yo" back at him as they picked up the menus and examined the selections they had both memorized years ago.

Over Rub's right shoulder, Nathan could see his dad's welding business through the window. It was a strange feeling being back in the same place after so much time and change.

As the two young men sat drinking sweet tea, Rub opened up. He talked about college and his new role as a black activist.

He talked about the dreams and goals of Dr. Martin Luther King Jr. and Malcolm X. Rub told Nathan about marching and protesting and almost getting arrested.

Rub's current roommate was an organizer from Columbia University. He was taking some time after graduation to help organize a Tennessee State University chapter of the Afro-American Students for a Democratic

Society (AASDS). It was an activist organization for changing American culture.

Rub and his roommate, Alex Holder, had organized a five-day occupation of an abandoned ROTC building. The AASDS was demanding the University donate and rename the building the Malcolm X Library in honor of the late Malcolm X. It would house books and information on the black movement and also offer a gathering place for black students.

Rub was very excited about almost getting arrested! He had gotten away by escaping into the crowd, he said.

"Things are going to change quickly," Rub told Nathan.

"With the rise of black consciousness," he said emphatically, the future belongs to the black man."

Rub wanted to finish while he was on a roll. "Except for you, I don't socialize with white folks anymore."

"White folks got nothing I want and ain't givin' them nothin' I got," he concluded.

Rub watched Nathan closely for a reaction. Nathan just nodded and asked, "Are you still in engineering?"

"For the time being," Rub replied with a frown. "I'm not really into academics at the moment."

Nathan didn't want a repeat of the last meeting or the meeting before that so he changed subjects quickly. "Have you finished your Christmas shopping?" Nathan asked.

Rub twisted in his seat and stared out his window towards 4th Street. His eyes were dark and intense, "I have something for Mom and Sis but I am not going to stay around for Christmas. Christmas is a white man's invention. There ain't no God and there never was any little, white, baby Jesus. Christmas is another way that rich white folks take money from the poor and put it into their white pocket."

Nathan looked at Rub carefully. God only knew what those eyes had seen in Nam. Once again, at a critical moment, Nathan was lost for words.

Nathan was thinking that maybe Rub was still simply trying to shock him. He had been popping off about his lack of faith for several years. They had corresponded in detail but had never aired it out in public.

Rub knew Nathan was a Christian. A bad Christian maybe, but a guy who attended church regularly. He probably also knew that Nathan was not a big fan of Malcolm X.

Nathan didn't want confrontation. He smiled and told Rub that his mom would kick his ass if he left town before Christmas and she would kill him if she heard any of that talk about Jesus.

Rub laughed and said, "You're right!" The moment lightened. Nathan wanted to know more about Rub's time in Vietnam. He said he didn't talk much about it, but he went ahead and told Nathan some stories. Some were funny and some were awful. They laughed about the "package" he had sent to Nathan at school. Nathan let out a secret, "I still have it," Nathan shared: "I have been waiting for the rest of the body so we can do a proper burial." They laughed so hard they cried.

Woody prepared the restaurant for the next day while the two young men sat and ate apple cobbler with ice cream, and drank sweet tea, and pretended nothing had changed.

Rub told Nathan that Nathan was training to be a capitalist pig.

Nathan said that Rub was a Marxist. They laughed. Time passed quickly. They both hated to say goodbye.

Chapter 37

"If it wasn't for my lawyer, I would still be in prison. It went a lot faster with two people digging."

—Joe Martin, *Mister Boffo*

-

To Rub, the Vietnam War was a white war fought by black soldiers. To Rub, the war was an example of injustice where the poor, and especially poor black men, were drafted while the rich white boys went to college.

His facts were not totally accurate, but they weren't totally inaccurate either. The debate still rages. Over 86% of the deaths in the Vietnam War were white. On the other hand, more young black men did not go to college and therefore did not receive a college deferment. The black population had a much higher percentage of draftees than the white population. However, because of their lower population numbers, their totals were also less.

Between 1965 through 1969, African Americans formed 11 percent of the American population yet accounted for 12.6 percent of the American soldiers in Vietnam.

The unpopular war made the ground fertile for Rub to recruit angry black men to the causes he supported. A target being explored was a large army base northwest of Nashville and home to the 101st Army Airborne.

Rub and his associates stayed away from the active duty soldiers. A few had drifted into the group but it was dangerous to push onto the base. That would draw too much attention. It was better, at the moment, to stay stealthy until they had the numbers necessary to punch hard and make a monumental statement for black power.

The large Army base straddled the Kentucky/Tennessee state line. Rub came to Clarksville, Tennessee with fellow students, professors and others who supported the anti-war movement, the civil rights movement, and the Black Power agenda. They were all from the Nashville area. Most were young and black. They generally represented the target group they sought to recruit.

North of Clarksville was the small Kentucky town of Hopkinsville. Rub and Leon, another member of the group, had been invited to speak at a church on the northeast side of town. The invitation was a direct result of their networking success and the efforts being made into the area's black community.

No one at the church knew that Rub was an atheist. He didn't say anything or do anything to lead anyone to conclude he was anything but a fine young Christian black man. He delivered his well-rehearsed and refined speech about freedom and the need for equality. Having logged hundreds of pew hours himself, he knew how to use his voice and his message to elicit the desired emotions and responses he desired. Rub spoke to a crowd that included many young black men; all hungry for the hope and future he promised.

Unknown to Rub and to many in the church, there were black elders who feared what agitation of the black masses might bring to the black community. Although half of the city residents were black, the entire police department and all of the sheriff department employees were white (except for the janitors). Every single elected official, including the judges, in both the city and county were white. Whites held all of the law enforcement, justice system, and political power.

It was true that the Civil Rights movement was in full swing in other places. Most everyone knew of the Civil Rights Act of 1964. But Hopkinsville was <u>not</u> other places. The young were restless alright, but most of the older blacks were afraid of losing the small gains and the limited power they had already achieved.

After the church service ended, there was a short social time with members of the congregation. Rub and Leon felt welcome. Many of the young men took information on how to join the cause or how to support it in other ways. Both visitors were in good spirits as they left the church.

When Rub pulled the blue and white Chevy station wagon out onto Hwy. 41A, they saw the flashing blue and red lights of the police car almost immediately. The police car quickly came up behind Rub's wagon.

He looked over at his associate and their eyes met. They both knew they had been "had".

*

Sergeant Prittchet and officer Williams had been patiently waiting for the appearance of the blue and white Bel Air station wagon. All sides had agreed that there was not going to be any nigger uprising in "Hoptown." Not tonight anyway.

Rub and Leon were schooled on what to do and say when stopped by the police. They were polite, respectful, and obeyed the officer's request to get out of the car. While officer Williams guarded and talked to the suspects, Sergeant Prittchet searched the car.

"Well, well, what do we have here?" a smiling Prittchet asked. "Looks like we have done found ourselves a couple of nigger pot-head dealers."

Rub jerked around to look at Leon. Leon dropped his head and refused to make eye contact with Rub. Leon knew better. He had ignored the rules and now his stupidity put them both in serious deep shit.

*

Monday morning, a young bright attorney walked into his office on the corner of 6th and Main Street across from the Christian County courthouse. His father had practiced law there for many years. His grandfather was a physician but Petey chose the law. He shared the two-story office building with his father.

Woodsin Ernest Rogers III was young, smart and handsome. He had graduated a few years earlier from Vanderbilt Law School in Nashville. His future was bright in both politics and in law. Everyone called him Petey. He was already active and a rising star in the local Democratic Party.

The attorneys in town rotated their obligation for pro bono work. They shared the duty of representation for anyone arrested who could not afford an attorney. It was Petey's turn when he got the call from Judge Watson's office. It seems he had a new client in the Christian County jail by the name of Victor Wells.

*

The jail was down the street from the courthouse so Rogers walked over after lunch to meet his new client. He had read the police report. It looked like a thousand other police reports he had studied. There were a few questions, but first he needed to hear his client's side of the story.

A guard unlocked the door and Petey entered the small room at the jail where his client waited. Rub stayed seated. His anger was controlled but obvious.

Petey stuck out his hand to Victor. "I am W. E. Rogers. I have been assigned to represent you." Petey spoke with a smile. Rub hardly responded.

"Are you well? Have you been mistreated in any way?" Petey asked.

Both Petey and Rub were trying to quickly detail the other. Rub had not yet spoken so Petey was at a disadvantage.

"I am fine," Rub responded. "I talked to my old roommate. He told me those cops didn't have a search warrant. They had no goddamn business searching our car."

"So you admit you had dope in the car?" Petey responded.

"I admit it was in the car. I don't admit it was mine," Rub said.

"Your accomplice is probably saying the same thing," Petey informed Rub.

"Maybe, if they weren't hick small town cops, they would have noticed whose suitcase held the dope," Rub said while rising slightly in his seat.

"First, you need to keep your butt planted in that chair," Petey quickly told him. "You need to settle down and listen to me. You are facing serious charges that could send you to prison. Possession of over five ounces of marijuana in Kentucky is a felony. You had a five-ounce bag in a car you were driving."

Rub had no idea how much Leon had in his bag. He quickly realized his situation.

Petey noticed a subtle change in Rub's facial expression. Was it because of the information about the level of the potential charge or was it because of his ignorance of the amount of pot in the car? Ignorance would mean he really didn't know about the dope. Petey mentally filed the information for future reference.

Petey pulled out a legal pad and took a pen from his coat pocket.

"We are set for a preliminary hearing before a judge tomorrow morning. The judge will listen to the charges and evidence and determine if there is enough evidence to go to trial. He will also set bail. I assume you don't have bail money yet. First things first. Why don't you tell me your side of the story?"

For the next thirty minutes, Petey listened to his client. He was impressed with the obvious intelligence and poise of the man. After he completed his story, Petey asked about his past and his family.

At the end of the meeting, Rogers knew his client was more worried about his mother than anything the judge would do to him. Petey rarely trusted his clients. He knew many of the local families but this Victor fellow was from Russellville by way of Nashville. Petey wasn't buying anything until he had a lot more information. It had to be information he could confirm.

Two things bothered Petey about the arrest though. First, what was the probable cause for the original stop by the police. The suspects were not cited for any moving violations and the automobile was apparently in good working order.

Second, his client was correct. The police did not have a search warrant to search the car. "Something smells fishy about this case," Petey thought to himself.

*

Petey decided it would be a good idea to call the other attorney representing the potential co-defendant. Leon was represented by Frank Pitts. Frank was past President of the Kentucky Bar Association and a respected local attorney. Outside of Hopkinsville, he was better known as a Thoroughbred horse breeder and poker player with an appreciation for Kentucky bourbon whisky. Frank was one of those men who was loved, respected and feared by most, but, he had made his share of enemies along the way too.

In his conversation with Frank, Petey learned that Leon had spilled his guts about everything. He had also given his opinion about the police being tipped off that he and Rub were in town. Frank said he would snoop around and see what he could find out. Both attorneys agreed to talk in the morning before the hearing, if not sooner.

*

At 5:30 that afternoon, Petey was closing the door to his office when the office phone rang. Petey answered and was surprised to find Frank on the line. In his usual style, Frank was blasting from both barrels. Petey could imagine his arms waving even though he couldn't see him.

"It was a set-up, Petey. Those sumbitches set up our boys. The police had been tipped off and were waiting for them to leave the church. The pot bust was a bonus but it doesn't matter cuz there was no reason for the stop and no warrant for the search. That pot is not, no way, no how, admissible evidence!"

Petey asked the obvious question: "What set up, Frank?"

Frank immediately launched into his teaching mode. "My wife makes me go with her to Nashville to the damn ballet. You ever go to the ballet, Petey?"

"A few times. No not really," Petey mumbled more confused than ever

"This whole thing is a ballet," Frank said.

Rogers laughed. "What the hell are you talking about, Frank?"

"Think about it Petey. A ballet is a dance with a story. Dancers hop around a stage to the music of some great composer and the audience is supposed to figure out the plot. And that is exactly what we have here," Frank explained.

"Sorry Frank but I still don't get it," Petey admitted.

"You are going to be a great lawyer Petey, but there are things around this county you need to learn. This is how the powers dance when trouble comes to Christian County."

Frank continued, "The local black youths needed to believe they were involved in the civil rights movement so they invite some "B" player civil rights activists to town for a little talk. The Negroes who really run things in the Negro community, tipped off the police. The police set up an ambush. The stop is bogus but they find some pot."

"Let me know when you hear the music," Frank laughed.

Petey didn't say anything.

Frank continued. "Everyone knows the judge is throwing this out tomorrow. The police set it up to fail. They just wanted to keep the local blacks happy and scare off the outside agitators. If we do our job in court, the whole thing goes away. No harm, no foul."

"Who all is in on this?" Petey wanted to know. "I can't believe the police were the only players in this ballet."

Frank was expecting Rogers to ask. It was probably why he had been assigned to represent Leon. The powers knew that the rookie would need some "guidance."

"You young lawyers are always full of piss and vinegar, aren't you? You want to change the world. Well, go ahead, but whether you like it or not, after tomorrow, you are as much a part of the problem as you are the solution."

"How does that make you feel?" Frank was still laughing. "Let it go, Petey. See you in court." He hung up the phone.

W. E. Rogers III sat back in his chair and rubbed his eyes. He tried to absorb all that Frank had told him. His mind whirled with the information. Petey wasn't naive. He had heard stories but he thought those days were all in the past.

Frank was "dead on" though. Petey had a job to do. His first obligation was to his client so his path tomorrow was set in stone. It didn't matter about the big picture. His client came first.

Chapter 38

"All that is necessary for evil to prevail is for good people to do nothing."

—Carlton Smith, *Hunting Evil*

Rub sat on the cot in his small cell. He seldom went out into the common area. There was no one he wanted to hang with out there. He didn't feel like recruiting convicts into the black power movement. Just about everybody in jail was black though. Rub had spent two sleepless nights in the hell hole known as the Christian County Jail. This entire mess was just bull shit.

He was tired. A jail has to be the loudest place on earth. Rub was having trouble concentrating.

Rub's training in Nam came in handy during his jail time. Rub knew he was as tough as anyone in there and his confidence kept the bullies at bay.

"A fantasy consumed him that maybe some big lawyer in the black power movement would come to his rescue. The lawyer would roll into town and blow these mothers out of the water. Maybe get a little payback."

Then he thought about that damn pot in Leon's suitcase. "Nah. Fat change of any help after a drug bust. Nobody wanted to get in the middle of a drug story. It didn't help the cause and it was bad publicity."

Rub spoke every day about freedom for black people. He had thrown that word *freedom* around in all manner of ways and places. Today he realized that freedom is just a word until you lose it. Now, his entire life and his entire world was about only one thing — freedom!

The guards took Rub to a holding room in the courthouse to wait for his attorney to arrive. The hearing was set for nine o'clock but he had heard that it was some kind of cattle call. There would be a dozen or more prisoners appearing in front of the judge with that same assigned date and time. Each would have to sit and wait for their turn.

Early that same Tuesday morning, Petey was at the office and then on his way to the jail.

The young lawyer walked into the courtroom and found his client. The two men sat and talked about what Petey had learned, how the hearing would proceed and how Petey thought it would go.

Rub's numbness softened his anger. His attorney was the only hope he had. Trusting a white lawyer was not his nature, however.

Rub wanted to know what his attorney was going to do about the injustice of his arrest. It wasn't enough that he would soon be free. "Who is going to pay for my two days in jail?" Rub wanted to know.

Unfortunately, at best, all Petey could prove against the police was two counts of stupidity. Rub wasn't the first person arrested without cause or searched without a warrant. Petey could insist on an investigation but nothing would ever come of it. Frank's comments flashed through his mind.

Petey looked across the table at Victor Wells. "I can't fix the system overnight, Victor. The system is bigger and older than both of us, but I tell you what. After the hearing, if all goes as expected, they will process you out of jail. When you are out, you come to my office. We will sit a spell and look at some options."

Rub was too tired to argue.

"Okay," Petey said gesturing to a bench. "Take a seat and remember to keep your mouth shut unless I tell you otherwise."

*

When Victor's name was finally called, the Commonwealth's Attorney stood up, gave a brief summary of the Commonwealth's case and stated that the two defendants would be charged together. He asked that bond be set at $25,000 each because the defendants were from out of state and they were a flight risk.

The judge then turned to Rogers and Pitts and asked how their clients pleaded. Petey asked to approach the bench.

Victor watched from his chair as Petey and the Commonwealth's Attorney argued back and forth. It only took a moment for Frank Pitts to join the discussion. Shortly after Frank arrived, the judges voice got louder as more and more papers were passed around the bench.

After about ten minutes, all three attorneys turned and went back to their seats. Frank motioned for Leon to join him beside Petey and Rub. Leon had been seated on a bench not far behind.

The judge banged his gavel to stop the chatter. Frank put his hand on Leon's shoulder. The bailiff asked Rub and Leon to stand.

The judge looked down at both defendants. "This court has found that the defendants' rights were violated when the police pulled over their vehicle without probable cause on the night of their arrest. The rights of the defendants were further violated during a search of their vehicle without a warrant to conduct such search."

The judge continued. "The evidence found in the car was obtained illegally and therefore is not admissible as evidence in this court. There being no admissible evidence that any crime has been committed, all charges against the two defendants are hereby dismissed. The defendants are free to go."

Everyone at the table turned, smiled and shook hands. Leon was in shock and speechless because Frank hadn't told him anything before the hearing.

Both post-defendants were escorted back to the jail to change clothes and pick up their belongings. Frank Pitts slipped Leon a one-hundred-dollar bill, took Leon to the bus station and told him to go home and to please stay away from Christian County for a while.

*

Rub walked out of the jail, took a deep breath of free air and then walked over to the office of W. E. Rogers III. He checked in with Nancy at the window and took a seat in the waiting area. The last two days were like a dream. Rub had been in combat and fought bloody battles but he had never felt as helpless as he had felt in the Christian County jail.

Petey studied the FBI report on Victor Wells. The judge was livid when he discovered what had happened. Apparently he was not a part of the ballet that Frank talked about. He demanded that the Commonwealth's

Attorney take up a private collection to pay for Leon's bus ticket home. He demanded they do something similar for Victor.

Petey had requested an FBI background check on both men. It usually took a couple of days. This time, Petey had the report in hand in less than two hours.

Leon had a criminal history as a juvenile but was clean so far as an adult. The report on Victor was amazing. He had an IQ of over 140. He was a war hero with a bronze Star and two Purple Hearts. Honor student in high school, Dean's List every semester in college. And no prior arrest.

Petey closed the file and walked out to the waiting area to greet Victor. As the two men strolled down the hall to a large conference room, Victor saw a wall covered with law books.

"You read all those books?" Victor asked.

"Yep," Petey answered.

Rogers motioned for Rub to have a seat.

Petey looked seriously at Rub. "I know you have had a long hard couple of days, but I need to ask you a question."

"What the Hell!" Rub thought as he nodded his approval.

"From here, this moment, what exactly do you want to do with your life?"

"You think about that for a moment while I get us a couple of Cokes."

Petey returned to the room with two Cokes and a sack of sandwiches. "We figured you might be hungry," Petey said.

Rub took the food and drink, suddenly realizing he was starved.

"Well?" Petey said.

"Well what?" Rub answered.

"What do you want to do with your life?"

"You know, maybe it's none of your goddamn business," Rub answered with the anger he had kept stuffed for several days.

"Petey took a sip of his drink and pushed back a little from the table. "I guess the bigger question is whether you are going to stay an angry hard ass or are you going to do something important."

"Like what?" Rub said with a frown.

Petey had no formal training on how to handle angry young black men, but he did have experience reading people. Petey read something in Rub deeper than his words indicated so he took a chance.

"I have taken a look at your records. You are a smart young man. I somehow don't see you in engineering school. Have you ever thought about the study of law?"

"How did he get a copy of my file," Rub wondered. A chill went down his spine. The feeling of helplessness was increased by knowing the system could get anything it wanted. The little guy was truly powerless.

Rub tried not to show his fear. "Nah, I never gave law any thought," Rub replied.

Petey leaned forward. "Did you enjoy the past few days? Wouldn't it be nice to know the law and work on the other side of the table?"

Rub looked down and didn't answer. He wanted to ask a thousand questions, but he didn't want to give this white guy the satisfaction.

Rogers stood up. Having done all he could think to do, he reached into his coat pocket and removed an envelope.

"They are bringing your car around to the office. They have already sent Leon home on the bus so you are free to go in any direction you choose."

Petey continued. "In this envelope are a few dollars to get you somewhere. I suggest you leave Christian County immediately and stay gone for a long time. Also in the envelope is my business card with my home number on the back. In the envelope there is a letter of introduction to a contact person in Nashville who will give you guidance, should you choose to pursue a law degree. Your contact is a black attorney and a professor at Tennessee State University. Let me know when you are ready to drop your attitude and move in a positive direction."

Rub managed a growl.

The phone rang and Petey answered it.

"It appears your car is here," Petey said as he hung up the phone, stood and shook Rub's hand.

"Good luck and God bless you," he said.

The attorney smiled and walked Rub out the door.

*

W. E. Rogers III watched as Victor drove away then stepped back into his office and closed the door.

"That Victor was a tough bird to figure out," he thought. His anger unnerved Petey. He rubbed the bridge of his nose and sighed. If he was going to be a criminal lawyer, guess he better get used to it.

Rogers picked up the phone and called Frank.

... "Yep, he just left," Petey replied.

... "Yes, I gave him the envelope. Do I need to call the Chief and the Commonwealth Attorney and thank them for their donations?" Petey said laughing.

Frank was happy that Petey had called. He wondered how long Petey had waited for his package.

"The envelope and the money got to my office about an hour after the Chief and Commonwealth Attorney left Judge Watson's office. I would have loved to have been a fly on the wall during that meeting."

... "Well sure, Frank! The Commonwealth's Attorney should never have taken the case. They had to have been in on it. I gained a lot of respect for Judge Watson today though."

"I pitched a couple of dollars into the pot," Frank admitted.

"I threw in a few bucks myself, so he is good to get home," Petey added.

Frank gave Rogers a rare compliment. "You did a good job in there today, boy. I look forward to working with you again one day soon, ya hear?"

... "Any time, Frank. See you later."

Petey hung up the phone, closed the door and headed for the house. He needed to move along. Jeannie would have supper on the table soon.

*

It was late afternoon when Rub slid in behind the wheel of his Bel Air station wagon. Rub was only 35 miles from his hometown of Russellville. Maybe he would just drive over and make a surprise visit on his mom. Maybe she would have some warm cornbread and beans on the stove. Maybe he could get a shower, sleep for a day or two and think about all that had happened.

It felt good to be free. Even the Jefferson Davis Monument was not going to upset his happiness. Jefferson Davis was the President of the Confederate States of America and he was born in Fairview, Kentucky.

Fairview is a small community between Russellville and Hopkinsville. The towering obelisk rose out of the horizon miles before it arrived out of his passenger window. In size, it rivals the Washington Monument in Washing D.C. Normally, it made Rub's angry every time he drove by, but not today. Today he glanced over and kept on rolling towards home. His mind elsewhere.

He felt the envelope in his pocket. Slowly, he opened it. There were 10 twenty dollar bills, a business card and a letter. Just as Mr. Rogers had said.

Rub dropped the envelope into the passenger seat and kept the car headed east on Hwy. 68/80. He looked over at the envelope and at all it represented. He was still angry about what happened, but also conflicted. Why would white people put him in jail and then try to help him get into law school? It made his head hurt.

Chapter 39

"The trouble with some women is that they get all excited about nothing and then marry him."

—Cher

Over the next couple of years, Nathan would occasionally see Rub as he passed through Birmingham on his way to or from some march or protest or sit-in. Rub was totally consumed by the "movement." He could talk of little else.

To Nathan's amazement, Rub's life had recently taken some new directions. Rub was admitted to law school. He would start next fall as one the few African Americans ever enrolled at the Vanderbilt Law School in Nashville.

Rub thought of his new adventure as both an honor and a challenge. He was happy to finally be at Vanderbilt. He never completely recovered from the disappointment he felt after his father died and he lost his opportunity to attend Vanderbilt University.

Rub knew that Nashville was still part of the old South. He had accepted the racism that he was sure to face as the only current black law student. In Rub's own way, he looked forward to it.

As an activist, his goal was to confront racism and expose it. As one of his school's first black law students, his mere presence would be a form of confrontation.

Rub's goal was to survive the racism and emerge on the other end with a law degree. Much the same way he survived Vietnam. It was a law degree that would open doors to his future. He knew he had to keep his eye on the prize.

Rub had watched many of his African American friends fall victim to the stress of achievement. Some used drugs or alcohol to numb their fears and cope with challenges that are unique to African American students. Rub understood why his friends dropped out of the battle, but he was determined that he would not be a statistic for failure. With the same determination his father Samuel had felt when he left Logan County, Rub had no option except to succeed. He had survived and even thrived in Nam. He was confident he would survive the small white world of the Vanderbilt Law School.

*

"Blacks can't trust white honky lawyers!" Rub told Nathan during one of their "get togethers." "That's why I'm in law school."

Even if forgotten, the "seed thought" planted by W. E. Rogers III, had fatefully grown and blossomed.

"I figured if we are going to change the world, the change must begin at the courthouse. Those goddamn crackers aren't goin' to change on their own," Rub laughed.

"Speaking for crackers everywhere, I wish you the best of luck," Nathan said with a smile.

Rub looked at him and frowned. "Weaver, sometimes I ain't sure when you are kiddin'. Anyways, what is going on in your sorry white-ass life?" he asked.

"Thanks for asking," Nathan answered sarcastically. I'm getting my white ass married and if you weren't such an asshole, I would ask you to be in the wedding."

Rub blinked! "What? Is she black and pregnant and you need a reference? What kind of stupid bitch would marry an ugly prick like you?"

"Your sister!" Nathan said laughing, then moved the conversation back on subject.

"She is a nice girl from Indiana. She has a BSN degree from the University of Evansville. She is working on her master's at UAB."

"Really? She have a name? Is she blind?"

"Her name is Melinda. No, she is not blind but she will knock your eyes out. I have told her about you but she still wants to meet you. I was wondering if you have any outstanding warrants in Indiana? That is where the wedding will be. Dad is going to be best man. I have a couple of fraternity brothers who will be there and I want you in the wedding party also. Can you behave long enough to mix with regular people?"

"White people you mean?"

"Will you quit the white shit for God's sake? You want to be in the wedding or not? If you don't want to be in the wedding, you are still invited."

"I don't know nothin' about being in no freakin' wedding, especially with a bunch of Bama rednecks! Do I have to wear a monkey suite?"

Rub was dancing around and waving his arms in the air. "This ain't really my thing man. I don't want no pictures of me standin' around lookin' like some fool with a bunch of white folks who don't want me there. What if I was to rape one of the white bridesmaids or somethin'?"

"Rub, dammit, you've got a real attitude, you know that? Just forget it! Or you can let me know. I don't care anymore! If I don't hear from you, I'll find someone else."

Rub stood up and put out his hand. "Well, congratulations anyway. I'll let you know in a couple of weeks. Let me check my schedule, ya know, before I commit to anything."

Nathan took his hand and they shook on it. Rub reached up for Nathan's elbow and Nathan did the same.

The two men stood facing each other in silence for a moment before breaking the odd embrace. Rub needed to get on the road back to Nashville so they said their farewells and he departed.

In a couple of weeks, Rub called. "I'll be in your stupid wedding but I think you're crazy for askin'."

"No truer words were ever spoken!" Nathan told him, "but we want you there anyway."

The wedding went off without a hitch, and Rub even wore a tux!

*

It was only a little over a year later when Rub called and requested that Nathan return the favor. Nathan and Melinda drove up to Nashville to

212

stand with Rub and his bride, Diana. It was a small wedding. In fact, there were only four in the wedding party plus a judge.

Rub and Diana had been living together for several months. They were hopelessly in love, but keeping their living arrangements secret from Patricia and Diana's parents was getting to be a burden.

Diana and Rub met in the summer before Rub's second year of law school. They were both attending a reception for the opening of a new black history museum on the campus of Tennessee State University.

Diana had come to Nashville from Atlanta. She had a master's degree from Spelman College in Art and Design. It was her knowledge of art and her experience with other designs that brought her to Nashville as project director and finally curator of the museum.

Normally, Rub would have been too shy to approach a woman with so much beauty and class. As the night progressed, he watched and circled her. Like a moth drawn to a flame, he moved closer and closer with every flickering of her light.

Diana saw him out of the corner of her eye. She pulled her best friend close and asked who he was. It took some investigation before his identity was confirmed as a single law student and civil rights activist.

When the distance between them became so small that they could not avoid contact, Rub managed a big smile followed by a weak "hello." When they finally started talking, they couldn't stop.

The meeting at the museum led to a lunch date, and then a dinner date, and then another and another. Rub was smitten.

Diana was infatuated with Rub but held the keys to her heart in check. She saw a loving, kind and generous human being until Rub showed his angry side. She worried about his demons.

Days turned into weeks and weeks into months. Rub and Diana talked about everything, including Rub's past. She loved him, but was scared to commit. They spent so much time together that they decided to move in together.

Over the next months, some of the anger in Rub started to melt. There was something about the unconditional love of a woman that softened his outlook on his life and on the world in general. Or maybe he just didn't dwell as much on himself anymore. Maybe he found something, or someone, more valuable than the anger he had carried for so long.

Rub graduated law school with honors. He took a job working as a junior counsel for the Tennessee chapter of the NAACP and also the Urban League. He was active in the Democratic party and thinking about running for office as city commissioner sometime in the future.

Meanwhile back in Birmingham, Nathan was organizing campaign events for local Republican candidates in Alabama. Most of the doctors in the clinic were Republican. Although Nathan was active, politics was not the center of his life

Rub and Nathan knew they were on opposite political sides. They took great pains to stay away from political discussions. When they failed, it was not pretty. Eventually their wives would learn to step in and stop them as soon as they started.

Chapter 40

"Beware of false knowledge. It is more dangerous than ignorance."

—George Bernard Shaw

"Freakin' pine trees! I hate pine trees," Victor thought to himself. "They are ugly and messy and they don't provide any shade. And, God knows they must harbor evil because the pine is the tree you see everywhere in the South."

To the casual observer, the pines simply blend into the greenery. Sure, the deep South had its beautiful majestic live oak trees, but it was the pine that usually lined the highways.

Zip, zip, zip they passed by the window of the bus in a near hypnotic fashion. Tree farm after tree farm. Row after row. Tree after tree. Thank God it wasn't hot. The windows were pulled back and air flowed inside. It was November. The bus had left Columbia, South Carolina early that morning in route to Greensboro, North Carolina for a day of marching and protesting.

It seemed there was always another march or demonstration somewhere, and that usually meant a bus ride. The white South was fighting the civil rights movement. Parts of the North were also fighting against civil rights, but the North was more subtle about it. The South was visible, vocal and sometimes violent.

It was the Klan, the old KKK, who was back in business and stirring up trouble in the South again. Today, Rub would join a group who was taking a stand against the Klan. Today, the world would see that Negros were not intimidated by the KKK.

215

The bus pulled into the parking lot of the New Calvary Baptist Church. About 30 young black people and a peppering of older blacks and whites stepped out of the bus. Dr. James Waller called everyone over to circle up.

James Waller, M. D. had quit the practice of medicine at the top of his career. He was currently the head of a textile union. He worked with the "*Death to the Klan March*" and the *Communist Workers Party* to organize mostly black industrial workers.

Victor Wells was a new attorney but an experienced activist in the Civil Rights Movement. He was concerned, however, with media coverage that might, because of his presence, link the civil rights movement to the Communist Party. The two groups were not partners in any fashion, but, his presence today was evidence that they might work together in a common cause.

It was a cool November day. November 3rd to be exact. The skies were cloudy. There had been some rain the day before and the ground was still wet in places. Protesters had been out early. They had signs and bullhorns. Most of the people in the rally were shouting, "Death to the Klan." The action was centered around and near the intersection of Carver Street and Everitt Street.

Unknown to Victor, fliers had been distributed locally, calling for violence by the protesters. A call had gone out for armed self-defense against the Klu Klux Klan. The Klan had learned of the call for confrontation and was eager to comply.

Victor was in Greensboro to observe and lend legal support if required. His Nashville office had arranged for him to accompany Dr. Waller to the rally. He was to observe and report back to the NAACP office in Nashville where he was now junior counsel. The NAACP was not officially participating in this demonstration.

The Morningside public housing project, located nearby had been a hotbed of unrest. It was in this mostly black neighborhood that many of the protesters lived. They lined both sides of Carver Street.

It was middle afternoon when a procession of old trucks and autos appeared several blocks away as they topped the hill. They rolled down Carver Street and slowly approached the protest area. The Klan had decided to confront the protesters openly. As the caravan of Klansmen began its invasion of the crowd, marchers began to pepper the vehicles with rocks and beat the cars with the picket sticks that held their signs.

Victor and Dr. Waller were walking over toward Carver Street as the action unfolded. No one is sure who fired the first shot. Evidence indicated there were handguns and other weapons in the protest crowd. The Klansmen, however were much better armed. Very quickly after the first shots were fired, the caravan came to a halt. Doors flew open on both sides of every car and truck as white men exited their vehicles. Weapons were pulled out of belts, pockets and holsters. Shells were pumped into the chamber of shotguns and the warlike clicks of bolt-action rifles signaled the first sounds of battle. People would later say that it sounded like firecrackers. Suddenly, smoke, noise, and the smell of gunpowder filled the air as fire was laid down, in lethal doses, on the crowd of protesters.

The entire incident was filmed by four TV camera units covering the rally. The videos would document, for all time, the carnage of that horrible afternoon in Greensboro. Bodies started dropping immediately. Screams could be heard from all directions. Every puff of smoke signaled a bullet had been launched towards a human target.

The video clearly showed Dr. Waller running towards the gunfire. Odds are he did not know that Rub had been hit. He ran towards the other victims. His first instinct as a doctor was to help the wounded. A Klan member saw the doctor advancing. His 12-gauge rotated as he spun and fired. Bam! Bam! Two shotgun blasts hit Waller square in the chest. He was dead before he hit the ground.

Rub felt the bullet hit his left leg, his leg collapsed, and he dropped to the ground. A review of the video tape evidence would indicate that Rub was probably wounded by a stray bullet from a handgun.

Rub kept his head down but he could hear the sound of gunfire as it popped around him. He had been in battle before. Rub knew the sounds, smell and feel of war.

Rub recognized immediately that this was not a fair fight. The suspicious absence of police told him all he needed to know about any immediate rescue. Rub laid face down and totally still until he heard the caravan members start their engines and pull away. Only then did he raise his head and survey the carnage around him.

He could see Dr. Waller on his back in the grass not far away. It was not immediately apparent he had been fatally wounded. The appearance quickly changed when Victor crawled closer to his bloody body. A shotgun wound from short range is not a pretty sight. Victor slumped over the body of his new friend and cried.

This was not the first time Rub had been wounded. He had been awarded the Purple Heart twice for wounds in Vietnam. And, this wasn't the first dead man he had cried over. He fought back the memories and trauma of the past, and felt the anger about what he had just witnessed. The greater shock was that he thought his bloody war days were behind him. He thought he would never again be covered with the blood of a fallen brother.

His tears joined the mournful wailing of those who knelt over the bodies of the other dead and wounded. Their sorrow filled cries of pain and grief rose upward into the heavens and begged for answers from a silent God.

Victor, however, cursed through his pain. He cursed a universe that allowed such hatred and death. He cursed and spat on the ground of a nation that, he felt, protected and often nurtured hate. And he vowed to use all his energy, knowledge and power to fight it.

Five died that day in Greensboro. Another thirteen were wounded.

After a two-day stay in the hospital, Victor went back to Nashville and recovered from his physical wounds. Victor would spend much of the next twelve months back in North Carolina in an effort to find justice for the victims and their families. There were two trials. Both trials resulted in the acquittal of all defendants by all white juries.

The massacre in Greensboro was a turning point in the career of Victor Wells. It became crystal clear to Victor that the states could not or would not change on their own. Change would have to come from the top down. Change would have to spring from the federal courts. Victor, therefore, changed gears, changed direction and refocused his energy. His shifted his legal efforts to cases that could be originated or moved to the federal court system.

Chapter 41

"I busted a mirror and got seven years' bad luck, but my lawyer thinks he can get me five."

—Steven Wright

Nathan was sitting in his four-position, high back, reclining leather chair watching the nightly news when suddenly there he was. A television report showed President Jimmy Carter after a meeting with Andrew Young, his Ambassador to the United Nations. Also in the group was Julian Bond and standing behind Mr. Bond was Rub.

Nathan hollered, "Melinda, Come quick!"

Melinda rushed to the scene of what she assumed was a crisis. Unfortunately, she missed the shot because the nightly news waits for no one.

Nathan wasn't surprised to see his friend on TV and in the company of power. Rub was smart and he had the education and experience to contribute to any cause or party. What Nathan couldn't believe was that he actually knew an "insider" in the Carter administration. Or maybe, more bazaar was that someone in the Carter administration knew little ole Nathan!

Over the next few years, Rub became a regular background figure in both politics and in civil rights. He was the "go-to-man" when there were marches or events of civil disobedience. He would be waiting at the jail with papers in hand to file for every person arrested. He usually had his clients out of jail and eating supper before the arresting officers had finish their reports.

Rub actually became the kind of "super attorney" he once dreamed might come to his rescue in the Hopkinsville, Kentucky jail.

The new Victor Wells was much refined from the angry hippie activist who attended Tennessee State University. Rub now wore expensive suits and his hair was cut short.

Because of Rub's never-tiring effort to keep the friendship going, Rub and Nathan grew closer as the time went by. Both families were getting larger as children were added to the mix. Rub would plan something and coax Nathan into joining him. During the summer months, both families would meet near Decatur, Alabama and get a cabin on Wheeler Lake for the weekend. It was a convenient mid-way location between Nashville and Birmingham. Sometimes they rented a houseboat with a slide for the kids.

Rub and Nathan made extraordinary efforts to stay away from political debate. Family came first.

During Christmas break one year, they tried skiing in Utah. Melinda and Diana were frozen solid after a one-hour introductory ski lesson. The ladies spent the balance of the trip reading books, shopping and going to the spa.

Melinda and Diana also became close friends. Both women shared an interest in art and interior design. There was mutual respect and sincere affection between them.

*

In the spring of 1987, Rub was in Atlanta for a meeting. Nathan was also in town. They met at the Peachtree Towers Hotel for dinner. Rub brought along an associate by the name of Jerry Baker. Jerry was the local director of the Office for Community Development. It was a private venture funded by federal grants and private donations.

Rub and Jerry wanted to pick Nathan's brain on some general accounting issues. They were trying to implement good accounting practices and procedures, however, the process had become overwhelming because they were activists, not accountants.

Nathan tried to explain but there were no simple answers to their complex questions. Finally, he offered to take an extra day after his meetings and give the operation an accounting review.

It ended up taking not one day, but two days; plus, several hours on the phone over the following weeks. The good news was that the accounting was eventually certified and the integrity of the organization was saved. Even better news was that the board approved a budget that included a consulting CPA and a yearly audit.

Rub appreciated the work that Nathan had done. Nathan had seized the opportunity to work with Rob in an area where they found common ground. Accounting is not political. Finding common ground was the secret to their relationship.

*

Presidential election years were always a difficult time for Rub and Nathan's friendship. It was the time when political emotions ran higher than in other times. The situation was made worse because of political party trash talk. In spite of pledging not to get into heated discussions, it happened now and then.

Rub called himself a "Socialist Democrat." Nathan laughed and said that the term "Socialist Democrat" was redundant!

Rub said Nathan's joke wasn't funny. "What joke?" Nathan replied.

And then suddenly, the argument was on!

Rub wanted a tax system that took wealth from the wealthy and redistributed it to those who had less.

Rub also hated big business. Especially big oil.

Nathan was a conservative capitalist. He thought The War on Poverty was a failure. "The percent of people in poverty never changes!" Nathan would shout during a heated argument.

Nathan didn't necessarily like *all* big business, but, he didn't want to destroy capitalism as a method of fixing capitalism.

The arguments were often brutal. Nathan never understood why Rub cared what he thought about issues. It seemed important to Rub that Nathan understand why he believed what he believed. There was always hope, in Rubs mind, that Nathan would someday finally see the light. Nathan never bent and Rub never quit.

By his actions, Rub was the better friend. He remembered all the birthdays and anniversaries. He even sent birthday cards to Nathan's children. Rub's Christmas card and gift was early every year. His thoughtfulness amazed all who knew him.

Rub knew that Nathan's experiences as a white man had shaped his beliefs. Nathan knew that Rub's experiences as a black man had shaped his beliefs. It was the racial element that was the first difference between them. It was the color of their skin that was the most obvious contrast between the two men.

It would have been easy. Most people would have expected it. In the emotion of the moment, it is common to say something that is regretted later. Rub and Nathan never crossed the racial line.

Oh, they came close a few times. During Rub's angry years, there were certainly moments.

If one of them had broken the unspoken rule, the other might have also pulled out the stops. The situation was similar to the cold war stalemate of mutually assured destruction. The world was never destroyed by nuclear weapons because both sides understood the consequences of reckless behavior. It was understood between the two men that neither had a choice in their skin color. It was not subject to criticism.

Race was often a topic of discussion, however. In fact, race was probably the most common topic because Rub was a civil rights activist!

Rub knew racism and he was sensitive to subtle bigotry. In Nathan's ignorance, he sometimes stepped on Rub's sensitivities. Rub would turn and give him a quick look. It was a look of, WTF are you saying?

Nathan would "hum" and "aha" and smile and apologize and explain that he didn't realize how his comments sounded.

On occasion, Nathan would tell him that he was too damn sensitive. He would try to explain that, in the real world, it happens that sometimes a cigar is just a cigar! "There is not a racial link to every word in the dictionary, he would lament.

With Nathan and only with Nathan, Rub usually shrugged it off. He was so smart and so well read that he had an advantage in every discussion. Nathan did his best, but often lost the debates on points. It didn't matter because they weren't keeping score and there was no prize in the end.

Chapter 42

"If we find ourselves with a desire that nothing in this world can satisfy, the most probable explanation is that we were made for another world."

—C. S. Lewis

Nathan visited Rub's mother, Patricia, from time to time. The visits were usually hasted by a family wedding or some other event that brought Nathan back to Logan County.

Patricia was proud of Rub. She had a scrapbook of newspaper clippings and photographs that she kept on the lamp table next to her chair in the living room. She had autographed pictures of all kinds of famous people.

A favorite picture was of her and Rub and Gladys Knight. It was taken in Las Vegas. Rub had taken his mother with him on a trip and gotten backstage passes.

Rub often invited Patricia to events, but she seldom left Logan County. Her hip bothered her some and she didn't like to fly. Patricia was, however, very active in her church. After Samuel died, she threw herself into God's work. It kept her busy and gave purpose to her life.

On one of his trips home, Nathan ran into Patricia at the local Cracker Barrel Restaurant. He recognized her immediately and went over to her table. She was on an outing with her Sunday school class.

"I can't make biscuits any better than this and there is no mess to clean up," she admitted while she laughed and talked to Nathan.

"I have eaten more than a few of your biscuits and I rank then up there with anybody's. I'm here because I can't cook at all!" Nathan joked back.

Patricia was now in her mid-seventies. Nathan told her how young she looked and she said she thought he was losing weight. Nathan was telling the truth but Patricia was lying!

"Seen Victor lately?" she asked.

"No, well I saw him about three months ago but no, not lately," Nathan answered.

"Well, he doesn't look good to me. He has lost some weight and I worry about him." Then Patricia motioned for him to come close so she could whisper in his ear. "Rub told me a few years ago that he is an atheist. I think that fool has lost his mind or something. He must be lying to me, but why would he lie about something like that? What do you think is goin' on in his head?"

"Mrs. Wells," Nathan said, "I remember when Rub sat with you and Mr. Wells in church every Sunday. Rub may have rebelled against God, but I do not believe that God accepted his resignation. God is still with him."

Patricia wiped her eye with a tissue. "I hope you are right. It keeps me up nights. I just don't understand the why of it all."

Nathan continued, "Rub is a good man. He has conducted his life as well as any good Christian I know. You are a wonderful mother and you did your best for him. I doubt very much that God is finished with Rub."

Patricia smiled. She held Nathan's hands in hers and patted them. Her eyes were getting older but they still sparkled. Patricia looked at him.

"You and Rub are something else, I swear," she smiled. "I remember you when you were knee high to a grasshopper in my kitchen; you and Victor both, stealin' my cornbread." She closed her eyes, raised her arms while shaking her head and laughed.

"Thank you for not killing us when we deserved it," Nathan told her. She put her arms around his neck and hugged him. Nathan told her she was his second mother. They chatted a short while longer and then it was time to walk back to his table.

It was hard to say goodbye. Nathan knew she wanted more convincing about Rub's spiritual status. Fact is, Nathan never understood it either. Faith is a personal thing and Nathan simply accepted Rub's choices. What was hardest to figure was that Rub was in the church and then left it. How did he lose his faith? Could anybody lose it?

That was it! It was the fear that, if Rub could fall from grace, it could happen to anybody. Was there a big trap door waiting for unsuspecting

Christians? Could anyone accidentally step on the trap door and fall into an abyss of lost faith?

Rub thought that religion was invented so people didn't have to take responsibility. He said Christians did not want to face the realities of life. He said he understood that some people needed for there to be a God. Rub said he wasn't one of those people.

Although Nathan knew some of the answers, his general feeling was that we know what we know, but there is much more to God that we understand.

So, regarding Rub, ... *God's job!*

Chapter 43

"Politics is the art of looking for trouble, finding it everywhere, diagnosing it incorrectly and applying the wrong remedies."

—Groucho Marx

Samuel Wells died in 1968. Charles Weaver died in the spring of 1991. Patricia passed away in 2005, six months after Nathan's visit with her at the Cracker Barrel Restaurant. Nathan's mother was the only parent still alive. Sadly, her memory had failed her and she didn't recognize Nathan anymore.

Rub was doing very well in life. A long list of big corporations hired Rub as their civil rights legal counsel. It was a signal to everyone that the corporation was open to better opportunities for African Americans and other minorities. It was a win-win situation. Rub received large retainers and the corporations avoided civil rights unrest that hurt profits.

He was also the lead council in a number of high profile legal battles. He had taken two cases all the way to the Supreme Court and had argued before the court in both. Most cases involved racial discrimination in education and employment. His name was in the news regularly because he was the public face and voice for his clients and the causes he represented.

*

Meanwhile, out of Illinois, a presidential campaign was taking shape. The junior senator from Illinois was making news because he was young and black and had remarkable communication skills. Rub was hired by the O'Bannon campaign in early 2007 right after his announcement for

President. Rub went to full-time status two months later. Rub was a key player in the early endorsements. He was well known in the circle of players who could never be king, but who were the makers of kings.

One day in mid-April, Nathan's friend called him. Nathan answered the phone and Rub started talking immediately. "Senator O'Bannon wants a national healthcare product," What do you think?" he asked Nathan.

Nathan could tell that Rub was stressed but focused. "I think the time has come to do something about the problem, Nathan said. "Healthcare was once affordable but the costs have risen so much that it is no longer something people can do for themselves. Like highways and higher education, we need to come together for common solutions."

"How would you do it?" he wanted to know.

"That was too big a question," Nathan thought.

"We have the best healthcare system in the world, but it is not available or affordable to some. We need to solve the latter without destroying the former," Nathan told him.

"Would you fly up to Chicago and meet with some folks? We want to put something on the campaign platform but we need help pulling it together."

"Are you crazy?" Nathan suggested. "After fifteen minutes, they would throw me out of the room, and probably fire you for bringing me in."

Rub laughed. "They already know all about you. They know you are a redneck, racist, hillbilly Republican. They also know that you know the administration and supply side of healthcare. You are going to make the arguments we need to be prepared to answer. And you may have some influence on the final product. What do you say?"

"Why don't you come to Birmingham?" Nathan countered.

"No, we need to do this where we can pull together the most staff. It will be an informal gathering. Just a few people around a table."

Rub hardly stopped to take a breath. "The Senator is scheduled for an appearance on *Meet the Press* Sunday morning. He wants something for an announcement. He needs a few talking points. I have a private plane leaving Chicago in two hours. That gives you time to get home and put some things together for the trip. Bring Melinda along. I have you booked at the Drake. The best shops in Chicago are a few steps away. The future President of the United States is eager to meet you. Nathan, do this for me, please."

Wow, what a salesman, Nathan thought to himself. He couldn't remember the last time Rub had asked for a favor so this must be important to him. "What kind of plane is it?" Nathan asked, just being an asshole.

"A Gulfstream I think. It probably has a bar but no flight attendants. It belongs to a supporter. You will find the experience much better than flying commercial. I promise."

What could Nathan say? Oh boy, there would be hell to pay at the office. He worked in the vortex of Republicanism. His mind calculated the up side and down side of the situation.

The wheels turned in his head. Nathan wasn't agreeing to work for this O'Bannon person. He wasn't agreeing to vote for him. He rationalized the trip as a preemptive shot at saving healthcare from socialism.

Melinda and Nathan were comfortable middle class. Their life-style certainly did not include flying on private jets! They did not use limos or stay at the Drake when in Chicago. They had saved and gotten all four children graduated from the University of Alabama without student loans and had a retirement plan going. That was about it.

Their modest home in Vestavia Hills, a suburb of Birmingham, was never going to make the cover of *Southern Living* magazine, but the mortgage was almost paid off. To put it bluntly, they were not part of the "Jet Set"!

Nathan finally agreed to make the trip. He called Melinda and told her to pack some bags. They were going to Chicago. In answer to her question, he didn't really understand why they were going, either.

When Nathan and Melinda arrived at the airport, there was no security! No lines! Nothing. They drove to a private terminal. The pilots were waiting and helped with the luggage. They introduced themselves, helped their special passengers on board, then zip! Down the runway and into the air. A small bar was packed with plenty of food and drink. In no time, they were landing at an executive airport just outside of Chicago.

As Melinda and Nathan enjoyed the luxury of the private jet, they wondered how they were ever going to want to fly any other way. "It is easy to see how power and wealth could change a person," they thought.

The jet came to a stop near a small hangar. The copilot opened the door of the plane and there stood Rub and Diana. They were standing by a large black thing with wheels. It wasn't a stretch limo. It was a big Suburban with tinted windows.

Rub ran up and hugged Melinda then warmly shook Nathan's hand. He excitedly welcomed them to Chicago.

Rub noticed Nathan eyes cutting over to the car and a big grin came onto his face. "The Secret Service was concerned about the Senator's safety so they had arranged protection that included the car." He thought Nathan would enjoy riding in a version of the "Beast" used by the President.

Nathan thought it was the coolest thing he had seen since the airplane! "What a lovely day!" he thought.

Diana and Melinda quickly started talking about their shopping plans. Diana had lots of ideas for sightseeing with Melinda.

Rub told Nathan they would meet for breakfast. There were other teams working on other pieces of the project. Their job was to put together a basic outline of a plan to insure every American citizen. Nathan listened, nodded his head, and took deep breaths.

*

Breakfast at the Drake was great but the Cracker Barrel was more Nathan's speed, he thought.

To Nathan, on that cold wet January day, the University of Chicago seemed a massive academic collection of dark Gothic structures. The sky was gray and a light rain fell as they walked across campus. Nathan wondered, "What the hell am I doing here?"

A bright warm room and the smell of coffee lifted Nathan's spirit. There were probably twenty people sitting in small groups of four or five. He recognized a few faces. Daniel Axle was leading Nathan's discussion group. Valerie Galla leading another group focused on the economy. Senator O'Bannon led a third group with a goal to nail down Iraq War talking points. "Is this what Rub calls a small group around a table," Nathan grimaced.

Other staff people, who would later become very well known, were moving around the tables and joining in from time to time. Rub introduced Nathan. There were several Ph. D types in his group. Nathan was smart enough to keep his mouth shut for a while.

Axle started them off with an overview of what the Senator wanted. Rub then took over. He would be keeper of the notes and general moderator. "What does a national healthcare system look like?" he asked. The discussion was off and running.

Everyone at the table, except Nathan, wanted a single payer plan. They saw an expansion of Medicare to cover everyone as the best solution. The Department of Health and Human Services would manage the plan. Enrollment would be mandatory. It was the basic European model.

Nathan's ideas focused more on cutting cost. He wanted healthcare, not necessarily health insurance. He wanted to allow insurance companies the ability to offer policies across state lines. That strategy was effective in other kinds of insurance. The cost of life insurance, for example, had dropped significantly through deregulation.

He pushed strongly for a common healthcare computer language so patient information could flow from provider to provider. And, of course, Nathan favored many of the other Republican proposals, including tort reform.

All of the participants were polite. No one stormed out of the room when Nathan spoke. What Nathan saw was more of an attitude that they had "heard it all before."

Valarie Galla and Nathan smiled at each other but never had a conversation. She knew who he was, what he was, and why he was there. She knew they would never be friends and didn't see any reason to invest her time in diplomatic chit chat.

Axle on the other hand, had been the one who approved Nathan's invitation. Axle was a liberal, for sure, but he had several notches on his belt. His specialty was in packaging black liberal politicians in ways that won elections. He had been successful in Illinois and in Oregon and even in Canada. He was a street fighter with the skills to develop successful strategies

Axle knew this group assembled in Chicago was not going to design a national healthcare system. What he wanted was enough talking points to give the impression of a plan, but lacking the details that would launch specific opposition on points.

By lunch, Nathan was mostly an observer. He was amused as he watched a side of Rub that he had never seen before.

Rub worked the room like a pro. People came to him. They sought out his counsel. He was the consigliere, the adviser with no fear. Nathan was impressed!

*

Lunch was catered. Rub and Nathan sat talking when Axel came over and joined them. "Mr. Weaver," he said.

"Here it comes," Nathan thought. "You are out of here, dude!"

"Mr. Weaver, we appreciate your coming up here on short notice. You have some excellent ideas and you obviously have a good grasp of how healthcare works at the ground level."

Nathan waited for the hammer to drop.

Axel continued, "Here is what we would like to do. Let us complete some work on our end. Give us some time to put together some preliminary ideas."

"Tonight, the Senator would like to go to dinner with you and Victor and your spouses. He wants to hear your thoughts first-hand. Tomorrow morning, come back here for a meeting with a smaller group to lay down the draft of a proposal. How does that sound to you?"

They both knew it did not matter a tinkers damn how it sounded. Nathan was going to play along because he was a long way from Alabama without a ride home.

Actually, they could have knocked him over with a feather.

Nathan thanked Mr. Axle and accepted the invitation. Rub had a hard time controlling his excitement. His grin was bigger than his face.

*

Reservations were made at a small Italian place just off Rush Street. The big Suburban pulled up in front of the Drake. A hotel doorman rushed to the car and opened the door, as Melinda and Nathan slipped inside. Rub, Diana and the Senator were already in the car. Introductions were made all around. They did some small talk as the big car made its way to the restaurant.

231

Once they arrived and exited the car, a crowd formed immediately. A mob descended upon them instantly. Lights from TV cameras made it look like high noon.

Rub had been in that situation before. He took the arm of Diana and Melinda, looked at Nathan and said, "Follow me."

They made their way into the restaurant. A man with a bug in his ear appeared and escorted them to a small private dining room. In a short time, the Senator arrived.

Senator O'Bannon more or less plopped down into a chair and took a deep breath before speaking. "Sorry about the mob back there. That's why Michelle doesn't go with me half the time. We have small children at home, too. She has so little time to be with them lately."

Diana and Melinda nodded their heads in an understanding manner.

Senator O'Bannon grabbed a beer, loosened his tie and sat back. "Victor has told me all about you, Nathan. You guys go way back, I understand."

It was easy to see why he was popular. Nathan had never met anyone with so much charisma. They talked about universal healthcare and college football. He sat patiently listening to Nathan's healthcare ideas. Nathan bragged on Rub and Rub bragged on Nathan.

Before the end of the meal they were chatting like they had been friends for years.

O'Bannon said, "I am going to get your vote." He had that big and soon to be famous smile going.

"You have some work to do but we'll see," Nathan told him.

He laughed.

Rub was as happy as Nathan had ever seen him. Nathan was happy too. Happy he hadn't made too big a mess of things for Rub!

Finally, it was time to leave. Rub, Diana, Melinda and Nathan left the restaurant first. They were sitting in the beast before the Senator left the dining room. Security came out of nowhere to escort him to the door of the car. Once in the car, another car came alongside. Two cars rolled in procession and followed the front vehicle to the Drake.

Nathan and Melinda were back in Birmingham by dark on Saturday. Sunday morning, they skipped church to watch "Meet the Press." And there he was. O'Bannon was talking about the need for everyone to have health insurance. Nathan wished he had said healthcare instead of health insurance. Still, it was exciting to watch.

Rub called immediately after the segment ended. He was all excited. "Did you see it? Did you hear what he said?"

"He used one of your cost saving ideas. The one you suggested to get computers talking to each other. How cool is that?"

"It was great, Rub. So, I guess you still have a job?" Nathan asked.

"Yeah, so far. I don't have much time though. I just wanted to make sure you had seen him on TV. Thanks for coming up."

"Melinda and I had a blast. Can I borrow some money? That shopping cost me some real cash. By the way, who paid for dinner?

"The restaurant got a lot of free advertising so they comped our dinner. Every local station carried it on the 10 o'clock news. The campaign thanks you for your service to the next President of the United States." Rub said. "And I especially thank you for your help. I will see you after the election."

And just like that, Nathan's political career came to an abrupt end.

Chapter 44

"I predict future happiness for Americans, if they can prevent the government from wasting the labors of the people under the pretense of taking care of them."

—Thomas Jefferson

It took a few days to come down from the trip to Chicago. It was left to Melinda to clue Nathan in on the true purpose of his adventure.

At dinner, she sat him down and gave him the facts. "Rub found the perfect niche where he could plug you into his world, she told him. "Rub wanted to give you a look and a taste of his life. He wanted to show off some, and give his friend a peek at what real power looks like. I don't get it," she said. It was the same observation she had made many times before. "Rub is still looking for your approval."

Well there you are. That was it! Mr. "Alabama Cracker" goes to Washington. Nathan had to laugh. Talk about a duck out of water!

Rub, on the other hand, swam with the sharks like he was armor-plated. He had certainly found his mission in life. He was living his dream.

*

The early primaries were a close battle. Axel worked his magic in the caucus states where the other candidates were poorly organized. Soon, the numbers started to shift. The momentum was with the O'Bannon campaign.

234

Rub made a call to an old friend from his college days in Nashville at Tennessee State University. She was now a big TV success in Chicago, and the entire nation. Hope Reynolds was delighted to hear from him. He made an appointment to meet with her at her studio where she was taping her afternoon TV program. Hope was already a big fan of Senator O'Bannon. She had supported his Illinois campaign for the Senate.

Two weeks after Rub's meeting with Hope Reynolds, Senator O'Bannon made his first appearance on her program where she introduced him to her "Hope national family." Within a month, Hope had publicly endorsed his campaign for president. Other big endorsements quickly followed.

Poor Mary Clayton, the original bet to win the nomination, never knew what hit her. She came in second in Iowa and never caught fire.

Rub worked the southern primaries like an organizational machine. He got out the vote for O'Bannon as they won state after state.

Rub continued to shine as an organizer in the general election. His natural enthusiasm was contagious. His leadership was effective.

That old expression, "if you love your work, you never have to work a day in your life" was true for Rub. He had finally put the horrors of war and all his other demons behind him. Victor Wells was destined for greatness as a political consultant or in the civil rights movement or in whatever he wanted to accomplish. If Senator O'Bannon won the general election, Victor Wells' name would be golden.

Senator Barry O'Bannon did win, and Rub was a key member of the transition team. His name was mentioned for the position of Solicitor General. He ultimately took a job as general legal counsel to the president. Nathan asked him what that meant. He told him that his job was to do the will of the president, whatever that was! Nathan thought that was funny. Rub did too – a little.

*

Nathan was a member of the Birmingham Downtown Rotary Club. He got Rub booked as a speaker to give an update on the Administration's goals for the next four years. Although the room was packed, it was unusual for a key White House official to speak to a small gathering such as a Rotary Club. Especially the Rotary Club in a state that the candidate did not carry in the general election.

Rub did a great job. He received a warm welcome from the crowd. It helped that he was from the South and had attended several Alabama football games. After Nathan's introduction of Rub, it would take years to convince his associates that Nathan was truly a Republican!

*

Rub and Nathan talked on the phone and exchanged Christmas cards but Nathan did not see him again for a couple of years. Life in the fast lane was all- consuming. And he was living in the fastest of all lanes.

Nathan was happy to be bumbling along in his relatively slower lane. Slow compared to where Rub was driving anyway. More like a dirt road.

Things did get exciting in healthcare. Nathan had more than a few calls from doctors he knew asking him to see if he could do something to stop "O'Bannoncare."

Nathan knew that the healthcare horse had left the barn long ago. The Republicans were caught out of position and they stayed on their heels during the debate. They did not have the votes to stop O'Bannon's plan. Neither did they have a well-constructed counter-proposal to take to the public. The administration was a year ahead of them in planning and they had the momentum of a strong showing in the election.

O'Bannon ran on a promise of change. The first change came in the form of an overhaul of the national healthcare system.

Chapter 45

"Friendship is born at that moment when one man says to the other, "what, you too?"

—C. S. Lewis, The Four Loves

Rub and Diana were the toast of Washington. They also traveled the world. Nathan and Melinda got post cards from every continent.

Rub and Diana were always inviting Nathan and Melinda to Washington. The best entertainers in the world were streaming through the White House. Nathan never accepted. He didn't own a tux and he didn't see the need to spend a fortune so he could say he had been there for a party. They did accept an invitation for a special tour of the White House while the President and family were out of town. That was something Nathan would never forget.

The typical political battles raged on in Washington. There were legal battles too, and that was where Rub would always be standing front and center. Congress thought that the President was exercising too much power. Powers reserved, they believed, with Congress.

Few in Washington knew Victor by the name of Rub. That was his "Kentucky" name or the name reserved for "Old" friends. He was now Victor Wells, Chief Counsel to the President of the United States.

Many a Sunday morning he would be on the talk shows defending the President's action on one issue or the other. He was so much a common guest on TV that Nathan could not watch them all anymore. His friend was a star!

Rub's life was on a roll. It seemed nothing could stop him from even more greatness.

*

Nathan came out of a business meeting and stood outside his office door going through his messages. His executive assistant hit the hold button on the business phone and said, "Mr. Weaver, it's the White House on line two." "Really?" Nathan said.

Rub usually called him on his cell phone. This was maybe only the third time he had ever called through the White House phone exchange.

Nathan walked around the corner to his private office and picked up the phone. "What's up, Bro?" Nathan asked with a smile.

Nathan knew something was wrong in the first word he spoke. He had known Rub too long, but maybe he was wrong. Maybe it was something in the connection or maybe his radar was off.

"Houston, we have a problem," he said.

"Yeah, what's goin' on, friend?"

"My doctor just told me that I have prostate cancer."

The smile drained from Nathan's face. He knew he needed to speak without hesitation and with confidence.

"No problem," Nathan replied with his most convincing voice.

"We will just cut that sucker out or kill it with radiation or do whatever we need to do. Prostate cancer is one of the most treatable of all cancers."

"I agree," Rub said. "I've done some research this morning. I would like a second opinion. Have any ideas?"

It just so happened that Nathan's meeting that morning was on the installation of new radiation equipment using protons instead of photons. It would take several more months to install at the University Hospital, but one of the most successful uses of proton therapy were treating prostate cancer.

"What exactly did your doctor tell you?" Nathan asked.

Rub's voice sounded controlled. "They are a little concerned that we didn't catch it earlier. They are suggesting surgery, radiation and possibly some chemotherapy."

Nathan was taking in the information and making notes on a pad. "How do you feel?"

238

"I have some back pain. That was what finally drove me to see a doctor. I hadn't seen a doctor since I left the Marine Corp. The first thing they did was order a ton of tests. It turns out that my blood pressure could use some work and my PSA was high."

Nathan found out later that Rub had left out a lot of details on his blood work. His lipids were awful too.

"How high?" Nathan asked as he kept up the questions.

"I don't know. I don't remember," Rub tried to recall. "The doctor ordered a biopsy. No surprise that my biopsy came back with the bad news. I met with my urologist who did the biopsy. He went over some options with me, gave me some literature to read, and said he wanted to consult with his partners to put together a plan. He wants to schedule surgery as soon as possible."

Nathan absorbed the information while searching for words.

"Okay, I hear what you are saying. If you want, I will be happy to have one of our urologists take a look at your chart. You can come down here or see what is available in Nashville. Your call."

"How about Vandy? You know anything about what they have?" Rub questioned.

Nathan could tell that Rub was looking for answers. He was out of his element.

"Tell you what, why don't you call your doctor and tell him that I will be contacting his office. Let me get a copy of your chart. I will get with our doctors and call you back with some recommendations. We have several Vanderbilt Medical School grads here. I will check that out for you too."

"Done! Thanks Nathan. I don't know what to do and Diana is all worried about me. She suggested I call you."

A picture was starting to come together. Nathan would call Melinda as soon as this call was over. He would fill her in on the situation and then she could call Diana. It sounded like Diana could use some support too.

"We'll get you fixed up like new," Nathan said. "Just take it easy and stay calm until I get back to you. Give me a few days."

Nathan was trying to stay positive and not show his concern.

He hung up the phone and put his head down on his desk. He wanted to cuss and needed to pray.

First he told Melinda the story. Then he went over to the urology department and gave them the information to get Rub's chart.

*

By 4PM, Nathan sat in a conference room with three of the best doctors and friends he had. All three physicians were Board Certified teaching professionals. Dr. Mike Soppet was Chair of the Department of Urology at the University of Alabama, School of Medicine. Dr. Lawrence W. Long was Board Certified in radiation oncology and also carried a Ph. D in physics. Dr. Kelly Tate was a Board Certified medical oncologist and a leader in medical oncology research. Each had completed Fellowship and had a wall full of certificates and honors.

Dr. Soppet spoke for the group.

"Your friend has prostate cancer. They have preliminary staged it as T-4. They will be more confident in their diagnosis when they get in there and check the tissue around the area of the gland.

Nathan removed his glasses and rubbed the bridge of his nose. "So what does that mean and what advice should I give him?" he asked.

Dr. Soppet was the best urologist in Alabama. People came from all over the state and neighboring states just to have a consultation with Dr. Soppet. He had great outcomes and also a low infection rate. That's what makes a great surgeon. It was simply a plus that Mike was a really nice person. His patients loved him.

Dr. Soppet sat back and combed his hair back with his hands. This was also the same Mike Soppet who had answered the phone at the fraternity house many years ago when Rub called to tell Nathan he had joined the Marines.

"All we have is the one chart. We lack a bigger total picture of his general health. I would encourage him to start treatment soon. If he wants to come here or go to Vanderbilt, we will help him any way we can," Dr. Soppet offered

Drs. Long and Tate agreed. They had met Rub a few times at social gatherings with Nathan, seen him on TV, and had also heard Nathan's stories about Rub.

Dr. Tate took a deep breath. "Nathan, this is not what I like to read in a patient's chart. His Gleason score is high. I am concerned about his back pain in combination with the test results we are seeing.

Ordinarily, your friend Rub would have a number of choices. I believe his choices are now limited. In my opinion, he needs surgery right away. The surgery will tell us a lot because they can look around in there, take some tissue samples and get a better picture of what he is up against.

Dr. Long nodded his head in agreement. "I like to follow surgery with some radiation and then use chemotherapy if it has jumped out of the box. His urologist should work with the radiologist and oncologist to put together a treatment plan. We can get him set up at Vanderbilt but he needs to get on it. I have a good friend in Nashville who would probably work him in next week."

Nathan stood and shook the hand of each physician. These doctors dealt with life and death every day. They were on the front lines of medicine.

Nathan was a bureaucrat. He stayed on the business side at arm's length from the patients. Nathan was not well prepared to handle the stress of patient contact. Especially if the contact was practically, family.

"I will call Rub now," he told his friends at the table. "Give me a moment."

Nathan dialed Rub and he answered after just a couple of rings. He gave him the details of his meeting.

"So, what should I do?" Rub wanted to know.

"It's your call," Nathan told him. "Do you have any questions while the doctors are at the table?"

Rub asked a few general questions. The physicians were all three experienced at guiding patients through the emotions and perils of cancer.

After about fifteen minutes of Q&A, Rub made his decision to go to Vanderbilt Medical Center in Nashville. It was his home and it was close to his family and support system.

The doctors said their "goodbyes" and "well wishes" and left Nathan's office. Rub remained on the phone.

"It looks bad doesn't it, Nathan? What did Dr. Soppet say about my chances of a cure?"

"Honestly Rub, he didn't say," Nathan told him. honestly. You will know more after they get in and look around. Prostate cancer is a very treatable cancer. You have been in tough battles before. You always come out on top."

Nathan could tell Rub was concerned. "I don't know what to say to Diana. What am I going to say to her?"

"Tell her the truth, Rub. Tell her the tests came back positive for prostate cancer and they are going to aggressively treat it. Tell her you are going to whip this thing."

When three physicians call in favors at the same time, the odds go up for a good result. Rub was scheduled for an appointment at Vanderbilt the next week.

Rub had kept a home in Nashville. He and Diana always planned to go back there at some point. They used the home as a place to get away from the hurried pace of Washington. Rub also wanted a Tennessee residence in case he decided to run for office.

Melinda and Nathan decided to go up to Nashville and spend some time with Rub and Diana. Rub was tense but seemed to enjoy the visit.

Rub went into surgery at the end of the next week. He lost a lot of blood but he recovered. They removed the prostate and the lymph nodes near it. The pelvic area was positive for cancer.

The fight was on.

Chapter 46

"I have offended God and mankind because my work didn't reach the quality it should have."

—Leonardo de Vinci

As treatments progressed, the Marine Corp sergeant started to show his toughness. Rub approached cancer like it was a military assault or a political campaign. He organized his resources, took calculated risks, and went all out for a victory.

The radiation treatments went easily. He started while he was still healing from the surgery. Nathan was impressed. He knew that attitude plays an important role in recovery.

After eight weeks of radiation, Rub started chemotherapy. The chemo went well for another couple of weeks and then he started getting really tired. Rub lost his appetite and started to lose weight. The goal of chemotherapy is to destroy cancer without killing the patient. Chemo is a brutal process.

Three weeks into chemotherapy, Melinda and Nathan traveled back to Nashville to check on Rub and Diana. Rub was sitting in a chair watching MSNBC. He was staying on top of the political situation and cussing Republicans with all the strength he could muster.

He had been receiving calls, cards, and flowers from friends on both side of the isle in Washington. There was an outpouring of encouragement from across the nation and even the world. Diana took a carload of flowers to the hospitals and nursing homes every day. There wasn't room in the

243

house to put them all. The President had called twice to check on him. Michelle O'Bannon sent regular notes.

Rub lost his hair. He wore a Vandy baseball cap. Nathan didn't remember seeing him wear a cap before. It was obvious he had lost weight. Rub told him that if he couldn't put on a few pounds, they might put him in the hospital and build him up a little.

Nathan tried to laugh and act as if this visit was like any other. But Rub's eyes were sunken and his arms were thin. He looked awful. Nathan was worried about him.

Rub, however, projected a positive attitude. Nathan didn't know how he did it. He actually inspired others.

When they were alone, Rub pulled Nathan close and asked him to pray for his sorry butt. Nathan faked a look of shock. "Who am I supposed to pray to Mr. Atheist?"

"I have been praying," he said, "All I'm saying is that if there is a God, heal me. If I am to die, let me die without pain and with dignity. Take care of my family."

It was difficult for Nathan to speak for a moment. He cleared his throat to cover the lump that had choked him.

"There is a God," Nathan promised him. "He has always been with you and he is with you now. I think he would enjoy it if you continued the conversation."

Rub flashed Nathan his big grin. The two men sat and talked for another hour or longer. None of their differences seemed to be a problem anymore. Finally, Nathan told him it was time to get back to Birmingham. Nathan hated driving at night anymore, he told him. "My eyes aren't as good as they used to be."

Diana had always kept her faith. She attended church services regularly throughout their marriage. She had prayed and patiently waited for Rub to come back to God. Nathan ignored any pretense of confidentiality and told Diana about his prayer. She couldn't control her emotions anymore. They all decided to have a good cry.

During the next few days, Rub's emotional state continued to improve. He was getting more and more confident that he could beat his cancer. The spirit is as much a healer as the medicine. In Rub's case, his pain was less than it had been in months. He was also sleeping much better.

However, Rub, also, continued to lose weight. After another week or so, Diana called Melinda and told her that Rub was going to go into the hospital to get some fluids and start something to help put on some weight.

He was not getting enough calories.

Nathan checked on Rub later that evening by phone. His voice was a bit weak but his spirits were still high. He told Nathan that the last three months were like a blur. He said he was anxious to get in and get out of the hospital as quickly as possible. Rub talked about the possibility of a meeting with his treatment team to see if exercise would help with his appetite.

"If I can get past being so damn tired, maybe I could get some exercise. Maybe use a treadmill or something," he lamented. "Maybe I could get stronger."

Nathan liked his attitude and he told him so. "Keep up the fight and I'll be talking with you in a day or so."

*

Nathan jumped. The sound took a few seconds for him to process from a deep sleep. His phone was ringing. Nathan sat up in bed and did that thing people always do when they are awakened in the night. He looked at the clock. It was 4:30 in the morning.

Nathan fumbled to find the light switch and the phone before it went to voice mail. Grabbing the phone, he saw the caller ID was Diana. He knew immediately that Rub was gone.

The cancer never got him. It was his heart.

*

Diana had been asleep in a chair near Rub's bed. Before she dozed off, she and Rub talked. They had always been a close couple. They enjoyed the time spent every day sharing the important and unimportant pieces of their lives.

Rub told her that he wanted to go on a nice vacation when this mess was behind them. They discussed some ideas. Did they want a beach or the mountains? He told her that he would let her decide.

245

Rub told Diana how much he loved her and how much he enjoyed their life together. That was not unusual. It was something he told her every day.

She kissed him, he rolled over and very soon, she heard him snoring.

Diana woke up a few minutes after midnight, she looked over at Rub. He was still snoring.

At a little after three in the morning the nurse came in and turned on the over-the-bed light to check his pulse and blood pressure. Diana woke up but didn't move. The intrusion was routine by then.

This trip, however, the nurse was taking longer. Diana sat up and turned on the light. The nurse's eyes met Diana's eyes. Diana watched closely and read the lips of the nurse as she mouthed the words, "I'm sorry."

Diana felt a wave of heat wash over her. "No! This is a bad dream. How could this happen? Why? Please God, No! Oh Jesus," and then she collapsed in anguish.

Soon, a staff support team arrived to help Diana. A doctor was there in short order, too.

Rub's prayers had been answered. He had died in his sleep of a heart attack. The chemo had come too close to his limit. His heart and all of the support arteries were not strong enough to pump through the stress of his treatments.

There had not been time to address his potential heart condition. Rub knew the risks but it was, "damn if he did and damn if he didn't." He decided to go for the cure.

With pleading eyes, Diana asked the doctor, "How do you *know* he died in his sleep? How do you *know* he went peacefully? You don't *know*! You are just trying to make me feel better!"

"Look at his hands, Mrs. Wells, the doctor said reassuringly. "See how they are relaxed and not clinched. Most importantly, look at his eyes. They are closed. I assure you, your husband felt no pain."

Diana put her hands over her heart and looked upward.

"Thank you Jesus. Thank you Jesus. Thank you Jesus. Thank you."

Chapter 47

"I plan to live forever. So far; so good!"

—Steven Wright

The First Emmanuel Baptist Church in Downtown Nashville, Tennessee was the largest Afro-American church in the South. Preparations were underway for Rub's memorial. The service had been delayed for several days so the President of the United States could deliver a eulogy.

Diana worshiped with a smaller congregation but that church would not come close to handling the crowd expected to attend the event now being planned and organized. She reluctantly agreed to move it downtown.

In some ways, the whole scene was a blessing. Diana and the two children chose a casket. Everything else was being handled by the Secret Service and the White House.

Diana thought it was ironic that Rub's last appearance, even in death, had become a political event.

Valerie Galla called Diana the day after Rub passed. She was very nice on the phone. Valerie told Diana that the President would be honored to say a few words at Victor's memorial service. "How do you feel about that?" Valerie wanted to know.

Diana was still in shock but she knew that Rub would have loved to have the President say something at his funeral.

"The honor would be ours," Diana replied.

Valerie was always prepared. Like her or not, everyone agreed she worked hard for the President. "I know this is a difficult time for you, Diana," Valerie continued. "We all loved Victor. We have resources to help you get through this stressful time. You understand the enormous preparations involved when the President travels. Subject to your approval on everything, of course, I hope you will allow our people to make the arrangements and handle the details of the services."

And so it was settled. The funeral for Victor Wells was going to be a memorial, a media event, a campaign speech, and a fund raiser, all in one package. Rub would have loved it.

Nathan's feelings and motivations however were simple. His friend had died. He selfishly would have preferred a small service so he could mourn in private.

*

Melinda and Nathan arrived in Nashville late afternoon. No one had gotten much sleep. Diana looked like a woman who had been up all night suffering with grief and the pain of loss. She was physically exhausted and emotionally drained.

Melinda immediately took Diana by the arm and led her away. When they reappeared, Diana still had tears in her eyes, but she also wore a weak smile and a touch of makeup.

Everyone piled into the car to go have some private time and say their personal farewells. Rub's body lay in a beautiful casket at a local funeral home.

Nathan was able to spend time alone with him. He told him that he would miss him. He told him he would help Diana and that he and Melinda would not abandon her or their children. Nathan knew he was not actually talking to his old friend. He knew Rub was gone and this was only what remained of Rub. But, he needed to tell him a few things before he said goodbye for the last time.

*

Two days before the funeral, Diana and her entire family, plus Nathan and Melinda, were moved to the Vanderbilt Ritz Carlton Hotel. The President was scheduled to arrive in Nashville the day before the memorial. He had a speech planned at Tennessee State University and a fund raiser the evening prior to the service. The President and his staff would stay overnight at the Ritz and then attend the funeral with the family the next day.

Diana also asked Nathan to say a few words at the memorial service. He was nervous about speaking at such a large event but was honored at the opportunity to speak about Rub.

Nathan was returning to his room after going to the desk to get an extra room key. He was about to exit the hotel elevator when the elevator door opened and there stood Valerie Galla. "Well, well," Nathan thought to himself. "I guess she had been wrong back in Chicago. We did meet again!"

Valerie stepped back, and did not enter the elevator. "Oh Mr. Weaver! Nice to see you! I am so sorry for your loss. By the way can we talk a moment. I need a copy of what you are saying tomorrow at the eulogy. If you don't mind, would you get me something by early tomorrow morning?"

"It is nice to see you too," Nathan lied. "Sorry, but I am not speaking from a script. I have nothing to give you."

"I see." she said in a thinking tone. "Then why don't we just meet sometime after breakfast. We can talk and you can give me a summary of what you are thinking."

Nathan took a deep breath. It was an involuntary response to a mix of emotions. He kept his voice calm.

"We can talk now, if you like. Tomorrow I am burying a friend, so for me, tomorrow is not a good day for meetings. I hope you understand."

Nathan looked for signs of agreement and thought he saw some understanding in her eyes. He continued, "My words tomorrow will be about my friend Rub. I am going to talk about friendships and about the best friend I ever had. My eulogy is not political unless you consider love, friendship and loyalty to be political."

"I see. Yes, that is fine," she said. "I know your feelings for Victor. But there are several speakers. We want to arrange everyone in the best order possible. It helps to know what each speaker is saying. That way, no one steps on another's comments."

"I am speaking first after the opening prayer and scripture reading," Nathan said.

She jerked her head back a little and sort of blurted out, "We haven't set up the order yet.

"Look Ms. Galla, I was asked to do this. I didn't request the opportunity." Nathan could tell his true meaning did not go unnoticed. "I am not foolish enough to follow a President of the United States, who is one of the best speakers of all time."

"I asked Diana if I could go first and she agreed. You can speak with her. I will support her wishes."

Nathan stood silent for a second or two before he spoke again. "For the family and friends, this service is about Rub, or Victor, as you know him. For Diana and the family, it is an important step in the healing process. I hope everyone on the White House team will remember that."

"Sure, good, okay then. I think I have enough information. You go ahead and plan on going first. That will work out well actually. We had been thinking of going with comments from the pastor with just you and the President giving eulogies. That is going to work out fine. Thank you, Mr. Weaver and please excuse me. I have a lot of work to do yet tonight. See you tomorrow."

With those words. Valerie pushed the elevator button to continue her original journey and Nathan headed towards his hotel suite.

*

Melinda, Nathan plus Diana and children were relaxing in Diana's suite having some cheese and wine when there was a knock at the door. Diana's daughter Ella rose, opened the door, and stepped back in shock. There stood President O'Bannon and his wife, first lady, Michelle.

He put his arm around Ella and walked into the room - then turned and hugged Diana. Greeting were made all around the room. Spirits were lifted as the President told stories about Victor, on the campaign trail and at the White House. It was obvious the President really liked and respected the man.

Nathan and Melinda stayed a few minutes then excused themselves. They pleaded fatigue but actually they wanted to give some space to Diana and her family, and to their visit with the sitting president of the United States.

Nathan and Melinda left Diana and the President and retired to an adjoining suite. A bar was set up in the room that separated the two suites. It wasn't a mini-bar. It was a full bar with a mirror behind it, a sink, a small refrigerator, and an ice maker. Nathan had never been much of a drinker. He was a control freak and alcohol is not a tool of control!

Tonight, after the loss of his friend and a pending speech - a speech where he would share the podium with President O'Bannon - a drink seemed appropriate.

Melinda went off to bed so Nathan sat alone with his thoughts and a single malt while listening to the quiet. It could have been an hour or even longer before the sound of a ringing telephone startled him back into the moment. He hesitated until another ring confirmed the connection between his ears and his brain. Eventually, he leaned over and picked up the receiver of the hotel phone.

"Hello," Nathan answered.

"Mr. Weaver?"

"Yes, it is," Nathan answered. He wondered who would know where he was and could be calling him on a hotel phone.

"This is Cece Russell, special assistant to the President. The President would like to meet with you for a few moments tonight. Could you possibly come upstairs to his suite in about a half hour?"

Nathan accepted the invitation without hesitation. Nathan was from a generation that respected the office of the President. A personal call from a President was the same as a personal call from the nation itself; regardless of politics and party. If the President calls, you go!

Nathan knew, from stories Rub had told him, that the President was a night owl. He looked at his watch. Rub was right again.

The Secret Service ushered Nathan past security and into a sitting room in the presidential suite. Looking around the room, Nathan was impressed. He thought he had been transported into a French palace. The President entered a moment later. Nathan stood and they shook hands.

The president began. "Valerie tells me that you may be a little upset. Val is my right hand. She looks after me and she does the best job of anyone who has ever held her position. Her attention to details can sometimes put people off, though. She hopes you will accept her apology," the President said.

"Damn these guys are smooth," Nathan thought. His instincts, however, said it was best to acknowledge and move on.

"Mr. President, you and I do not agree much on politics but I think we share an admiration for Victor. I always called him Rub."

Nathan received a nod of agreement then smiled and continued, "Nothing would have made him happier than having you here at his funeral. That is what Rub did. Rub brought people together."

The president returned Nathan's smile and leaned forward. "You are spot on about Victor. He *did* bring people together. Why don't we follow his example, work together, and send ole Victor off in style? How about it?"

"I'm in," Nathan eagerly replied.

All of the resources of the Executive Branch of government came together in support of the two men as they worked together to honor their friend's memory. They spent the next 90 minutes writing their tributes to the man and to the life of Victor (Rub) Wells.

*

Morning came early. First, it was a late night with the President, then Nathan had trouble sleeping. He wondered how Rub was able to keep the pace so long.

It was, thankfully, late morning before it was necessary they arrive at the church. Nathan and Melinda sat with Diana and her family, the President and first lady.

A large choir sang hymns as background to the events unfolding in the service. The music took Nathan back to the memory of Samuel's funeral. In this service, however, there would be no spontaneous, spirit-inspired, outbursts.

The closed casket was front and center. Rub had arrived long before anyone else. Although Diana had been informed that Rub's body was already at the church, her knees buckled when she saw it. Her children were by her side and steadied her steps as they made their way to their assigned pew.

After the pastor's prayer, Nathan rose and walked to the pulpit. He prayed he would be worthy of the man he honored that day. He felt a sudden peace as he remembered why he was there.

Nathan told some of the story of Samuel and Patricia. He talked about Rub's early life in Logan County. He recited the story of how he came to be called Rub by his Kentucky friends. Nathan described their friendship and of Rub's passion for life and for what he believed was important. He spoke about a man who was always the smartest person in the room, but who still asked questions.

Nathan concluded with a tribute to the man who brought people together for important work in order to accomplish great things. Nathan said that, in many ways, "this service was both an example and proof of Rub's success."

Nathan returned to his seat. He felt relief wash through his body. He was now free of his responsibilities so he could focus on his grief and his farewell to Rub.

The President then rose from his pew seat and approached the pulpit. He stood for a moment waiting for the clicking sound of cameras to end. He then reminded everyone that Victor was born just a few miles north of where they stood that mournful day. He reminded everyone that Victor's father's grandfather was a slave.

The President spoke of a war hero who came home and graduated, with honors, from Tennessee State University and Vanderbilt Law School. He spoke of a man who was determined to achieve.

"Victor," he said, "was always mindful of all who were denied opportunity. In the past, as well as the present. He chose to serve his country to insure a better future for those who follow him in life."

President O'Bannon's eyes focused on those seated in the pew directly in front of the coffin. "As I look down at Victor's wife Diana, and his family, I want to express, on behalf of the nation, our gratitude for his exceptional service to our nation."

"Starting as an activist for the rights for the poor and the helpless, he finished his career as Chief Legal Counsel to the President of the United States. In between, he fought for justice on the streets and in the courts; sometime, all the way to the Supreme Court!"

"I can tell you without hesitation, no one ever served this nation with more courage, more dedication or worked harder to make the nation a better place - for everyone!"

As the President spoke, Nathan looked over at Diana and the family. There were tears but there was also pride. The grandchildren were young but they were on the edge of their seats. There, just a few feet away, stood the President of the United States as he praised their grandfather! The expressions on their faces spoke volumes.

Nathan wished Rub could see it. Maybe he was looking down. Nathan hoped so.

Nathan was brought back from his meandering thoughts when he heard his name.

Nathan focused his eyes upward to see the President pointing at him from the pulpit. "Victor's old friend, Nathan, and I sat together last evening and shared some Kentucky bourbon and memories of the man we honor here today."

The President looked directly at Nathan, "I must now confess to Nathan why I called last evening and requested we meet at such a late hour."

"What Nathan didn't know was that Diana mentioned, in one of our many conversation, that Nathan and I are the two men who Victor loved and respected the most.

"Victor would be proud, knowing that you and Nathan are the ones saying goodbye tomorrow," Diana told me.

The President paused. Partly for effect and partly to collect himself.

"I was somewhat surprised at Diana's words. After Michelle and I returned to our hotel suite, I couldn't stop thinking about it. Frankly, I could not see that Nathan Weaver and I had much in common outside of our separate friendship with Victor."

O'Bannon paused again before continuing. "Something was missing, and I was driven to get to the bottom of it. I needed to understand what connection united us in Victor's mind and in his heart."

"As Nathan and I talked last evening, and we shared our separate experiences with Victor, the answers came to me like an epiphany! It occurred to me that Victor had evolved past us all! He did not see the color of our skin or the politics of our party! He simply saw us as two old friends. As two individual men. Victor saw the common values and virtues. He ignored the differences."

"I am blessed to be here today and to admit that, as much as I admired and respected Victor, he was a far greater human being, adviser, friend, husband and father than I ever knew or understood. Victor Wells has inspired me, even in death. And, he should inspire all of us to approach others with a focus on the values we share, rather than differences that divides us."

The President looked down at the coffin, "Thank you, Victor," the he concluded. "Thank you for your service to the nation and for the lessons you taught us through the example of your life.

Chapter 48

"What you leave behind is not what is engraved in stone monuments, but what is woven into the lives of others."

—Elizabeth Cady Stanton

The long funeral procession wound its way north on Gallatin Road to the Veteran's Memorial Cemetery. Victor Wells was laid to rest with full military honors, including a horse drawn wagon that carried the casket to his final resting place.

There was a short prayer, followed by Taps and a twenty-one-gun salute by cannon fire.

Diana, clinching an American flag, leaned forward and kissed the casket. Nathan and Melinda stayed with Diana until she was ready to leave. Thankfully, transportation had been arranged to take them all back to the hotel. Nathan had to admit, Valerie Galla knew how to organize an event!

The press coverage of the funeral included a video clip from the President's speech. The local news was wall to wall with coverage of the President's visit to Nashville.

A few weeks later, Nathan received an envelope from the White House. Inside was a copy of the entire eulogy with a note attached from the President. His note was very kind.

*

Diana continued to live in Nashville. She received several offers to serve on this board or that board but she decided to focus only on the causes she felt strongly about. Her children and her grandchildren kept her busy too. Melinda and Nathan stayed in close contact.

Nathan returned to work the week after the funeral. He was famous for about a month and then everybody forgot about it.

The next December, Nathan received a Christmas card from the President. He thought it was nice that someone put him on the Christmas card list, even if he shared the honor with a million other people. It was an outstanding conversation piece.

There was some hate mail and he had some problems with phone calls. Nathan turned the mail over to the FBI and they put something on his home phone for a few months. The calls and letters stopped almost immediately after the FBI got involved. Nathan thought, "Those guys are scary!"

One day Nathan got a call asking if he would like to run for the Alabama State Senate. Nathan thought it was a joke. The man swore he was serious.

Nathan respectfully rejected his proposal, still believing that only the best of minds with the highest character should hold office.

Rub was certainly qualified to run for office. Had he run, he would have, undoubtedly, been the best qualified person for the job. Since Nathan and Rub didn't agree on political issues, what a dilemma that would have been for Nathan. No question however, he would have supported him.

That was their story. Their differences were the consistent thread that ran through every day of their lives as friends. One of them was always trying to figure out what to do about the other.

One thing is for sure. When Samuel Wells put on his first pair of new shoes that late summer day long ago, he never imagined that his son would, one day, sit at the table with the most powerful man in the world.

But there was only one Victor Wells. If there were a million more of him, the world might be a far better place.

People from all cultures and views were simply drawn to Rub and united by common admiration. The simplicity of his attraction should be easily duplicated, but sadly, it remains elusive. Victor Wells set the bar so high that even his friends could not comprehend the scope of it. It was more altitude than attitude. They couldn't reach that high!

*

Nathan didn't realize how "large" Rub was in his life. It was only after he was gone that Nathan noticed the giant hole where Rub had been.

Nathan visited Rub's grave every few months. He would sit on a bench in the shade and look at Rub's marker. His thoughts drifted. It was a time of reflection, meditation and prayer.

Sometimes, during his visits, Nathan thought he heard Rub's voice in the wind. Or maybe it was God; or maybe it was simply his own thoughts searching for answers to the big questions of life. Or maybe it was nothing at all.

It was in those quiet moments that Nathan thought how easy it is to look back in time and see what we should have done. Will we look back at the present and shake our heads again? Will we repeat our mistakes?

Nathan sat and pondered the questions. "Is it the curse of every generation to miss the point, and later, make the same old excuses?"

A sudden feeling of frustration swept over him. Nathan looked over at the small marker, paused for a few moments and then spoke in a loud voice to make sure Rub could hear him.

"I don't have the damn answers, Rub! And you're too dead to help!"

*

Victor "Rub" Wells and his memory lives on in Diana and his children and in their grandchildren. He lives on in the foundation that carries his name and in the nation, where his court battles changed the course of history.

And he lives on in the small museum in his hometown of Russellville, Kentucky. The house where Victor and his family lived is now a library filled with pictures writings and the history of Victor Wells. Michael Morrow will show you around. He is an expert and a wealth of knowledge on African American history in Logan County.

Almost every minute of Rub's life is now documented and organized. There are thousands of both small children and elder scholars who know the biography of Victor Wells and all he accomplished.

During a recent Logan County Tobacco Festival, Diana was in town with her children and grandchildren. Nathan and Melinda had their whole clan together also. The two families had jointly rented the "Washington House on 9th Street. The home was so named because it had once been owned by a member of the George Washington family.

The parlor was in constant use as dignitaries arrived at appointed times to have a word with Diana. She was hosting a forum on women's issues at the high school on Friday evening. Hope Reynolds was attending as co-moderator and the whole town was abuzz about it.

Diana came out to take a break onto the side porch where Nathan and Melinda were having an afternoon snack. Melinda had just been commenting on how strong and confident Diana appeared. It was amazing how she picked up Rub's torch and made it her own.

Diana sat down with a cup of tea and a few chocolate chip cookies. "Nathan," she said. "I have finished going through all of Victor's personal belongings. The museum has several of his professional documents and the Smithsonian has taken many of his papers from the White House years. I was wondering though if there is anything you would like to have. I can't remember anything he ever gave you of a personal nature."

A number of thoughts ran through Nathan's brain in rapid succession. "Yes, I do have something but it's an EAR! Where is that damn ear? I need to find it and get rid of it, and I need to recover quickly and give Diana an answer."

Nathan managed to get out a few words, "That is very nice of you Diana. I gave the museum copies of many of the pictures I have, so I kept those treasures. If I had known he was going to be so famous, I would have started collecting things early." Diana and Melinda laughed at his lame joke.

Nathan put his hand over Diana hand resting on the table. "If you see something that you think I might like and it is not important to you or your children then sure, I would be honored to have it."

At that very moment, Marc, Nathan's oldest grandson and Makenzie, Diana's oldest granddaughter bounced onto the porch. Both were freshmen in high school. Marc in Birmingham and Mackenzie in Nashville.

"We're walking downtown to see what's going on. Be back in a couple of hours," they shouted as they passed through the porch.

"You all be back here by dark because we are going out to eat, you hear?" Diana shouted back.

They both waved backwards as Marc and Mackenzie headed out the screen door towards Main Street.

Diana looked at Melinda and Melinda looked at Diana. "Well, how about that", Diana chuckled. "Now wouldn't that be something…"

Nathan had no idea what the ladies were talking about. It probably wasn't important and if it was important, somebody would tell him about it eventually. Melinda and Diana were still giggling and whispering as they elbowed each other and filed out of the porch and into the kitchen.

Nathan took a sip of his hot apple cider and inhaled the cool autumn air. He was happy to be home in Logan County with the people he loved. Almost fifty years had passed since Nathan left Russellville for college and Rub joined the Marines. It seemed like only yesterday.

The future, he thought to himself, was in the hopes and dreams of the grandchildren as they walked down the same sidewalks that Victor and Nathan had walked many years before. The present was secure in the sweet taste of homemade cider, and the smell and feel of a wonderful fall day. The past was what it was.

*

Homecomings, such as Logan County's Tobacco Festival, link the past with the present. Old friends come to watch grandchildren march down the same streets in the same parade where they once marched.

Everything, the streets and the building, they all look very much the same as they did in years past. It was, after all, the community and the common history that brought them together every year. It is a history that was good and bad, and just and unjust, but, nonetheless, it was their shared experience. To some degree, most have come to embraced it.

And so the pilgrims congregate each year. Their common history being as much their identity as their genetics. With the mellowing that comes with age, and the collective wisdom that evolves with time, there are subtle signs of change.

People are beginning to understand that cultural foundations are simply an opportunity platform that can launch them anywhere they want to go in life. It is a starting place. They realize that *"the way it was"* is not their only option for the future. *"The way it will be"*, shows great promise. As long as there is liberty, there is an opportunity to make the future a better place.

The End

About The Author

Nelson Weaver's roots are solidly planted in the South. He was born and raised near the Kentucky/Tennessee border in Logan County, Kentucky and he is a graduate of the University of Alabama.

Nelson enjoys spending time on his small boat or at the beach. Other interests include music, golf and college football.

The Weaver family travels frequently between Kentucky and Ormond Beach, Florida. Nelson and his wife Mindy have four children and two dogs.

Acknowledgments

First, I am blessed to have a wife who allows me to disappear into a laptop for hours (days) at a time. She is smart, beautiful, an excellent writer, and artist in her own right. The cover art for this book is her work. She is also an outstanding editor. Thank you, Mindy.

A special thanks to Reverend Bruce Russell-Jayne. Bruce is my brother and friend. Bruce is the friendship model for Rub. Phillip West is inside some of the young Rub up to the time of Vietnam. Phillip was kind enough to help me better understand the life of a black Kentucky teen during the late '60s. I will forever be indebted to Phillip. A big thanks goes out to another dear friend, Cathy Holmes. Cathy helped with research and supported this project from the early stages. Patricia Wells Ashby was important as a source of information on black women during the '60s, the black community in the South, and a good friend during the writing of this book. Michael Morrow is a positive role model in the Russellville black community. He was generous with sharing his time and knowledge. It was Michael Morrow who gave me my first Logan County Black History lesson. A big thank you to all of these people

To Jim Turner for his support and for providing an outlet to test my early writings. Evelyn Richardson is a Logan County community treasure. She took the time to drive me all over south Logan County and brought its history to the present. Her encouragement was invaluable. Mrs. Richardson and Marc Griffin are outstanding resource assets at the Logan County Library. A big thanks to Tom Noe for the lesson on the Logan County political history. I am thankful for Jim Young who gave me an enormous amount of insight into R. E. Stevenson. Dent Morris brought me a wealth of knowledge about the Andrew Jackson duel.

Thanks to Don Neagle because sometimes it is good to talk about it.

I am grateful for Al Smith for many reasons, including his creative encouragement and his perspectives on life in Logan County.

The best history lessons, however, come from the mouths of those who were there or who learned firsthand. A special thanks to Lt. Colonel Heath Twichell, Jr.

What is life without technical, moral and family support? I am proud to have Joe Bill Schirtzinger, Michelle Singleton, Marc Weaver, Janet Stanley, Martha and Butch Carter on my team. Thank you.

The memory of Russellville native, Leonard Vick, is alive in the character of Rub and in the story on these pages.

To Larry Long, Fletcher Long, W. E. Rogers III, and countless others, thank you!

Thanks to all the families who are a part of this story.

And finally, yes Virginia, there is a Logan County. To the people of Logan County, both past and present, you are many and you are special. Thanks for the support and encouragement.

Made in the USA
Columbia, SC
02 August 2018